I0572177

ARCHMAGISTER

ROBERT M. KERNS

KNIGHTSFALL PRESS

Copyright © 2020 by Robert M. Kerns

All rights reserved. No part of this publication may be reproduced, stored in a retrieval system, or transmitted in any form or by any means--electronic, mechanical, photocopying, recording, or otherwise--without the prior written permission of the publisher and copyright owner.

This is a work of fiction. Any resemblance to any place or person (living, dead, or reanimated undead) is unintended and purely coincidental.

Published by Knightsfall Press
PO Box 280
Mineral Wells, WV 26150

ABOUT THIS BOOK

Think your job is bad?

The Archmagister of Tel wields complete and total authority over the Society of the Arcane and the Kingdom of Tel. Tel is fractured. The Royal Line and its sycophants abused the people for over six hundred years. Brutal taxes for the common folk. Uneven (or outright nonexistent) justice. Nobility trained across generations to be harsh and unforgiving.

The Society of the Arcane is filled with elitists who have spent generations carving out their fiefdoms, sniping their opponents, and dominating their 'lessors.'

Oh...and let's not forget all the other countries. The ones clamoring for war over King Leuwyn's treatment of non-humans.

As the newest Archmagister, it's Gavin's job to fix all this.

Will Tel be overrun in a multi-front war? Will Gavin survive his new office?

Read Now to find out!

TYPOS

Typos and little slips in grammar are the bane of any author. Unfortunately, they are almost impossible to eradicate completely. I can show you many traditionally published books—twenty years old and more—that have a 'whoopsie' here and there.

That being said, if you find a typo or something that seems to be an error in grammar, please do not hesitate to contact me at typos@knightsfallpress.com.

I will periodically collate any emails and produce an updated PDF and eBook files, and I'll make an announcement in my monthly newsletter when the updates have been published.

CHAPTER 1

The moon shone brightly from its perch in the night's sky, tracing its lazy path from horizon to horizon. For many, that specific night would be a peaceful time, used for contemplation perhaps or intimacy with a loved one. But in the siege camp on the outskirts of Vushaar's capital, the night held no peace.

A mere two days ago, every slave mark vanished, and any who had used slave brands died horrific, agonizing deaths. In the wake of that, the former slave conscripts of Ivarson's army attempted a rebellion of their own. Many were loyal Vushaari, after all, taken by slavers and pressed into service. Soon, the siege camp devolved into chaos as officers and security personnel tried to restore order...and had yet to succeed.

No one noticed the moving shadows that crossed the camp's perimeter.

HER COLLEAGUES KNEW her as Cyn. Her mother knew her as Cynthia, Cynthia Dawn when vexed, but Cyn hadn't seen or spoken with her family in a very long time. She started down a new path in life when she robbed a warehouse of the Guild of Shadows. Now, she was a protégé eager to please her mentor on her first assignment: capture General Sclaros Ivarson. She would only get one chance to succeed, just one chance to impress her mentor, and failure—otherwise known as discovery—meant death.

The sounds of fighting and dying swaddled her as she moved from tent to tent. Smoke, food, alcohol, and other far-less-savory scents wafted on the light breeze. She kept her awareness on the moment, on her immediate surroundings, as she picked a path to her destination.

SHE HEARD them before she saw them. People—several people, at least—moving her way. The rattle of weapons and clink of armor alerted her, and they were close...as she could hear them over the background cacophony. With only seconds to decide, her eyes flitted around, scanning. There, a collection of barrels less than ten feet away. The map she'd memorized indicated the nearby tent was a cook-tent. The barest hint of a smile crossed her lips, and she moved, crouching between the barrels and the tent, pulling her hood as far forward as she could.

"This is all such a mess," one voice groused. "What in Lornithar's Abyss could make slave marks vanish? And did you see those other poor buggers? They had some kind of brand burned into their foreheads."

"It wasn't a brand," another voice said. "It's okay. You're not from Tel, but I know that symbol. It was the Glyph of Kirloth, and I'll tell you right now. I'd run for the hills as fast as my legs would carry me if I thought I could get through the sentries."

"Don't be such a girl," a third voice groaned. "Kirloth is ancient history."

"You're a damned fool," the second voice countered. "I was in Tel. I saw the battle-standards of the Great Houses myself. Kirloth is back, I tell you, and I want no part of that. If you want to live, you should run with me. Anyone who stays here is already dead; they just don't know it yet."

If they only knew how close to death they were. Cyn smiled at the thought. It would be a small matter to slip out and kill them; there were only three. But that was not her mission, not her focus. Until she reached Ivarson's command tent, she would be nothing more than one more shadow in the night.

Cyn waited until the three soldiers moved beyond her hearing. Pushing back her hood just enough to improve her peripheral vision, she slipped out of her hiding place and moved once more.

She slipped from cover to cover; sometimes a tent, sometimes a wagon. Any object large enough for her to blend into the shadows sufficed, and all brought her closer to her objective.

She dodged people on the move with ease, in some cases simply by stepping into a deep shadow and pulling her hood to hide her face. Her close brush with a group of soldiers was the most unnerving. She stood in complete shadow created by the moon shining against the far side of a tent. Ten soldiers trotted by, so close she could have pressed her elbow against them.

Cyn was just about to leave the safety of her shadow when a colossal fireball flared skyward, sending her matte black armor into sharp contrast against the tent's off-white canvas. She gasped—surprised—and dropped to the ground, pressing herself face down as close to the earth as she could, to be just a darker patch of night. She glanced at the tattoo on her left wrist as she waited for the light to fade. It was normal, barely visible in the night and not glowing. So, the flare wasn't magical, then...all-natural in origin, whatever that origin was.

People shouted and ran for the blaze, calling for water and help—all unaware of the danger that lurked so close by, a danger waiting for her night vision to return. Return it did, though far more slowly than Cyn would've liked. By that time, the blaze held the full focus of that section of the camp. Still pressed against the ground, Cyn raised herself up just enough to move and slow-crawled deeper into the night.

Cʏɴ ʀᴇᴀᴄʜᴇᴅ her destination just as the moon reached its zenith over the camp. Now came the most challenging part, to slip into Ivarson's command tent unobserved, drug the general, and signal for a teleport. It would be difficult—almost impossible—to retrace her path out of the camp with an insensate general over her shoulder...even if she were able to lift him.

Drawing a small knife, she made a slit at the bottom edge of the tent's canvas and pulled it back to peek inside. She resisted the urge to sigh. Fifteen officers—including Ivarson—sat around a table. It seemed the general was holding a late staff meeting.

Well, at least that would simplify her associates' tasks somewhat...

Cyn withdrew from the command tent enough to pull a simple sandstone disc from a belt pouch. Rubbing her thumb over the disc's texture told her in an instant she'd picked the correct one. Holding the disc between the index finger and thumb of each hand, she snapped it in half, waiting a couple heartbeats before returning the pieces to the pouch. That disc would summon any of her associates within a radius large enough to encompass the camp but not include the city, and Cyn settled herself in the shadow of an empty supply cart to await their arrival.

Tʜᴇ ғɪʀsᴛ ᴀᴡᴀʀᴇɴᴇss Cyn had of anyone moving around her was the faint scratch of a padded boot against the grass. Mere moments later, one of her associates was at her side.

"What?" the new arrival hissed in a hushed whisper.

"Staff meeting," Cyn replied. "I think over half your targets are in there."

More human shadows materialized out of the night as the first arrival looked toward the command tent. Others soon arrived and tried questioning Cyn, but she held her tongue; she didn't want to repeat herself multiple times. They could either wait or have a look for themselves.

They waited.

It took some time before all of her associates surrounded her, but once they did, Cyn said, "The general has fourteen officers in the command tent with him. I saw a couple captains, a major or two, and a colonel...but most were subordinate generals."

In the minutes that followed, seemingly random associates moved forward to peek through the small slit Cyn had made. Once everyone had looked, they sketched out a rough-and-ready plan to assault the tent. More rough than ready, really, but it was the best they could do in the circumstances.

At last, several nodded, and the group separated. Cyn went to the back of the tent, where Ivarson's sleeping quarters would be. Making another slit in the canvas, she verified it was empty. She pulled a small dart from her belt and a vial of sleep poison from her potion pouch. She flicked the top of the vial back to open it and dropped the dart inside, point first; nearly half of it stuck out the top. Cyn shifted the vial to her right hand, retrieved a dagger with her left...and settled in to wait.

She had no idea how much time had passed when the tattoo on her wrist glowed red and burned as if she were being branded. That was the signal. She moved. It took little effort to enlarge the slit in the canvas so she could slip into the general's quarters in time to hear a commotion erupt from the staff room. Cyn exchanged her dagger for her blowgun, retrieved the dart from the vial, and loaded the blowgun with practiced ease. She leaned through the drapes separating the sleeping quarters from the meeting space, took aim, and puffed air into the blowgun. Only then, did she glance around to examine the rest of the room.

Her associates filled the room, moving with lightning-fast precision and leaving dying bodies in their wake. Five of them moved through fourteen trained and experienced fighters as if they were angels of death amidst defenseless babes. Ivarson was just reaching for his alarm horn when the dart struck his neck, a perfect shot. By the time he pulled out the dart to look at it, he was already collapsing, and unconscious by the time he hit the ground.

Cyn secured the vial and returned it to her potion pouch; drawing her dagger once more, she moved to assist her associates. Ivarson's executive officer was closest to her, and she moved behind him without hesitation, opening the major arteries in his neck before pushing the soon-to-be corpse to rest on the table. A woman holding the rank of major was the next closest.

WHEN THEY LEFT, General Ivarson was nowhere to be found. They left his staff officers arranged around the table, all face down in their own blood, and snuffed out the lights. Perhaps the aide bringing the general's breakfast would find them.

CHAPTER 2

The landscape was bleak. No matter which window one chose, the view showed little beyond rocky, mountainous terrain with sparse vegetation. A sky that was once a vibrant blue with periodic clouds now existed as perpetually overcast. Nothing but a dismal gray.

Time and lack of maintenance had weathered the stone of the fortress at the center of this wasteland to a dull, boring hue. The courtyard that had once hosted training and inspections now contained a horde of undead, aimlessly shuffling and milling about.

This was Skullkeep, the fortress once entrusted to defend the old alliance against those who lost the Godswar.

THE ROOM WAS deep inside the fortress, several floors below ground level. Bookshelves lined several walls, and several workbenches held various beakers, alembics, and a multitude of other paraphernalia used in arcane research. The center workbench supported a mass of dead flesh, pieces of corpses on which the sole occupant worked to craft into a new form of flesh golem. It was slow, tedious work. There was no guarantee of success. Upon animation, the golem could easily attack its creator. But that was part of the thrill of creation; one never knew what the result would be.

The laboratory's sole occupant hummed to himself as he went about his work. He wore only a hooded black robe without runes, which had become his trademark. The world knew him as the Necromancer of Skullkeep.

A knock at the laboratory door drew his attention, interrupting a particularly vital train of thought. He was not pleased.

"Enter," he growled.

The door opened to reveal the lieutenant who was the designated messenger to deliver news to the fortress's master. He entered cautiously. Beads of sweat became rivulets and burned his eyes. Everyone knew the fate that awaited those who disturbed the master's work without good reason.

"Yes? What is it?" The Necromancer's tone harsh and unforgiving.

"Begging the master's pardon, we have received word. First, the royal family of Tel is dead."

The Necromancer scoffed. "That is unfortunate, but I am also tempted to say good riddance."

"Yes, sir. They died at the same time the slave marks vanished... seemingly everywhere that we can determine."

The Necromancer turned to face the lieutenant. "Interesting. Devote more resources to learn what happened."

The officer jerked a choppy nod and continued, "The last item is that the braziers on Tel Mivar's walls are burning."

"What? Why didn't you lead with that?"

"But...milord, it didn't seem important that the braziers started burning after all this time. No one told me that information was significant."

The Necromancer's hands clenched into fists. He stood silent, facing the officer for a terrifyingly long time. If he'd still had eyes, he would've been glaring at the man.

"You fool. The braziers burning is the most significant piece of information you could've told me. It means Bellos has selected a new

Archmagister. Summon my counsel at once. This requires an entirely new strategy."

The Necromancer pushed the officer aside as he strode from the room. The moment he crossed the threshold, every light in the laboratory snuffed out.

Once the officer was alone, he pulled a handkerchief from his pocket. Taking short, precise steps, he carefully navigated his way out of his master's workshop and closed the door behind him. He then leaned against the door and spent several moments dabbing the sweat from his forehead while giving thanks he was still alive.

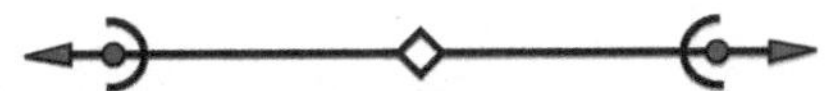

CHAPTER 3

A soft breeze blew through the window, tugging at Gavin's tunic and hair. He stood at the north-facing windows, looking out over the Vushaari capital and the terrain beyond. Even at this range, he could see the disorganized chaos Ivarson's siege camp had become, but that was the extent of the change he could identify. He wondered if anyone had found the dead officers in Ivarson's tent yet.

This was the second morning since he'd awoken, almost weaker than a newborn, and it was his first time out of bed. He didn't feel any different. He felt just like he remembered feeling before he invoked the composite effect to remove all the slave brands. But the armoire beside his bed put the lie to that. When Gavin had left his room to go to his laboratory, every robe in the armoire had been black with white runes, signaling an arcanist who put the Art before all else with no specialization and possessing the rank *Magus* within the Society of the Arcane. But now? Now, those robes were gold with black runes, and Gavin didn't recognize the rank runes at all. The gold robes were sufficient for him to guess his new rank. Besides, Gavin clearly remembered agreeing to take the position.

The faint squeak of a hinge needing oiled was the only indication the door had opened, and Gavin turned. He nodded his greetings to Declan as the bard pushed the door closed and latched it once more.

"It's good to see you feeling well enough to be up and around," Declan said, approaching Gavin.

Gavin nodded. "It's good to be feeling that well. How did it go?"

"Well. Very well, in fact. My protégé distinguished herself, by all accounts, and Ivarson is ready to be presented to the king. In fact, he is on his way here, now."

* * *

Since Gavin had not been seen since being carried back to his room, it was no surprise, really, that the Cavalier at the end of the corridor blanched and went rigid at the sight of Gavin striding toward the intersection wearing the gold robes of the Archmagister. As Gavin grew nearer, he could see her eyes were a little wild, too.

"Sir, forgive me, but are you aware that wearing gold is a capital offense across all countries of the old alliance?" the Cavalier asked.

"There is one circumstance in which it isn't," Gavin countered, a small smile curling his lips. "Are you aware of *that*?"

Any semblance of composure fled the Cavalier's expression at Gavin's question. "Y-y-you mean that—"

"Yes," Gavin nodded. "I am now the Archmagister of Tel. What can I say...Bellos made me an offer I couldn't refuse. I would ask, though, that you keep this to yourself until such time as a general announcement can be made."

The Cavalier snapped to attention, the formal pose they all were trained to assume at the passage of the king or princess. "Of course, Milord!"

A small, faintly sad smile escaped Gavin's control, and he nodded. "Thank you. Now, if you'll excuse me, I'm meeting some associates at the entrance to the throne room. I have a gift for the king."

. . .

By the time Declan and Gavin arrived at the vestibule to the throne room, the doors were already closed, signaling court was now in session. It was rare for the king to look favorably upon any arrivals or interruptions.

Three people occupied the vestibule. Varne, the Royal Herald, stood resplendent in his courtly attire, and two Cavaliers stood sentinel, one to the right of the door and the other across the corridor from the left side of the door. All three gaped at Gavin as he approached.

"Gavin," Varne said, his voice almost a scandalized hiss, "what are you doing in those robes? His Majesty will have no choice but to order your execution if he sees you like this."

Declan chuckled. "He'd better not. Bellos might not be too happy."

It took a heartbeat or two for Varne to truly process Declan's words. Gavin saw the moment the herald comprehended their meaning. Varne's jaw dropped, and any hint of color vanished from his face. In the blink of an eye, Varne dropped to one knee, his head bowed deeply, and the Cavaliers snapped to attention.

"Milord," Varne said, "please, forgive my shocking lack of courtesy and respect. I assure you the fault was all mine and should not reflect upon His Majesty or Vushaar in any way."

Gavin bit back a sigh. This wasn't something that had been discussed when Bellos offered him the position, and Gavin was quickly becoming fed up with obeisance being everyone's new default reaction to him. In some ways, he preferred the fear and unease over being House Kirloth instead.

"Varne," Gavin said, exercising effort to keep his voice even, "get on your feet, and face me like a man worthy of respect. I never wanted you to kneel to me before, and I definitely do not now."

"But...but, Milord...the Archmagister is the last of the Divine Emissaries," Varne replied. "You outrank *kings*."

Gavin cast a questioning look at Declan, his brow furrowed. Declan replied with a shrug and a nod. Gavin rolled his eyes and wished he'd asked Bellos for more explanation of the offer's 'fine print.' Wait...*fine print*?

When Gavin focused on what he was sure to be an expression from his past, the gray mists at the edges of his consciousness swirled through his mind, allowing no recall of the phrase's meaning. Gavin wanted to sigh at the latest expression of his hidden memories, but he knew neither the Cavaliers nor Varne would understand.

Having spent what little patience he had, Gavin leaned forward, grasped Varne by his shoulders, and hauled the man bodily to his feet.

Once he could look Varne in the eye, Gavin gave him a flat smile with no hint of any mirth or warmth, saying, "Well, if I do indeed outrank kings now, you may consider it an order that you will not kneel to me unless I command it. Good enough?"

Varne swallowed hard and jerked a choppy nod.

Gavin looked over Varne's shoulder to make eye contact with each Cavalier in turn before he said, "Stand easy."

The Cavaliers relaxed into their normal stance for watch standing. The Cavalier on the opposite side of the corridor from the throne-room doors looked at Gavin, his expression speculative.

"You look like you have a question," Gavin said, stepping around Varne to allow the herald to compose himself.

The Cavalier nodded. "Sir...er, Milord. There have been all kinds of wild rumors about what happened and why, regarding the slave marks. Is it true that you removed them and killed anyone who had used a slave brand?"

Gavin nodded. "Killing anyone who had used a slave brand was an unintentional side effect because of how I removed the marks. In all truth, though, I can't say I'll miss anyone who would support such a ghastly institution."

"So that was why you did it, then? You wanted to end slavery?"

Gavin allowed his mind to drift back to one of his earliest memories in this world. Kiri sitting in muck at the end of a grimy cul de sac in Tel Mivar's warrens, an expression of sheer unmitigated terror on her face as she saw the slavers arrive. He was so absorbed in the memory, he didn't see the Cavaliers' reactions as his expression shifted to one of distaste and sheer unadulterated contempt. But the expression vanished far more quickly than it appeared as Gavin's memories carried him forward in time to one where Kiri was laughing and dancing around the suite they had shared with Marcus.

Gavin pulled himself out of his thoughts and focused on the Cavalier once more. "Yes, it is true that I wanted to end slavery, and I suppose I should say that I wanted to end it because it harms anyone it touches. That's not the real reason, though." A soft, warm smile curled Gavin's lips as another memory of Kiri came unbidden to the forefront of his mind. "I wanted to end slavery so Kiri would be safe. So she could go home."

The two Cavaliers looked to one another at his answer and held it for several moments. Finally, they broke eye contact with each other, shifting their attention.

"Tell him, Varne," said the Cavalier standing beside the door. "He's the best chance we have of stopping it."

Gavin pivoted on his left heel to face the royal herald. "Is something wrong? Something in the throne room?"

Varne wet his lips and grimaced, swallowing hard once again. "Well, you see...there's a small matter involving Kiri—"

Gavin's expression shifted almost immediately into a hard glare, and his right hand curled as if holding an apple. A slight tightening around his eyes was the only warning before a gold-colored, iridescent mass of seething, roiling power the size of a honeydew melon appeared over his right palm. Gavin shifted his attention to the double doors controlling entrance to the throne room, and everyone present knew it was a matter of heartbeats before those doors no longer existed, quite probably in a very violent, very destructive manner.

"No! Gavin, no! She's safe! Her Highness is safe and well!" Varne said, his hands up in a stopping gesture. "Just give me a moment to explain."

Gavin shifted his attention to the herald, and when he spoke, his voice held the cold, unforgiving tone so many had come to associate with 'Kirloth.' "Don't waste your words, Varne. Explain. Now."

Varne took a deep breath and released it as a sigh. "Baron Torgunson—he's the first petitioner today." He glanced at the clock on the wall over the doors. "In fact, he'll be announced and called forth very soon. His petition seeks the hand of the Crown Princess in marriage. But...but Gavin...y-y-you can't go in there like...like that." Varne's eyes flicked to the golden iridescence hovering above Gavin's palm before returning to his face.

Gavin took a deep breath and closed his eyes. The orb was only a minor manifestation of the sheer volume of power Gavin held inside him, and it was neither easy nor pleasant to push it back. It was almost like the power *wanted* to be invoked through a Word to reshape reality. Certainly, invoking a Word would be the shortest and easiest path to divesting himself of it, but control and discipline were the true hallmarks of a master wizard. Over the course of several heartbeats, Gavin willed the power to recede back from whence it came. Gavin released his held breath as a slow sigh and opened his eyes. He flexed his right hand, now devoid of the seething mass of raw power, and let his arm hang at his side.

"Well?" Gavin asked, his voice now closer to 'Gavin' than 'Kirloth.' "How are we going to do this?"

Varne blinked. "We need a reason to interrupt His Majesty's court. Something that would be completely understandable and easily forgiven."

Just then, a group of Declan's associates rounded the far corner of the corridor, leading a man in chains with a hood over his head. Out of his peripheral vision, Gavin saw the Cavalier at his left shoulder tense.

Gavin waved to the two elite soldiers to remain standing easy, saying, "They're with me. The hooded fellow is a gift from me to His Majesty."

"With all due respect, Milord," the Cavalier at Gavin's left shoulder said, "how is a hooded captive an appropriate gift for His Majesty?"

Gavin smiled as he pointed at the hood and gestured as if removing it. The man at the captive's right elbow nodded once and whisked the hood away. Gavin turned to face the Cavalier who had spoken and grinned at seeing the man gape at the sight of a gagged and chained Sclaros Ivarson.

Varne turned to see what was behind him. The only outward sign of his reaction was his right hand taking a firm grip of the table at his side.

"Yes," Varne said, "I think that qualifies."

CHAPTER 4

The throne room was ancient, dating back to the Godswar at the very least. Colored slabs of marble in one-foot squares lined the floor, arranged so they formed the Muran family crest if one looked at the floor from the overhead galleries. Chandeliers hung from the vaulted ceilings, and combined with the windows, they lit the room well.

Along the right wall from the perspective of the public entrance and close to that entrance, one found the horns that played appropriate fanfares if visitors warranted such. The Royal Herald normally arranged those receptions in advance with the Master of Horns.

Further along the wall, there was a gallery where honored guests of the monarch could sit and observe court or even present petitions if they wished. Lillian, Mariana, Wynn, Braden, Telanna, Elayna, and Sarres—as guests of Kiri and her father—currently occupied seats in that gallery.

A raised dais lay centered against the wall at the opposite end of the throne room from the large entrance. A magnificent throne occupied the center of the dais, and a slightly less ornate throne stood to its right about a hand-span farther back. The thrones were once positioned equal with each other, years ago when the king and queen held court. Now, the reigning monarch occupied the center throne and his heir the other.

THE FIRST PETITIONER stood before the thrones. An older gentleman, the representative of the salt merchants' guild presented his associates' concerns over delivering their contracted amounts to the government, especially given the civil unrest gripping the country just then.

Putting forth a valiant effort to pay attention to the salt merchant, Kiri fought the black mood that threatened to overtake her. Yes, she was home. Yes, Lillian and Mariana and Wynn and Braden visited her often. Yes, her father had welcomed her with open arms and openly shed tears, even before Gavin removed the slave marks.

Gavin. It always came back to Gavin.

Grief clawed at her heart and soul, and Kiri calmly slipped her hands off the armrests to hide how she was clenching her left hand into a fist. She had the occasional good day now, at least when self-loathing for having the good day didn't swoop in and perch where her grief had vacated. But thinking of Gavin always brought her feelings to the forefront.

It was silly, she knew. She was the Crown Princess of Vushaar, the next in an uninterrupted line of monarchs that stretched back to before the Godswar, over six thousand years. She should be able to put one man out of her mind. Gods knew she never felt this kind of heartache over losing the young man she'd favored before the *Sprite*. But then, he had never given his life to return her to the life she knew, and she'd never truly loved him. That had been a heart-wrenching realization when combined with the knowledge that Gavin would probably never wake up.

The salt merchant concluded his remarks and received King Terris's assurance that he would not activate the penalty clauses of their contract. The merchant bowed his thanks and returned to the crowd.

Q'Orval deBentak stepped forward. Besides being her father's majordomo, Q'Orval also held the prestige of being the longest serving member of her father's personal retainers. He cleared his throat and said, "Your Majesty, Your Highness, I have the honor to present Joric Torgunson, Baron of Torstead, as the next petitioner."

Q'Orval stepped aside to allow a young man to approach the throne. He was slightly taller than Kiri but possessed a thin and wiry build like Wynn. His rather pointed, prominent nose and his preference for keeping his hair slicked back against his head with a glossy gel completed his resemblance to a rat or weasel.

Kiri tried to keep her face neutral. She wasn't sure she was supposed to have read the family journals and the various archives she'd read, but those archives and journals painted the Torgunson line as a perennial threat to the Muran family. Numerous times down through the centuries, the then-current Torgunson attempted to overthrow the king or queen, and each time, the perpetrator insulated the family so the line would continue. They played on the Murans' mercy and sense of justice time and time again. Baron Torstead was the last of his line. Unmarried and an orphan, he was all that remained of the Torgunson family. Kiri had a bad feeling about his petition.

Baron Torstead bowed at the waist, straightened, and began, "Your Majesty, I come before you today to discuss a matter near and dear to my heart. I have come to formally petition for the Crown Princess's hand in marriage."

A chorus of gasps moved throughout the audience like a wave. Kiri fought to maintain a neutral expression, all the while wanting nothing more than to burn Baron Torstead to ash where he stood. Reflecting on that thought, Kiri couldn't help but wonder if she'd spent too much time around Gavin.

"And what would such a betrothal provide the kingdom?" Terris asked.

"Your Majesty, forgive me for being frank," Baron Torstead answered, "but your family doesn't have that many allies left. A rather impressive army lays siege to the city, and were you to see your way clear to grant my petition, I would feel it incumbent upon me to call in several debts owed my family by General Ivarson and require him to surrender."

A silence so complete one could almost hear another breathe settled on the throne room. Most expressions Kiri saw displayed varying degrees of shock sprinkled with outrage, and as her eyes flicked to the gallery...oh, my. Lillian could barely contain her reaction; hints of contempt and fury chased each other across her countenance from moment to moment.

Just as the silence was drawing out into awkwardness, one of the doors of the public entrance opened just enough for a person to squeeze through, drawing both the king's and Kiri's attention. Varne, the Royal Herald, scurried through the small opening and approached the Master of Horns. They engaged in a whispered exchange for a heartbeat or two before Varne strode with hurried purpose to the dais.

"Varne, why have you disturbed our court?" Terris asked.

Varne bowed deeply and said, "Your Majesty, may I approach?"

Terris nodded, and Varne approached his left side—the side away from Kiri—and whispered in his king's ear. Kiri couldn't believe it when she saw her father's jaw slacken just enough for her to catch it, before he regained his composure and nodded once.

Varne nodded in response and hurried back to the position where he stood to announce prestigious guests. On his approach, he nodded to the Master of Horns and pivoted on his heel to face the court.

The Master of Horns gestured...and they played the fanfare for a visiting head of state. A visiting *head of state*. Kiri couldn't remember the last time there was a state visit anywhere, let alone in a realm choked by civil war. And how had they entered the city without anyone knowing?

The fanfare ended. Varne drew himself up to his court posture and called out in his booming voice, "Your Majesty, Your Highness, my lords and ladies, and people of Vushaar, it is my distinct honor to announce...the Archmagister of Tel!"

Every head in the room turned to the entrance faster than a finger-snap. Varne took the two steps necessary to reach the door and swung it wide. Kiri's eyes focused on the gold-robed figure who entered the throne room, and as she processed what—or perhaps who—she was seeing, the rest of the world ceased to exist.

It was only the fact that everyone was staring at Gavin Cross striding down the length of the throne room in the gold robes of the Archmagister that kept people from seeing the death grip Kiri now had on the armrests of her throne. She stared at the man who'd saved her and given her back her life, and her breath caught in her throat. Her heart thumped against her sternum like a condemned prisoner banging against the cell door, begging to be released.

Gavin stopped a respectful distance from the dais and nodded his greeting to Terris, saying, "Thank you, Your Majesty, for receiving me after court had already begun. I have no desire to interrupt proceedings or jump the line, but I would ask to be added to the list of petitioners today. I have a gift I believe you will find to be of some value."

Terris stood, and it was only her training ingrained across many years that drove Kiri to her feet as well. Terris led Kiri to step off the dais, whereupon he knelt with Kiri following suit. In short order, the entire crowd in the throne room was kneeling, including Gavin's former apprentices in the gallery. Only Baron Torstead remained standing.

Terris lifted his head just enough to glare at the baron, his voice almost a hiss as he said, "You will kneel before the last of the Divine Emissaries, or I will offer him your head as an apology."

Baron Torstead's descent to one knee was a bit choppy, as if he hadn't practiced much, but it was possible the threat on his life affected his composure.

"Please, stand," Gavin said. "If you had seats, please return to them. I don't need people to kneel to me."

No one was even going to think of standing until the king and princess did so first.

Terris pushed himself to his feet and extended a hand to Kiri, which she accepted. They returned to their thrones, and Terris shifted his attention to a Cavalier standing against the wall to the side of the dais.

"Would you please retrieve a chair for the Archmagister?" Terris asked before shifting his attention back to Gavin. "You are welcome to sit at our side, Milord, while we hear our people's petitions. The one before us currently is a proposed betrothal to the Crown Princess."

"Is that so?" Gavin remarked, shifting his attention to Baron Torstead.

"I am Joric Torgunson, Milord. Baron of Torstead."

A memory of a dinner party flashed across Gavin's consciousness. He recalled Count Varkas talking with this man as he said Kiri belonged on the floor of his bedroom, begging for mercy.

"Yes," Gavin replied, his voice shifting toward that of 'Kirloth.' "I remember you."

"Oh? I am flattered, Milord. It—"

Gavin's eyes narrowed, hardening. He interrupted the man. "You shouldn't be. Abject terror is far more appropriate."

If Gavin's statement unsettled Baron Torstead at all, he didn't show it. "May I ask why, Milord?"

"I can count on one hand and two fingers the people who stand out in my memory for *good* reasons," Gavin replied. "You, sir, are not on that list." Silence dominated the throne room for several moments before Gavin spoke again. "And just what incentive did you offer the king to consider your petition?"

Now, it seemed Gavin's sheer *gravitas* was starting to seep through Baron Torstead's veneer of superiority. Sweat beaded on his forehead as he answered, "Ivarson owes my family several debts. I am confident I can convince him to surrender and abandon the siege."

"Debts," Gavin repeated, his expression unchanged. "Of course, he owes your family debts."

"A-are you calling me a liar, sir?" Baron Torstead asked.

Gavin turned his attention to the king. "Your Majesty, perhaps you should receive my gift before you place any weight on this shyster's words."

Kiri was sure her father's eyes glittered with barely contained mirth, because she could hear the mirth in his voice as he said, "Milord, the Muran family is always willing to accept gifts from either

House Kirloth or the Archmagister of Tel. Both have been our staunch allies—and even friends—across the centuries."

Gavin lifted his right hand and snapped his fingers.

The doors of the public entrance opened once more, and another gasp wove its way through the crowd as the audience saw who entered. Kiri wanted to gasp, too, when she finally saw the new arrival, but her training was far too strong to allow her to do that. Baron Torstead, on the other hand, would need to wipe the floor where his jaw hit it; it was obvious he was not at all prepared to see a gagged and chained Sclaros Ivarson approach the dais under escort by two Cavaliers.

"Your Majesty," Gavin said, "I present to you the rebel general, Sclaros Ivarson."

"A truly invaluable gift, Milord," Terris replied. "Thank you. Cavaliers, see to the general's hospitality in the dungeon, and make sure no one guarding him ever served with him. It would be terrible if the Archmagister had to track down his gift all over again, if we lost him."

The Cavaliers took Ivarson away.

"Baron Torstead," Terris began, shifting his attention back to the man at Gavin's side, "in light of these events, we see no advantage in accepting your petition. Thank you for coming before us today."

But Baron Torgunson was not to be outdone. "Your Majesty, your guest slandered my honor, just moments ago, before your entire court. I demand satisfaction." He spun to look directly at Gavin. "I challenge you."

Kiri saw the twitch at the corner of Gavin's mouth, which would've become a sneer under other circumstances, as he asked, "To what? A knitting contest?"

"I'll have you know, sir," the baron answered, "that I am considered quite the accomplished arcanist in some circles. I have won several duels."

Gavin blinked. "A wizards' duel? *You* are challenging *me* to a wizards' duel?" Gavin now turned back to the king. "Terris, that's tantamount to suicide. Surely, you won't allow this."

. . .

TERRIS SAT on the throne in silence, considering the situation before him. His eyes flicked from Gavin to the baron and back. If he denied Torgunson the duel, he'd be leaving a family enemy alive. But would Gavin—or even more importantly, Kiri—understand? He turned the matter over in his mind a couple more times. He made his decision... and a mistake.

"WE FIND it is the baron's right to pursue a wizards' duel, Milord," Terris said.

Gavin's eyes narrowed just a bit as he regarded Terris. His jaw tightened briefly before he replied, "So be it."

Baron Torstead squared his shoulders. "Why should we wait? Let us finish this now."

The baron stepped back and lifted his hands. As his fingers wove through the necessary spell forms, he recited words in the language of magic.

Gavin frowned, listening to the man's pronunciation. It was almost unintelligible. In the end, he had to settle on using his *skathos* to determine what the baron was casting, and his eyes widened.

"Death magic?" Gavin remarked. "You're casting death magic in the presence of the king?" He turned to Terris. "Isn't that treason?"

Terris made a permissive wave with his right hand and said, "We give you leave to defend yourself, Milord."

Gavin scoffed. "Defend myself? The way he's mangling the language of magic, he'll be lucky if he doesn't conjure a canary."

Kiri watched Gavin's eyes flit across the scene before him. Moments later, she heard him invoke the Word, "*Irhys.*"

A faint tension around his eyes was the only visible sign of the pain the invocation caused, but Kiri didn't see any effect, either.

Gavin pivoted on his heel and approached the Cavalier standing nearby. The Cavalier stiffened as Gavin snaked out his hand to grasp the man's sword by its hilt.

"I need to borrow this," Gavin said as he drew the sword and walked back to the baron.

The baron was still casting, and Kiri didn't know how long the spell would take. She was a little worried that Gavin would take too long with his showmanship.

Gavin walked up to the baron, holding the appropriated sword. The baron continued to cast, but his eyes started to look a little wild around the edges. Without comment or flourish, Gavin gripped the baron's right shoulder with his left hand and slid the sword into the baron's torso at the proper angle to pierce the diaphragm and run through the vicinity of the man's heart. The baron froze. He tried to speak, but only blood came out of his mouth. The baron's spell fizzled. Gavin gave the sword a savage twist to break the suction and pulled it from the dying man's body.

Drops of blood fell from the sword toward the tiled floor but hissed into smoke a mere finger's breadth before touching the floor. Kiri knew what Gavin had done, then. He'd invoked an effect to protect the floor from blood. It was an excellent idea, really; the bloodstains would've never come out of the tiles. They would've had to be replaced.

Baron Torstead collapsed to the floor, the blood drooling out of his mouth and seeping out of his torso, creating a steady stream of smoke. Gavin stood motionless, watching the man die. When the light faded from the baron's eyes, Gavin leaned forward and wiped the sword on the corpse's pant leg. He turned and walked the sword back to the Cavalier, offering his thanks as he presented the weapon hilt first.

Gavin then moved to stand directly in front of the dais and looked the King of Vushaar right in the eyes and said, "I'm your friend, Terris, not your executioner. Remember that."

Gavin turned and walked out of the throne room without a backward glance, his footfalls the only sound.

CHAPTER 5

Gavin's trip back to his room passed in a blur. He wasn't aware of his surroundings or anyone who greeted him along the way. Anger and jumbled thoughts dominated his mind.

What does Terris think I am? Some kind of rabid dog? Yes...okay, I've probably killed a lot of people, but it isn't even a rounding error if you compare my body count to Marcus's. And it's not like I enjoy it or look forward to it. I'm not a psychopath.

He paced back and forth, working his hands but not really paying attention to what he was doing. The cascade of thoughts and emotions continued unabated.

Gavin had no idea how much time had passed when a knock interrupted his thoughts. Blinking, he scanned his surroundings and saw he was standing in front of the bed, his hands holding a set of trousers mid-fold. The bottomless satchel sat on his bed, open and waiting. Looking over his shoulder, Gavin saw the armoire was open and partially empty.

Another knock pulled Gavin's attention to the door once again, and he called out, "Enter."

The door opened, and a Cavalier in full ceremonial regalia stepped into the room. On the Cavalier's heels strode Kiri. As she entered, her expression and the set of her jaw indicated she had something to say...but then, she took in the scene before her.

"Y-you're packing?" Kiri asked.

Gavin held her eyes with his own for a moment before looking down at his hands.

"Yes, Kiri, I guess I am."

She blinked several times in rapid succession, her eyes possibly possessing more moisture than a few moments before. "Why?"

Gavin shrugged. "What's left for me to do? One minute, I hand your father the general responsible for the rebel army besieging the city, and the next, he arranges for me to kill his other enemy in such a way that he's totally blameless. From all appearances, my work here is finished...unless you're here to discuss starting down *your* list of enemies." Gavin's eyes flicked to the Cavalier standing motionless by the doorframe. "Besides, I wasn't aware our conversations were public fodder."

Kiri took a half step backward, blinking and shaking her head as if Gavin had just slapped her.

"With all due respect," the Cavalier interjected, "you should be glad Her Highness's entire travel team isn't inside this room. You caused a bit of a stir."

Gavin shifted his attention to the elite soldier, his eyes tightening. His expression wasn't *quite* a glare, but it was close. "There is a very short list of people I would give my life to protect and take as many hundreds or thousands with me as necessary to achieve that protection. Kiri is one of them. Do not question my honor or intent again."

The Cavalier paled. Gavin accepted that as a win and shifted his attention back to Kiri.

"That wasn't fair, Gavin," Kiri said. "Both what you said to me and what you said to her just now."

"Your father had me commit murder." Gavin paused, and Kiri took a breath as if preparing to speak, but he continued. "And before you stand there and bring up how many people I've killed, I do not deny those deaths. Yes, I've killed. In two specific cases that come to mind, I've killed on a mass scale. But I've never committed murder... until today. That man was no threat, Kiri; he was a mage."

"He may not have been a threat to you, Gavin, but he was most certainly a threat to my father and me."

Gavin finished folding the trousers in his hands and dropped them into the satchel. His eyes never left her. "How?"

"How what?" Kiri asked.

"You said he was a threat to you. How was he a threat?"

Kiri sighed. "He was the last of a long line that has engaged with my family multiple times down through the centuries. The most recent attempt to remove my family was a little over twenty-five years ago."

"What happened?" Gavin asked, stepping back to the armoire to retrieve the next piece of clothing.

Kiri gave a small, half-smile. "Marcus." Gavin almost missed a step as his eyes and full focus returned to her. "He became aware of their plot somehow, and he walked alone into the castle on their lands and laid waste to it. To this day, the castle is a mass of stones. Joric Torgunson was the only survivor. I-I'm afraid to consider what he would've done if Father had accepted his proposal."

Gavin sighed. "This didn't need to happen. I almost added Torgunson to the list of people to be...interviewed following Count Varkas's comments. I regret now that I didn't." he sighed again. "But we can rectify that now."

He dropped the trousers on the bed and said, "The Catalogue of Power," as he plunged his right hand into the satchel. He withdrew his hand immediately and brought a thick tome bound in gold leather.

Kiri frowned. "Gavin...what are you doing?"

"I'm going to question Torgunson," Gavin replied, setting aside the gold-leather-bound book and shrugging into a gold robe once more.

"But...but he's dead."

Gavin nodded. "Yes. But that's not the obstacle it would normally be. I just hope they haven't moved the body far."

Scooping up the tome, Gavin strode around the bed and approached the door. He noticed Kiri hadn't moved as he took hold of the latch. For that matter, the Cavalier looked a little wild around her eyes, too. Giving a mental shrug, Gavin opened the door and left.

He was halfway to the corridor intersection when he heard footfalls behind him and Kiri calling out, "Gavin, please wait."

* * *

FOR THE FIRST time since he'd believed Kiri lost at sea, Terris couldn't focus on the petitioners who'd come to court. His thoughts swirled around the mistake he'd made with Gavin, and he feared Gavin would paint Kiri with the brush of her father's action. His immediate surroundings came back to him, and his eyes settled on the small girl half hiding behind her father.

The man's name was Walsh, and he was from Thartan Province. He was here because he thought Terris to be his last hope of saving his daughter's life. His daughter was a wizard who had used her power—much like Gavin—but had not received training in mastering it. Terris could see the man's worry and fear as he stammered through the account of the provincial academy refusing to accept his daughter.

Terris did something unprecedented. He stood and stepped off the dais and approached Goodman Walsh.

"I nearly lost my daughter," Terris said, "and I am beyond thankful to have her back. I don't know how to help—"

The massive doors to the throne room opened once more, and Terris looked up. A weight lifted from his soul as he saw Gavin stride into the room with purpose, Kiri at his side.

"—but here comes someone who just might," Terris finished.

Gavin arrived at Terris's side, his eyes on the space Torgunson's body had occupied. He looked at Terris.

"We need Torgunson's body brought back here," Gavin said. "Kiri explained to me that he was a threat, and I want to ensure the threat died with him."

Without saying a word, Terris turned to the Cavalier at the edge of the dais, the same one whose sword Gavin had used to kill Torgunson. "See to it the body is returned at once." Terris turned back to Gavin. "As long as we're waiting, Milord, I'm currently hearing a petition that I feel is outside my purview. Would you consent to hear the matter?"

Gavin took a breath and released it slowly. He looked Terris right in the eye and said, "You addressed me as 'Gavin' not so long ago. There's no reason to stop. But what could possibly be outside your purview in Vushaar?"

"An issue with one of the provincial arcanist academies," Terris replied.

"Ah," Gavin remarked. "What is it?"

Terris turned to Walsh, saying, "Forgive me, but would you care to repeat your petition so the Archmagister could hear it directly from you?"

At the word "Archmagister," the man started trembling. He started to look at Gavin but quickly jerked his eyes to the floor.

Gavin took the two steps and put himself directly in front of the man. "My name is Gavin Cross. Despite the first impression you may have of me, I do not routinely go around killing people. How you conduct yourself not only reflects on you and your family; it also reflects upon Governor Zentris and your king. So, square your shoulders, and look me in the eye."

The man took a deep breath and released a shuddering sigh. He slowly did as Gavin bade, squaring his shoulders and lifting his gaze to meet Gavin's.

Gavin nodded once. "Good. Now, what's going on with the arcane academy in Thartan?"

"W-Well, it's my daughter," Walsh said. "My wife and I thought she was ill, so we saved our coin and took her to the temple in Thartan. The priest there said she was a wizard and needed training if we didn't want her to die. We sent an application and...and received this." Walsh lifted his hand, showing a folded letter.

Gavin accepted the letter and asked, "Did the priest keep your money?"

"Oh, no, sir," Walsh replied. "The priests at Thartan's temple are honest folks."

Gavin nodded and opened the letter with a smile on his face. The smile faded, the more he read of the letter. The missive was very polite and respectful, but the gist of its message was that a farmer's daughter was not the type of student the academy sought.

"I see," Gavin said at last. He shifted his attention back to Walsh, holding up the letter. "Sir, may I keep this?"

Walsh jerked a nod.

"This offends me on a fundamental level," Gavin continued, "but what I need to know is what you and your daughter want."

"I...never really thought about it," Walsh said. "I just don't want my little girl to die. Coming here to petition His Majesty was my last hope. And if we get a miracle? I want her to have a better life than I've had."

Gavin knelt and waited. Soon enough, a little girl with honey-gold-colored hair peeked out from behind her father. "And what do you want? I can help you if you'd like. Would you like that? To be a wizard like me?"

The little girl fiercely shook her head. "I want to be like her." Then, she pointed off to Gavin's left. Gavin turned and saw she pointed right at Lillian. Gavin smiled.

"You want to be like her?" Gavin asked, turning back to the girl.

She nodded.

"There's a lot to learn to be like her," Gavin said. "Are you prepared for that?"

The girl was quiet a moment, then said, "No, but I'll do it anyway."

"That's the spirit," Gavin said, nodding once. "My name's Gavin. May I know yours?"

The little girl's eyes hadn't left Lillian. "Holly."

Gavin stood and gestured for his friends to join him. As soon as they arrived, Gavin squared his shoulders and spoke in a hall-filling voice, "Under the authority vested in me by Article 23 of the Arcanists' Code and before these witnesses, I hereby take Holly Walsh as my apprentice...as was in the old ways."

Walsh's jaw dropped. "Oh...uhm...sir...Milord, you don't have to do that. We're just simple folk."

Gavin held up the folded letter. "This letter is an affront to everything the Society stands for. Every application this Theobald Fletcherson has denied will be re-evaluated, and I will ensure he remains in the Society just long enough to greet your daughter as a full member."

Just then, a group of Cavaliers arrived bearing the linen-wrapped corpse of Joric Torgunson.

"Lillian, would you and the others take Holly and her father to my suite, please? I'll be along as soon as I can, but there's another matter that requires my personal attention."

Lillian curtsied and nodded. "Of course, Milord."

That 'Milord' struck Gavin more than anything else that had happened. He wanted to deal with it right then, explain that he would never be 'Milord' to Lillian and their friends, but Terris's throne room wasn't the place for that, especially when there was a squad of Cavaliers holding a cooling corpse.

"Thank you," Gavin replied.

As Lillian and the others led Holly and her father out of the throne room, Gavin passed the tome he was carrying to Kiri and began directing the Cavaliers in the placement of the body. As Terris and everyone in the throne room looked on, Gavin went about the task of arranging the corpse in as close a position as possible to how it lay when Torgunson died.

After a few moments, Terris returned to his throne and prompted Kiri to do likewise. After several minutes, he said, "Gavin?"

A few heartbeats passed before Gavin turned, saying, "Yes, Terris?"

"What are you doing?"

"I'm trying to arrange the body to be as close to where it was before it was moved as possible," Gavin replied, returning to his work. "Ideally, we would've done this before the body was moved, but I think we'll be okay."

"And just what is 'this'?"

More silence passed before Gavin nodded and stepped back from the corpse. "Well, I think that's as close as we're going to get. I'm sorry, Terris; did you say something?"

"I asked what 'this' is that we'll be doing."

"Oh. I'm going to attempt calling Torgunson's spirit back to question it. Kiri said his family has been a threat to you down through the years, and I want to be sure any threat died with him."

Gavin held his hand out to Kiri, and she passed him the tome. He opened it and began flipping through its pages. About halfway through the book, Gavin stopped and concentrated on the pages before him. After a few moments, he nodded once and snapped the book closed, and held it out toward Kiri. Kiri took it, and Gavin stepped back. He took a deep breath and exhaled slowly, then drew just enough breath to speak one Word, "*Mysphaex*."

No one in the throne room felt the resonance of Gavin's power as he invoked the Word of Interation, but they certainly saw its effect. The corpse slowly lifted from the floor until it hovered in a standing position a few inches off the tiles. A gray cloud resembling a thick fog bank coalesced around the body until all that remained was a smoky, man-shaped form. The shape looked more like classical drawings of a ghost, a torso that narrowed down to a rounded point, much like the tail stub some dogs have. Its arms had no apparent hands, and there was no neck between the rounded shape atop the torso and the torso itself. Gradually, the shape took on even more definition, forming legs and hands and a defined but featureless head. Gavin knew the process was complete when two pinpricks of light appeared where eyes would've been.

"Why?" a wispy voice said. "Why have you called me back here?"

"I would question you, shade," Gavin said. "In life, you had information I want."

The man-shape was silent for several moments, then replied, "I know you now, Planes-walker. You were not born here."

"I didn't call you back to tell me something I already know," Gavin said. "Now tell me, who worked with you in your bid for the throne?"

"Why should I help my murderer?"

Gavin's mouth quirked in a faint half-smile. "Because if you don't, I'll bind you to the throne of Vushaar so you can watch in impotence as the family you despise leads Vushaar to greater and greater heights of prosperity. Across the millennia, you'll slowly go insane from watching the world of your life, unable to affect it."

Silence reigned.

"Very well," the shade almost spat. "Ivarson worked for me. Even if the king ordered his execution, as the Crown Princess's betrothed, I would've been well-positioned to spirit Ivarson away to lead our master's armies."

"Who is your master?" Gavin asked.

"The Necromancer of Skullkeep," the shade replied.

Gavin nodded, turning to Terris. "Is there anything you would ask?"

"What would've happened to Kiri if I had accepted your proposal?" Terris asked.

"The moment she bore me a healthy child to secure my dynasty, she would've died. I would have administered the poison myself."

Gavin regarded the shade for a moment before he turned to Terris. "I don't regret killing him now, Terris. I apologize for my reaction earlier. Do you have anything else to ask?"

Terris shook his head.

Gavin turned back to the shade. "I release you. Be on your way to whatever fate you face."

The shade faded until not even the corpse or its clothes remained.

In the silence that settled on the throne room, Terris stood and stepped to the edge of the dais. "This has been a most unprecedented day. As you all know, it is our custom to hear petitions only until the midday bell, which will soon ring. For this day only, we will hold court until the evening bell and offer respite to any who wish to remain." He shifted his attention to Gavin. "May I impose upon you to dine with me and my daughter?"

Gavin nodded once. "I think I can manage that."

CHAPTER 6

Gavin followed Terris and Kiri into the common room of the massive suite that made up the Royal Apartments. Exquisite tapestries and artworks adorned the walls, and area rugs warmed the floors. Midday light streamed through impressive windows, lighting the space.

"I'll return shortly," Kiri said, already tugging at her mantle as she headed toward what Gavin assumed to be her rooms. "I want out of this—this torture."

"You'll just have to put it all back on again," Terris said, a hint of amusement in his voice.

Kiri did not deign to give him a reply.

Terris chuckled, but he too began undoing the fasteners of his outer court garment. "Make yourself at home, Gavin. I'll be just a moment."

"Thank you," Gavin said.

By the time Terris returned a few moments later divested of most of his court attire, Gavin was standing by a plush armchair across which he'd draped his gold robe, leaving him in the simple—though exquisitely crafted—tunic and trousers he preferred.

Terris nodded at the robe, saying, "You wear it well."

Gavin chuckled. "I hope so. The thought of what it represents can be...daunting."

"Do you regret accepting it?"

"No," Gavin answered, shaking his head. "If I hadn't, Tel would be thrown into even greater chaos than it was in already."

Terris frowned. "How so?"

"I have it on very good authority that the royal family died when I destroyed the slave marks, just like anyone else who had ever used a brand."

"Oh," Terris vocalized. "So, Tel would have no leader right now."

"Technically, Tel's constitution empowers the Conclave of the Great Houses to appoint a regent in that case, but since I'm in Vushaar, the Conclave can't convene. Yes, I could've teleported back... but not in the state I was in."

Terris nodded and heaved a sigh. "I'm sorry, Gavin. I—"

"No. Do not finish that thought. If I had acted on my thought to order Torgunson picked up along with Varkas, none of what transpired today would've happened. It is I who should apologize to you."

Terris chuckled. "I'm not certain I recognize a need for you to apologize to me. Perhaps we should just consider the matter settled."

"Sounds fair," Gavin replied.

Just then Kiri returned, and as Gavin turned to greet her, every thought in his mind evaporated. She was wearing one of the dresses he'd bought her in Tel Mivar, the blue dress with silver trim, which left her shoulders and arms bare. Gavin's gaze moved from her eyes to her left shoulder, and he smiled at seeing unmarred flesh where once the slave mark had existed.

"Father, I want you to propose a betrothal between Gavin and me," Kiri said, her words pulling Gavin out of his reverie. "As he is the Archmagister, it would constitute a dynastic marriage, so the talking heads will be satisfied. Even if he were not the Archmagister, I highly doubt they'd raise too much fuss over the Crown Princess marrying Kirloth."

By the time Kiri finished speaking, Gavin had already turned the matter around in his head several times. In truth, he welcomed the idea. He couldn't deny caring for Kiri more than he probably should, and the thought of returning to Tel and leaving her in Vushaar didn't sit well with him. But as much as he wanted to accept the idea, the very desire to accept was why he couldn't.

"No," Gavin said, drawing both surprise from Terris and hurt from Kiri. In fact, Kiri's expression told Gavin he could not have hurt or betrayed her more if he'd slipped a knife between her ribs. Every fiber of his being shouted at him to take it back, to say he'd made a mistake, to tell her how much he wanted to accept. But he couldn't. He kept his face expressionless and soldiered on. "Kiri, you're just recently returned home after two years I wouldn't wish on my worst enemy. You need to get settled back into this life. Put distance and healing between you and those experiences. I think it's best you take some time, and if you still feel a betrothal is what you want, we can revisit the topic."

By the time Gavin finished speaking, Kiri's eyes glistened with moisture, and her jaw was clenched. Without another word, she pivoted and strode back the way she'd come. The first door she passed through didn't *quite* slam, but it was a near thing.

Gavin heaved a sigh and said, "I'm sorry, Terris. That was harder for me than you'll ever know." Gavin picked up his robe and draped it over his left forearm. "You should go to her. Don't give her the opportunity to think you choose me over her."

Without another word, Gavin turned and left the Royal Apartments.

* * *

Lillian knocked on the door of Kiri's suite. She wasn't sure she should be there, but Gavin had just returned to his suite a broken man, and she wanted to check on her friend. After a third round of knocking, Lillian knew she should leave matters be, but instead, she tried the door's latch and found it unlocked. She opened the door and entered, closing the door behind her.

. . .

LILLIAN WAS NO MORE than twenty feet into Kiri's suite when she heard sobbing. She followed the sound and found Kiri draped across her bed, shoulders heaving with each wracking sob. Watching her, Lillian felt her own heart break just a little.

She went to the bed and said, "Kiri?"

"Go away, Lillian," Kiri said—almost whimpered—between sobs. "I...I don't want you, of all people, to see me like this."

Lillian sat on the edge of the bed and reached out to Kiri. "You helped me when I didn't want anyone seeing how fragile I was, Kiri. Do you honestly think I won't be here for you now?"

"I thought you'd be going back to Tel."

Lillian shrugged, even though Kiri couldn't see it. "I can go home to Tel anytime I want. I know that estate like the back of my hand. Now, come here. Tell me what happened."

A fresh round of sobs erupted from her friend. "He...he rejected me, Lillian. I asked Father to propose a betrothal, and Gavin rejected me."

Lillian thought back to everything she'd seen Gavin do for Kiri and how he looked when he returned to his suite. The man she'd seen didn't look like he'd rejected Kiri; he looked like he'd carved out his heart with a dull piece of wood. "Tell me what he said."

* * *

THE MIDDAY SUN shone clear and bright, bathing the capital in its warm embrace. Telanna, Elayna, and Sarres walked among the few petitioners who chose not to stay for the expanded court hours. Walking back to the elven embassy, their mood was contemplative and silent. Telanna led them to the sitting room where she received guests and invited them to sit.

"This...complicates matters," Telanna said at long last. "Asking the Head of House Kirloth for assistance is one thing, but Gavin is now the Archmagister of Tel."

"Should we not discuss the matter of a dark elf ruling in the High

Forest with him?" Elayna asked. "There may yet still be some way he could assist us."

"I still say we could solve the matter by putting an arrow—or a dozen—in Nirrock," Sarres remarked, almost a petulant grumble.

Telanna and Elayna both turned to regard him, their left eyebrows quirked upward in a question. In that moment, their sibling resemblance was beyond uncanny.

Sarres sighed. "Yes, I know it's been discussed, and I know why the Synod decided against it...but that doesn't mean it wouldn't work."

"And just how many more lives would be lost in the consequences of that action, Sarres?" Telanna asked.

"You don't know it would spark a civil war," Sarres rebutted. "Put all the evidence before the people and see what they say. More would side with us than you think."

"Perhaps," Telanna allowed.

"And perhaps not," Elayna said. "There's just no way to know. At least if we had secured Kirloth's assistance, we could mitigate the worst of it."

A heavy silence ensued, and just as it was becoming truly oppressive, Telanna said, "We should return to Arundel. At the very least, the Synod deserves to learn of the situation."

Sarres and Elayna both nodded but maintained their silence. They stood with Telanna and followed her outside to the garden. Approaching a large oak, Telanna took Elayna's right hand in her left and placed her right hand against its rough bark. Elayna took Sarres's hand as Telanna whispered a series of words. Moments later, they vanished.

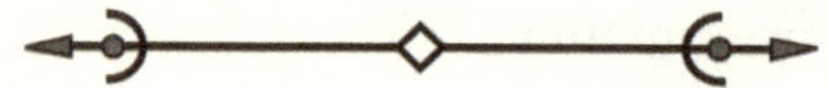

CHAPTER 7

Gavin stared at the door. He didn't know how long he'd been standing there. Now that he was here, he was nervous and afraid. He could always slink back to his suite. That idea galled him, though. No...the only way out was through. He lifted his right hand, curled his fingers into a partial fist, and knocked three times.

A few moments later, the latch released, and the door opened. For the briefest moment, Gavin saw shock flit across Kiri's face. As he watched her jaw work without saying anything, he noticed the puffiness around her eyes and the rosy tinge on her nose. Combined with how her eyes glistened, it was apparent to Gavin she'd been crying.

"Did Lillian send you?" Kiri asked at last. Her voice held a slight edge Gavin wasn't used to hearing.

Gavin blinked. "Why would Lillian send me?"

"Never mind," Kiri replied. "What do you want, Gavin?"

"I'd like to talk for a moment."

Kiri heaved a sigh. "Fine. Come in."

She stepped back and allowed Gavin to step inside. The door didn't quite slam as she closed it, but it certainly wasn't whisper quiet.

She crossed her arms over her midriff as she asked, "What do you want to talk about?"

Gavin heaved his own sigh. "Kiri, I didn't handle that moment as well as I should have. When you mentioned a betrothal, I...well...I was happy. I liked the idea."

"Then, why didn't you say that?" Kiri ask, her tone harsh enough to score stone as her eyes narrowed. "Do you have any idea how much you hurt me, Gavin? Do you?"

"No. I'm sure I don't," Gavin answered, "and I don't have sufficient words to explain how much it weighs on me that I hurt you. I never want to hurt you, Kiri. I'm sorry I did. It's...well, we just got rid of the slave marks. I don't want you rushing into something because you think it's what you're supposed to do or what I want or you think you owe me something. You can't convince me those two years didn't leave their own mark on you, and that's not something that just goes away in the blink of an eye. I'm not trying to control you or tell you what to do or anything like that. I just want you to step back and get settled before you make such life-altering decisions."

"Did it ever occur to you that maybe I *have* spent a lot of time thinking about it?" Kiri asked. "My hopes and prayers all came true, Gavin...until today.

"I'm home. My family is safe. I have new friends I never expected to have, who are also safe. And most of all, I'm not a slave anymore; no one's a slave anymore. But even before you brought me home, Gavin, you had already given me my life back. There was no reason at all for you to be different from Kalinor or the men before him, but you were. You're the only man, aside from my father, who I'm comfortable with...who I don't feel uneasy or unsafe around. Even Braden and Wynn...and Roth Thatcherson, too. It's nothing they've done or said; Roth would even give his life for me, and I know that. It's just they're *men*. You're the only man I feel safe with."

"Okay," Gavin said. "What do you want to do? I mean, can we fix this? Do you want to fix it?"

"There's a part of me that's screaming, 'yes, I want to fix it,' right now," Kiri answered, "but there's also another part that wants to slap you and yell that you don't get a free pass for hurting me. In all the time we've known each other, Gavin, you never hurt me...until today. It's still raw. I'm still fighting back tears. I don't know what to think, honestly."

Gavin nodded. "Okay. I'll leave it with you, then. Take all the time you need. Thank you for speaking with me."

Kiri nodded, and Gavin turned and left her suite.

* * *

THE MORNING after Gavin's arrival in Terris's court, he sat at the desk in his suite examining a collection of notes. In truth, he didn't know why he was still in Vushaar. The time had long passed for him to return to Tel.

A knock drew Gavin's attention. He set aside his papers and went to the door. Opening it, he found a young page in royal livery; he couldn't have been more than fourteen or fifteen.

"How can I help you?" Gavin asked.

"His Majesty asks if you have time to attend a strategy session of the city's defense counsel, Milord," the page answered.

Gavin considered the matter and mentally shrugged, saying, "When does the session occur?"

"With all respect, Milord, I will escort you there now if you agree."

"Well, there's nothing like advance notice," Gavin replied, grinning. "Let's go."

THE YOUNG PAGE led Gavin through the corridors of the palace, eventually delivering him to the doors leading to the war room Gavin had visited when he first arrived in the city. Gavin knocked twice and entered, the page following him. King Terris and several advisors were already present. As Gavin approached the map table, Terris gestured for the man at his right to make room for him.

"Please forgive the short notice, Milord," Terris said as Gavin arrived at the table.

Gavin smiled. "Think nothing of it, Terris. How can I help?"

"The main topic for the session today is what to do with the nest of chaos off the north wall. While we have sufficient soldiers to hold the city, we do not have enough to force the siege camp to surrender. I was hoping to get your unique perspective while we discuss options," Terris replied.

"And you don't want to risk an attack with the forces you have in case the new threat helps them get their act together," Gavin remarked. "Are there any other units of the Vushaari Army close enough to call?"

"No, unfortunately," a man wearing a staff officer's uniform answered. "Most of our units that are not garrisoned in the capital or province capitals are scattered all over the back of beyond trying to capture the rebel soldiers that have turned to banditry."

Gavin nodded, his eyes on the map table. He knew where Terris could obtain some shock troops...*if* asking for aid was permitted and *if* the Council of Clans would agree. He shifted his attention to the king, asking, "Was the old alliance ever repealed?"

"Not as such, no," Terris said. "It faded into the background, especially after the death of Bellock Vanlon."

"So, there is still a treaty to which all the signatories are bound?" Gavin pressed.

Terris shrugged. "I wouldn't see why not. No one ever specifically abrogated it that I'm aware of."

Gavin smiled again. "Do you happen to have a copy of it?"

"Yes, but not here. It's in the Royal Archives." Terris turned to the page who had escorted Gavin. "Would you please go to the Archives and bring Vushaar's copy of the old alliance?"

The page snapped to attention, nodding once. "Yes, Your Majesty!"

As the young man fast-walked out of the room, Terris turned back to Gavin, asking, "What are you thinking?"

Gavin shook his head. "Let's wait for the page to return. I don't want to get anyone's hopes up if I'm wrong."

* * *

THE PAGE TRIED NOT to run, but it was hard. So hard. Uncle Q'Orval had taught him to always make the best impression possible, and he wanted to get the book from the Archives as fast as he possibly could.

He smiled to beat back the sadness. Q'Orval wasn't his real uncle; he was an orphan. His parents had been killed by marauding troops back in the early days of the civil war. A really nice lady at the refugee camp in the city had brought him to Q'Orval, and Q'Orval had taken him in on the spot. That was months ago, now, and he hadn't been hungry or in danger since.

At last, the doors to the Royal Archives came into sight, and the page smiled. He increased his speed to something between a fast walk and a jog. When he reached the doors, he pulled one open so fast he didn't see the man stepping from between the reading tables with a stack of books.

They collided, and the books went flying.

* * *

HE STOOD at the edge of the main aisle. He'd long since forgotten his birth name amidst the many aliases and identities he'd used over the years. At the moment, he was Garth, an assistant archivist. The book he held in his hand was a long-sought prize among his fellows, for it was the sole record of the meeting that decided the hiding places for the foundation artifacts of his master's prison, who the world at large knew as Lornithar. His only problem now was to find a way to leave the Archives with it; there were banks that had less security over gold.

A commotion to his left drew his attention, and he smiled. A royal page had sent another archivist's armload of books in every direction. He quickly scanned his immediate area and saw everyone seemed focused on the books and the boy. Excellent.

He stepped further into the aisle between bookshelves and opened the book's well-thumbed pages right to the information he sought. The commotion was still loud and active as he ripped the pages from the book and stuffed them into his robe. He exited the aisle, placed the book on the cart laden with other tomes for re-shelving, and went about Archivist Garth's business for the last time. He'd slip out of the city that night with no one the wiser.

* * *

"Oh, I'm so sorry, sir!" the page gasped as he picked himself up from his stumble. "Here, let me help you."

The man looked to be about half Uncle Q'Orval's age, and he gave the page a kind smile. "I appreciate that, but you don't have to. What brings you to the Archives today?"

"His Majesty sent me for the copy of the old alliance," the page answered.

The man blinked. "Well then, you absolutely will not help me gather these books. We mustn't keep His Majesty waiting. One of the archivists at the circulation desk will help you find it."

"Are you sure, sir?" the page asked. "I feel rather poorly that I caused you extra work."

The man smiled again. "I'm fine. The books are fine. As long as you weren't hurt, it's okay. Besides, my wife says I don't get enough exercise anyway."

"Well...if you're sure," the page said and, at the man's nod, dashed to the circulation desk.

* * *

Everyone in the room looked up when the doors opened. The page hurried inside, clutching a scroll case as if his life hung on its care. He approached the table and held out his prize to the king.

"Your Majesty, I have the copy of the old alliance here," the page said.

Terris smiled, accepting the scroll case. "Thank you, young man. Have a seat and go back to your studies. I'll call if I need you again."

"Yes, Your Majesty," the page replied, snapping to attention once more before returning to his seat.

Terris turned and offered the scroll case to Gavin, who accepted it. Gavin wasted no time removing the scroll from the case and started reading. It took some time to wade through the flowery prose of the document that bound six societies in mutual defense and assistance, but Gavin eventually found the passage he sought. The alliance did indeed contain verbiage granting members in good standing the right to seek aid from other members. The members being asked for aid were under no compulsion to provide it, but the treaty guaranteed a hearing at least.

Gavin smiled as he read it and shifted his attention to Terris, saying, "So...want to go to Qar'Zhosk with me?"

The room erupted in pandemonium. Every councilor spoke, trying to talk over everyone else. The chaos lasted for a few heartbeats until Terris clapped his hands and called for silence.

"I will not have such chaos and disregard for order and discipline," Terris remarked, not quite glaring at his advisers. "Let's try that again, and this time, act like the adults I thought you were."

The councilors all looked to each other, as if trying to decide who would speak by telepathy or something.

"Your Majesty, attempting to go to Qar'Zhosk is a death sentence," one finally spoke. "No one has survived going to the dracon lands since they withdrew from the world."

"That's not entirely true," Gavin countered. "I, and those traveling with me, went to Qar'Zhosk on our way to Vushaar. As a matter of fact, the Crown Princess and my former apprentices were named *Drak'Thir*; I only agreed to go to Qar'Zhosk if they were protected. Come to think of it, one of my current apprentices is a dracon. She said she sought me out after our visit."

The councilors gaped at Gavin, and it took considerable willpower for him to keep his expression neutral when he really wanted to grin.

"Terris," Gavin continued, "if you are willing to ask the dracons for help, I guarantee your safety. I understand the King of Vushaar cannot go anywhere unaccompanied; you can bring Roth Thatcherson and one other. Between the three of us, your safety will not be in question."

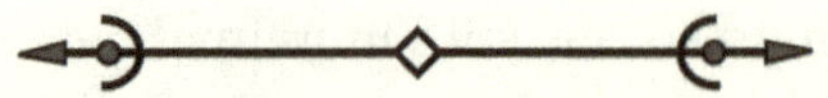

CHAPTER 8

Terris, Roth, and a Cavalier Gavin didn't know met him in the palace courtyard. It was a bright day, the sun shining down from a cloudless sky. Cavaliers along the fringes of the courtyard stopped what they were doing to watch.

"Are you ready?" Gavin asked.

Terris nodded. "You're sure they won't kill us? I know that sounds a bit cowardly, but I'm enjoying having my daughter back. I'd like more time with her."

Gavin shook his head. "They won't harm even a hair on your head."

"Let's go, then," Terris replied.

"We'll arrive at the gate to the Qar'Zhosk tunnel," Gavin explained. "Once we obtain permission or welcome or whatever you want to call it, I'll open another gateway to the facilities where they house visiting merchants. It will be a short walk to the Council of Clans from there."

Gavin focused his thoughts on the gate where they had gone into the Godswall Mountains, picturing it in as great detail as he could and pushing every other thought from his mind. His intent complete, he invoked the Word, "*Paedryx.*"

A sapphire archway of raw energy rose out of the courtyard flag-stones, and Gavin heard startled gasps from the watching Cavaliers. The moment the archway rose to its full height, the interior flashed and showed the gate to the Qar'Zhosk tunnel.

"Shall we go, then?" Gavin asked, leading the way himself.

Not even ten heartbeats later, Gavin, Terris, and the two Cavaliers stood about fifty feet from the tunnel gate. As soon as Gavin released the power holding the gateway, the arch vanished in a flare of light.

As Gavin traversed the short distance to the gate, Terris gaped as he looked all around him, his expression very close to that of a child filled with wonder. "That was amazing. Roth, how long would it take to travel here on horse?"

"Over two weeks with the siege, Your Majesty," Roth replied. "We would have to leave via the south gate and circle north once we made it out of the Sarnath Hills. If we could use the north gate, it would take maybe a week."

"And we just came here as easily as crossing the hall to another room," Terris remarked.

Roth smiled. "This is nothing, Your Majesty. I was not prepared at all for suddenly being in the palace courtyard when we had been standing in the wasteland of a slaver base with a company of Ivarson's army bearing down on us. There was no archway, that time. He just moved us—slaves and all—to the palace courtyard. And that was *after* wiping out over two hundred slavers."

Terris shifted his attention to the distant figure of Gavin speaking with the gate guards. "Just how powerful do you think he is...really?"

Roth shrugged. "I'm sure I don't know, Your Majesty. I knew Marcus, and the way Lillian and the others talk about Gavin lead me to think the only difference between them is that Gavin hasn't yet developed the instinctive awareness of his power that Marcus had."

Gavin turned from the dracons at the gate and looked at Terris and his party, gesturing for them to approach. Terris nodded once and began walking.

"It seems you will not be the first Vushaari to petition the Council of Clans," Gavin said as Terris arrived.

"Oh?" Terris asked. "How so?"

"It seems Kiri's uncle arrived yesterday on a mission to explore possible trading between Claymark and the dracons," Gavin said.

One of the guards regarded Terris and his Cavaliers for a moment before saying, "You and your party have been granted access to Qar'Zhosk on the recommendation of the Scion."

"The Scion?" Terris asked.

"Yes," Gavin said. "They insist on calling me the Scion of the Liberator, even though I've explained at least three times that I'm not a direct descendant of Kirloth."

"You are of his blood, however distantly related," the lead guard replied. "Plus, you saved our homes by repairing our sky. Some think we do not award you sufficient honor."

Gavin sighed. "I've also been over *that* with the Council of Clans, too. I don't want honor or accolades. Your people needed help, and I was able to provide it. I enjoy helping where I can; that's sufficient payment for me."

The lead guard grunted as if he had his own opinions but saw no reason to continue the discussion.

"Any problem if I use a gateway to take us directly to the city?" Gavin asked.

The lead guard shook his head. "No. You are always welcome in Qar'Zhosk."

* * *

GAVIN RESISTED the urge to grin at how Terris and his Cavaliers rubbernecked like tourists while they walked the streets of Qar'Zhosk. In truth, it didn't require much effort, as it seemed everyone wanted to greet him and offer thanks for all he'd done for them.

"Some of this construction looks reminiscent of dwarven architecture," Terris remarked as they walked.

"I'm sure it is," Gavin said. "This was originally a dwarven outpost, before the freed dracons needed a home. The buildings that look most dwarven probably date from before the arrival of the dracons."

They soon approached an open-air forum with a cupola that served as the meeting space for the Council of Clans. Once Gavin led them into the space, they found Paul Claymark in discussions with the Council. Paul gaped at the sight of Gavin beside his king for a few moments before dropping to one knee before his monarch.

"It is good you have returned to us," the ancient Councilor remarked. "Whispers of a very disturbing matter have reached us, and we cannot continue our discussions with Claymark until those whispers have been marked as truth or lies. Those whispers involve you."

"Oh?" Gavin asked, raising his eyebrows.

A number of the Councilors nodded, and Xask spoke, "Yes. We have received word that Patriarch Claymark banned you from his lands after you saved his life, his family's life, and the lives of his dependents. We chose not to raise the matter with his son, as it would be in his own best interests for those whispers to be false. What say you, Scion?"

Gavin heaved a sigh. "Yes, they're true. We found five Roensil agents among Claymark's guard force. We still had most of the country to travel, and I didn't think we could afford the knowledge that Kiri still lived getting out. I killed them. Natan Claymark was rather unhappy about that, and once he and those who depended on him were safe, he told me never to return to his lands. I ensured my people knew that the Claymarks were now fully hands-off, and we would do nothing further to protect them."

By the time Gavin finished speaking, several Councilors growled or hissed. They stood and gathered in a tight circle, speaking their own language as they discussed. The various gestures Gavin saw suggested none were happy. The sidebar took so long that Gavin almost wanted to ask they greet Terris as a matter of courtesy, but considering what they were discussing, he thought it would be better to hold off on that. There was no reason to put Terris in the middle of things.

At last, the Councilors returned to their seats. The ancient one spoke:

"Claymark, we cannot even fathom the audacity and callous rudeness your father displays in such treatment of Kirloth on one hand while entreating us for trade with the other. Unless and until the matter is rectified and Kirloth is provided appropriate reparations for the dishonor committed by your family, the sun will grow cold and dark before the dracons have anything further to do with you. Indeed, were it not for the respect and esteem in which we hold Kirloth, you would return with a declaration of war upon your family and holdings. More than one of us argued that our response should be your corpse, a written note optional.

"Leave. Leave now, and flee our lands as if your very life depends upon it. Do not sleep until you are safely inside Vushaar once more; you will not awaken otherwise. Serve our notice to your father that anyone wearing Claymark colors entering our lands will die until this matter is resolved, no matter the reason for the trespass."

Paul didn't move, but he did glance at his king. The Councilors hissed again, almost as one.

"Do not expect Kirloth to save you," the ancient Councilor almost growled, his voice harsh. "These lands are *dracon* sovereignty. Leave. Now. Or die. The choice is yours."

"You should go, Paul," Terris said, "and tell Natan to expect a summons from me."

Paul Claymark pushed himself to his feet and almost sprinted out of the forum.

The Councilors watched him go for several moments before directing their attention to Gavin.

"Thank you for clarifying that matter for us, Scion," the ancient Councilor said.

"Personally, I feel your response is a bit harsh," Gavin replied. "Like I said, I instructed my people to leave them alone, and I feel confident the decision would've caught up with the Claymarks sooner or later...with no actions on my part or anyone else's."

"Perhaps," Xask remarked, "but it was the response honor

demanded of us. Patriarch Claymark needs to learn his actions have consequences. No one stands alone. But this unpleasantness has taken too much of our time. You must have come to us for a reason."

Gavin chuckled. "I did, but I'm not sure that now is the best time to discuss it."

"Nonsense," the ancient Councilor countered. "Do not presume that our displeasure and anger with Claymark in any way carries over to you."

"Oh, it isn't that," Gavin said. "This man on my right is Terris Muran, King of Vushaar and Natan Claymark's son-in-law. Kiri—the young lady who was traveling with me when we met—is Natan's granddaughter."

The ambient temperature seemed to drop a little bit as the Councilors regarded Terris. The silence extended past the point of being ominous, and Gavin noticed Roth and his associate checking their surroundings out of the corner of their eyes.

"And just why should we entertain anything he has to say?" a Councilor asked.

"Well, for one thing," Gavin answered, "he had no knowledge of Claymark's actions, unless Kiri told him. I consider the matter to be between Natan Claymark and myself and, frankly, a non-issue. And second, Terris Muran is a good and honorable man who cares about being the best king he can be for his people. Third, it was *my* idea to ask for your help."

"You would stand with him even after his father-in-law and largest grain producer treated you so?" Xask asked.

"Yes, I would. He's good people."

The Councilors looked to each other for a few moments. The ancient Councilor asked, "What aid do you seek?"

Gavin began, "There's—"

"With all respect, Scion," the ancient dracon interrupted, "it's time for the Vushaari king to speak. We will hear his request out of respect for you, but that is as far as you can carry him."

If Terris objected to their perception that Gavin carried him, it didn't show. He squared his shoulders and said, "There is a large army encamped on the northern wall of the capital. It has been besieging the city, but so much of their force was slaves that it has devolved into little more than chaos with the destruction of the slave marks. Most of the Vushaari Army is involved in hunting bandits that thought the civil war provided an opportunity, and to be honest, I'm concerned for the former slaves' safety in the siege camp. I hoped to ask if you might be able to help us restore order to the camp."

The Councilors once more moved into a circle and discussed the matter in their language. This time, their deliberations were far briefer.

"We would be willing to assist you, were it not for the Claymark matter," the ancient Councilor announced. "Perhaps, it is short-sighted of us, but we hold the Scion in such regard and esteem that it feels beyond wrong to help Vushaar in any way while Claymark's dishonor remains. Once that is resolved, if you still need our help, communicate the resolution to us. If we find it appropriate, you shall have us."

"I don't want to seem like a villain here," Gavin said, "but what of your obligations under the old alliance? The siege camp existed because the Necromancer of Skullkeep manipulated people within Vushaar to attempt a coup. To me, that seems like something the alliance should cover."

"There may be some validity to what you say," the ancient Councilor allowed, "but the old alliance has been little more than an historical footnote for centuries. The Claymark of a thousand years ago would never have dishonored your family, Scion, and that Patriarch Natan did it so readily speaks to the rot that has become inherent in our societies. If Vushaar chooses to demand our assistance under the terms of the old alliance without addressing Natan Claymark's trespass, it would force us to convene a Grand Moot to discuss remaining a signatory to said alliance."

Gavin hoped his reaction didn't show on his face. He hadn't realized the dracons would throw down a gauntlet like that, and even more, he knew they were serious. Gavin could tell they felt *very* strongly about what Claymark had done.

"I wouldn't presume to try forcing your compliance with my wishes," Terris replied. "For one thing, it's not good diplomacy, and for a second, I'd rather have a chance at our peoples being friends, if at all possible. I give you my word that I will resolve the matter of Natan Claymark."

"Very well," the ancient Councilor said. "We will await word of your resolution."

* * *

THE COUNCILORS SAT in silence for a time after Gavin left with Terris and his Cavaliers. At last, one spoke.

"We should call a Grand Moot," a Councilor said.

"Yes," the ancient Councilor replied.

Xask frowned and asked, "Why? We should give the Vushaari king the chance to make this right."

"Not for the matter of Claymark," the ancient Councilor countered. "The Scion wore the gold robe. Bellos has at last named the Archmagister. It may be time for us to end our seclusion."

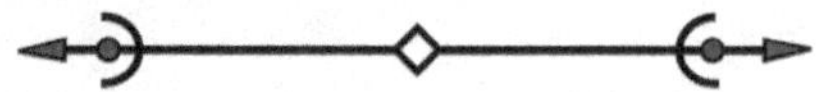

CHAPTER 9

K iri's brow furrowed as she approached her father's study. She knew he'd gone somewhere with Gavin but hadn't realized he had returned. In truth, his summons was a bit more urgent than normal, and that worried her. She stepped into her father's study and stopped. He looked...weary. What had Gavin done?

"You sent for me, Father?" Kiri asked as she approached.

Terris nodded and sighed. "Have a seat. There's a matter we need to discuss."

Kiri resisted the urge to work her lower lip between her teeth. Something *had* happened with Gavin. Still, she moved quickly to the chair beside her father and sat.

"What is it?" she asked. "What has Gavin done?"

"Nothing, actually," Terris answered, giving a half-hearted chuckle. "He was actually rather adult about the whole affair. The dracons, on the other hand, were rather incensed."

"I'm sorry, Father," Kiri said. "I don't understand."

Terris seemed to shake himself mentally before explaining, "Gavin and I went to ask the dracons for aid in policing up the former siege camp. Your uncle, Paul, was already there; apparently, Natan sent him to explore the possibility of trading with the dracons. Kiri, did your grandfather really ban Gavin from his lands?"

Kiri's eyes shot wide as she connected the dots in an instant. "The dracons knew?"

"Somehow," Terris said, nodding. "They did not hide the fact that it was only their respect and esteem for Gavin that stopped them from declaring war on Natan for his insult. A few of the Councilors even advocated sending back Paul's corpse as their response."

Kiri gaped and raised her hand cover her mouth.

Terris merely nodded. "Yes, I had a front-row seat to what I'm sure is one of the messiest situations I've ever faced as King of Vushaar. I'm going to have to discuss this with Natan. The dracons were prepared to leave the old alliance if I had tried to use it to force their assistance with this matter over Natan hanging out there." Terris heaved another sigh. "Kiri, I know you love your grandfather, but he has always been a cantankerous reactionary, and very rigid in his beliefs and values. My father never made much noise about it, but he told me privately that it was almost as much Natan's rigidity that created the Claymark/Roensil feud as Roensil's actions. If Roensil hadn't had anti-Crown leanings, there's a good chance my father would have sided with him in the dispute. I'm worried most about Paul, though; the dracons told him to flee their lands and not sleep. It's what...four, maybe five, days to the Vushaari border from Qar'Zhosk?"

"About that, I think," Kiri replied. "Father, I'm sure Lillian would help us get to Paul and get him out of dracon lands before he falls asleep in the saddle or founders his horse."

"Is it really a good idea to ask her? What if she hears why and agrees with the dracons?"

Kiri smiled. "Lillian's not like that, Father. Besides, she's much more diplomatically aware. Even if she personally agrees with the dracons, she'll see the value in preventing an incident with such implications."

Terris nodded. "Go ask her, please. If she's amenable, bring her to me, and I'll ask her for help."

* * *

KIRI FOUND Lillian sitting by herself in a corner of the dining hall set aside for palace guests. It wasn't quite time for the midday meal, but Lillian seemed to be using the space as a place to work. Papers covered almost the entire section of the table where she sat.

Lillian looked up when Kiri approached and smiled her welcome, saying, "Hello. How are you doing?"

Kiri realized that she'd been a sobbing mess the last time they'd spoken, and she offered Lillian a soft smile. "I'm better. Lillian, forgive me for disturbing you, but Father and I have a matter in which we could use your help."

Lillian nodded once and started gathering her papers. "Do we have enough time for me to drop these off in my suite?"

"Yes, absolutely," Kiri replied. "Thank you for dropping everything to help us."

"Not at all," Lillian answered. "It's what friends do."

SOON, Lillian sat across from Kiri and her father in the King's study. Terris had just finished bringing her up to speed on the situation, and she really hoped she didn't look as poleaxed as she felt. She never would have guessed the dracons would manage to find out about what Natan Claymark had said.

"Well, if they really did tell Paul not to sleep in their lands, they meant every word of it," Lillian said at last. "They're not ones for dissembling."

"I know," Kiri said. "That's why I thought of you. Do you think you remember Paul well enough to open a gateway to him and get him out of dracon lands before they kill him?"

Lillian grimaced. "I honestly don't know. Maybe? Gavin could use your thoughts and focus on your uncle, like when he teleported all of us to the courtyard."

Kiri glanced at her father, her lower lip held between her teeth for a moment, and said, "I'd rather not get Gavin involved in this anymore. It's nothing against him. I just don't know how my grandfather will react, but having Gavin involved won't help."

"Yes, I can see that," Lillian agreed. "I know Gavin basically swore off your grandfather. He wouldn't lift a finger now if the man was on fire. It's not that Gavin wants something bad to happen to him, just that he's largely indifferent to him now. I guess the thing to try is a scrying sphere. If I can scry your uncle, I can open a gateway to him."

"Would you please?" Kiri asked.

Lillian nodded, her soft smile returning. "Of course, Kiri. I'm happy to help."

She closed her eyes and focused on her memories of Kiri's uncle. Admittedly, those memories were a bit hazy, but they were the best she had. Once she felt her focus was sufficient, she drew a breath and invoked the Word, "*Klaepos.*"

A sphere of space in front of Lillian began shimmering and rippling, much like the surface of a still pond into which a stone has been thrown. The intensity of the rippling increased rapidly, until— in a flash of light—the sphere became a window overlooking a distant stretch of road. Paul Claymark was driving his horse at a heightened pace, though the pace was one a well-bred horse could maintain for hours, and he glanced behind him three times in the short time Lillian, Kiri, and Terris watched.

Without missing a beat, Terris stood and walked to his desk. He grabbed a piece of parchment with his left hand while dipping a quill into an inkwell with his right. He wrote quickly on the parchment, dripped sealing wax beside his signature, and pressed his signet ring into the wax as it cooled. He handed the parchment to Lillian.

"Please deliver this summons to Paul, asking him to accompany you back to the palace," Terris said.

Lillian stood and nodded once, accepting the parchment. "Yes, Your Majesty."

Lillian's brow furrowed as she concentrated on the image of the man in the scrying sphere. After a few moments, she took a deep breath, invoked the Word "*Paedryx,*" and vanished.

* * *

LILLIAN STEPPED out from behind a tree as Paul Claymark approached. She saw his surprise at seeing her, and he reined in his horse.

"Lady Mivar?" Paul asked. "What are you doing here?"

Lillian handed him the parchment, and Paul read it.

"I see," he said. "Well, we probably shouldn't keep His Majesty waiting."

"You might want to dismount," Lillian said. "Horses don't always handle manifestations of the Art well."

Paul nodded and did as she suggested. Once he was standing beside her with a firm grip on the reins, Lillian focused her thoughts on the palace courtyard and once more invoked the Word that formed the basis for the modern Teleportation spell. An arch of crackling energy rose up out of the ground, and once it was tall enough to accommodate the horse, it flashed and became a gateway.

* * *

TERRIS AND KIRI were waiting for them when Lillian led Paul into the study. When they reached a respectful distance, Paul knelt and bowed his head.

"Oh, get up, Paul," Terris almost growled. "Lillian has my permission to address me by name, so let's put aside all the royal playacting and discuss how to fix the mess your father created."

Paul flinched as he stood. "That...will be difficult, I fear. Father was incredibly offended that Gavin killed those men."

"And his granddaughter's safety meant so little to him?" Terris shot back. "Those five men could've had the whole countryside stirred up looking for Kiri. Do you think for even a moment that *I* wouldn't have killed them to keep her safe?"

"Your Majesty, I—"

Terris sighed. "For gods' sake, Paul, enough with the 'Majesties;' it's just us here. I have a summons for your father, which you will deliver. Lillian will take you home and bring you both back, and neither you nor your father will go home until we've sorted this out. We do not have the manpower to defend ourselves if the dracons decide to go to war over this, and what do you think the response would be if word reached the Society of *why* the dracons declared war against us? Do you think they'd just sit by and not want their own pound of flesh over the insult to their Archmagister?"

"If I may," Lillian interjected, "Gavin considers it a non-issue, and that means neither the Society nor Tel would get involved; they would need his approval."

"That doesn't mean individual partisans wouldn't hop the fence," Terris replied. "You are absolutely correct that Gavin could keep the Society and Tel from getting involved on the whole, but he can't control every single arcanist."

"It's a very busy time for the farms, Terris," Paul replied. "I don't know that Father will leave."

Terris lifted his eyes to lock Paul's gaze. "He can come with you and Lillian as my friend and Kiri's grandfather, or he can come when I send Cavaliers. But he will come regardless. There is too much going on right now to allow this to spiral into a major incident. You're going to have to explain it to him, Paul."

"I'll see to it he comes, Terris," Paul agreed.

"Good," Terris said. He turned toward his desk, retrieved a piece of parchment sealed with wax under his signet, and extended it to Paul. "This is an official summons. Don't use it unless you have to, because we both know that would just have him arrive with his hackles up. That won't help, no matter how you look at it."

"Can we bring Mother if she wants to come?" Paul asked.

"Of course," Terris answered, nodding. "I haven't seen her in years, and I'm sure Kiri would love to see her, too."

Paul nodded, and Terris returned it as he watched Lillian lead him out of the study. After the door closed behind them, Terris shifted his attention to Kiri.

"I am not looking forward to this conversation," Terris admitted. "Your grandfather has always blamed me for your mother's death."

"It wasn't your fault," Kiri countered.

Terris shrugged. "He argues she'd probably still be alive if she hadn't married me. She wouldn't have been Queen."

"Well, I guess he'll just have to let that go," Kiri replied. "You didn't make Mother marry you, at least not that I've ever heard, and I remember how happy we were. Besides, if she hadn't married you, he wouldn't have me. It'll be all right."

"That doesn't mean this will be in anyway pleasant, though," Terris said. "All right. Enough grousing and melancholy. Let's plan how we'll handle it."

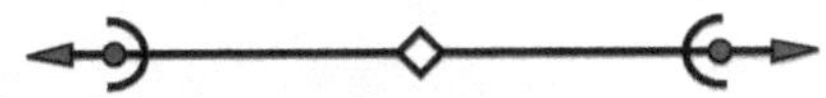

CHAPTER 10

Paul Claymark led Lillian into his father's office, where they found him at his desk surrounded by farm foremen. A massive map occupied most of the desktop's surface. Natan's father had paid handsomely to have as accurate a representation of the family holdings as possible, and as Natan added to the family holdings, he paid for updated maps.

"I'm not sure Field Number Four up near Stiller's Cave has laid fallow long enough, Mr. Claymark," one of the foremen was saying as Paul and Lillian approached.

Natan grunted. "If it hasn't, what does that do to our production schedule for the coming year? I thought we needed that field to meet our goals if we rotate Number Three out to a fallow season."

Now, Lillian saw Mrs. Claymark sitting at Natan's elbow, her quill scratching. She periodically glanced from her parchment to the map and back, before working the quill some more.

"I think we'll still have enough of a surplus to meet all our goals and commitments," Mrs. Claymark said, her eyes roving over the parchment. "We won't have quite as much leeway in case of a diseased field or some such, but with Roensil out of the picture, we don't need to worry about so-called bandits pillaging our fields."

Paul and Lillian arrived at the fringe of the group surrounding the desk, and Lillian saw that Mrs. Claymark's parchment was nothing but figures and math. In fact, Mrs. Claymark was the first to notice the new arrivals.

"Paul? I thought you went to Qar'Zhosk. Is everything well?" Mrs. Claymark asked.

Paul glanced at the foremen before saying, "We should discuss that. There were some unexpected developments."

Natan looked up and met Paul's gaze. His eyes narrowed, and he asked, "Unexpected developments?"

"Yes, Father...unexpected developments." With that, Paul handed the folded summons sealed with Terris's personal signet to his father.

Natan accepted the parchment and didn't even look at the seal as he unfolded it. He pulled his eyes away from his son and looked at the document in his hands, his jaw clenching as he read it.

"We will have to resume this discussion at a later date," Natan said. "It seems I have been summoned to the capital. Lady Mivar has agreed to expedite our journey."

Mrs. Claymark gasped. "Whatever for, Natan? Did he say what's going on?"

"He did not," Natan replied. "But on a personal note, he indicated you were welcome to come as well if you wanted to visit our granddaughter."

"Do you have any idea how long this visit will be?" Mrs. Claymark asked.

Paul and Lillian glanced at each other before Paul answered, "I really have no way of knowing."

"Very well," Mrs. Claymark replied. "Come along, Natan. We'll pack for three days. That will keep the baggage manageable."

* * *

LILLIAN'S first view stepping through the gateway to the palace courtyard was Kiri standing on the palace steps. She didn't grin or smile. She beamed. The moment the gateway faded, she ran forward and threw her arms around her grandparents. Both Natan and his wife let out little *oofs* as they arrested some of Kiri's forward momentum.

"Should the Crown Princess be acting like this in public?" Natan managed to ask.

"Don't care," Kiri countered as she buried her face in her grandparents' shoulders. "I spent two long, brutal years thinking I'd never see you or anyone I loved ever again. If some fop decides to comment, whoever it is had better be godlike in their job and not have an immediate replacement, or they'll join the embassy in Kyndrath."

"Now, Kiri," her grandmother began in a reproachful tone, "is that really the way the future Queen of Vushaar should act?"

Kiri broke off the hug and stepped back just enough to meet her grandmother's eyes. She took a deep breath before saying, "No, probably not, but I was a granddaughter long before I was Crown Princess." Her grandparents each gave her a smile with indulgent undertones. "Yes, yes...I was Crown Princess the moment I was born. I *learned* to be a granddaughter long before I learned to be Crown Princess. Better?"

"I think we'll have to accept it," Mrs. Claymark answered. "Do you know why your grandfather was summoned?"

Kiri's expression clamped down into complete neutrality. "I should let Father discuss that with Grandfather. He's waiting in his study. I'll escort you."

AFTER DELIVERING her grandfather to the door of her father's study, Kiri swept her grandmother off to the royal apartments, almost pulling the older woman into her suite. In no time, they were comfortably ensconced in Kiri's sitting room.

"Now that we're alone," Mrs. Claymark said, "why did your father summon Natan? He's never done that before."

Kiri looked down at the floor, working her lower lip between her teeth.

"Kiri," her grandmother said after several moments of silence, "you're starting to scare me."

"Gavin took Father to Qar'Zhosk to ask the dracons for aid under the terms of the old alliance. The aid involves rounding up the former siege camp outside and protecting any former slaves."

"Wait...*former* slaves?"

Kiri grinned. "Didn't you notice I'm missing something, Grans?"

Kiri watched her grandmother's eyes go to her left shoulder and saw her jaw slacken just a bit as she processed the lack of a slave mark.

"How?"

"Gavin," Kiri replied, shrugging. "I don't know exactly how he did it, but he removed every slave mark, ruined every brand, and killed anyone who had ever used a brand...all in one go."

"In the capital?"

Kiri shook her head. "Not just the capital, Grans...the world. There are no more slaves or slavers. Anywhere."

Mrs. Claymark paled. "By the gods...he really *is* Kirloth."

"He's the Archmagister of Tel now, too."

Mrs. Claymark gaped, and Kiri nodded.

After a few moments, Mrs. Claymark said, "So, back to the summons?"

Kiri winced. "Well, the dracons have learned that Grandfather banned Gavin from the family lands. They asked Gavin for confirmation, and from what Father said, Gavin tried telling them it was between him and Grandfather. The dracons didn't seem to care and pressed for an answer. Gavin confirmed it was true, and they are not happy. Father said more than a few wanted to send Uncle Paul's corpse back as their response...along with a declaration of war."

Mrs. Claymark gasped. "At least your father talked them out of it."

"He didn't," Kiri replied, shaking her head. "Gavin did. And from what Father told me, it wasn't so much that he talked them out of it as they knew he would never support it. But Father had no doubts it was solely because of Gavin that Uncle Paul left Qar'Zhosk alive. He said the dracons were ready to leave the old alliance if he tried to use the treaty to force their help with this hanging over everyone. The dracons also said that anyone wearing

Claymark colors who enters their lands will not return until this is resolved."

Mrs. Claymark sagged against the back of her seat. "Thank the gods we've always kept that buffer between our fields and the border. We can't afford to lose hands right now over border disputes, with everything else that's happened. This is such a mess. You know how well your grandfather admits he's wrong about something."

"That's just it," Kiri countered. "Gavin doesn't feel Grandfather's wrong. For that matter, Gavin doesn't care at all. He tried telling the dracons it was none of their business, but they wouldn't listen. He... uhm...he tried explaining that he'd informed his people that all Claymark holdings and people were no longer to be protected after Grandfather's decision, but the dracons didn't care about that, either."

Mrs. Claymark blinked. "Protected? What does that mean?"

"If Grandfather hadn't done what he did," Kiri replied, "the two of you and all your holdings and people would've been...well, for lack of a better term, protected by Gavin's people. Like if Roensil's assault started again, Gavin's people would inform him while doing all they could to hold it off until Gavin responded. I don't know a whole lot about Gavin's people, but I can't say what I do know. I know enough, and I'm not about to break that confidence."

* * *

TERRIS SAW the door open and forced himself not to let out a heavy sigh. This was not going to be pleasant, not at all. Q'Orval sat in an armchair to his right, near the hearth, and they had positioned a third chair to face them.

Natan stepped into the room, and as he approached, Terris gestured to the empty chair. Natan eased himself into the chair and didn't quite glare at Terris. Things had been strained at best between them since Rionne's death. Natan blamed Terris for it, arguing she wouldn't have been targeted by an assassin if she hadn't been Queen. Terris had never had the heart to tell him that the target hadn't been his daughter. No, the man had been sent to kill Kiri. At least, that was what the papers in his belt pouch had indicated.

"Very well, Terris. I'm here," Natan said, almost growled. "What do you want?"

"There's no good way to say this, Natan," Terris replied. "The dracons learned of how you treated Gavin, and they wanted to send your son's corpse back to you as their declaration of war because of it."

"If those scaly bastards want a war..." Natan's voice trailed off as he frowned. "Why didn't they? Send his corpse, I mean."

"Gavin," Terris replied and enjoyed seeing Natan flinch, though he hid it well. "They didn't do it because they knew Gavin would not approve. And with Gavin right there, there was a good chance he would've brought down Qar'Zhosk if that's what it took to save your son. He's the Archmagister of Tel now, also."

Natan reacted as if physically slapped. For all of his crotchety contrariness, he was no fool. He knew how it would look if word spread that he'd banned the Archmagister of Tel from his lands and given how most of the populace regarded the boy, it wouldn't be long before they made their opinion of his conduct known.

"I really stepped in a pile of cow dung, this time, haven't I?" Natan said at last, sighing.

"It wasn't one of your better decisions, no," Terris agreed.

Terris watched Natan while he stared at the floor. Finally, he lifted his head and met his king's eyes. Natan took a deep breath and asked, "How do we fix it? *Can* we fix it?"

Terris nodded. "I think we can, but I think we need to include someone else in the discussion."

Terris turned to Q'Orval and nodded. The majordomo pushed himself to his feet and left the study.

"By the way," Terris said, filling the silence while they waited, "did you notice Kiri's missing her slave mark?"

Natan blinked. "She is? How did you manage that?"

Terris smiled. "Gavin. He removed all the slave marks every-where. I don't know how he did it. Beyond the marks, every brand turned into blackened, twisted metal, and everyone who'd ever used a slave brand died. Slavery is over."

"He could wipe us off the face of the world for what I did, couldn't he?" Natan remarked. "Why didn't he?"

Terris shrugged. "Knowing Gavin, I'd say he didn't care. Your decision didn't threaten his friends in any way, and it didn't interfere with bringing Kiri home. And if we're honest, it's not like being banned from your lands was any great hardship on him. Beyond that, Kiri wouldn't have liked it, so with all of that combined, it doesn't surprise me at all that he just walked away."

The study door opened admitting Q'Orval and Gavin. Terris felt a bit surprised that Gavin wasn't wearing his gold robes. Terris and Natan both stood as they approached, and Terris realized the study only had three chairs.

"Forgive me, Gavin," Terris said. "I'll have another chair brought at once."

Gavin grinned. "No need." He placed his hand on the back of Natan's chair and invoked a Word, "*Nythraex*."

In the blink of an eye, a fourth chair sat facing the three, and it appeared to be a perfect replica of Natan's, who gaped.

"It'll disappear by morning," Gavin said, "but it'll do for now. I'm guessing you wanted to discuss the dracon matter."

"Yes," Terris answered, nodding as he gestured for everyone to sit.

Gavin almost flopped into his conjured seat, his expression shifting into a frown. "As far as I'm concerned, it's none of their business. The matter is between Natan and me, and quite frankly, I couldn't care less whether I'm banned from Claymark lands. It doesn't affect me at all."

"And it's not like Natan could enforce the ban if you decided to prove a point," Terris added.

Gavin shrugged. "Sure, if I wanted to be a bastard about it, I could walk through the gate to his manor house and dare him to make me leave. But again, what does that get me? I'm already on rocky enough shores with Kiri as it is; I don't need to add to the situation."

"Oh, so my reaction doesn't affect you?" Terris asked, his expression curling into a smile.

Gavin laughed. "Truth be told, any concern I have over how it would affect relations between Tel and Vushaar rank a distant third or fourth after Kiri's feelings on the matter. No offense, but I would like to ask your permission to propose one day. Hating the sight of me doesn't speak well for the odds of her agreeing."

"No," Terris agreed. "I don't imagine it would. So, how do we fix this?"

"I think we all need to go back to Qar'Zhosk," Gavin said after a couple moments. "We need to hash all this out with the Council of Clans."

"But Terris said they'd kill anyone wearing Claymark colors until this is resolved," Natan countered.

Gavin smirked. "I'd like to see them try to harm you while I'm around. If they won't see reason, that cavern of theirs isn't so structurally sound that I couldn't bring it down."

Terris locked eyes with Natan and said, "Told you."

"You would really kill all those people, just to keep me safe?" Natan asked.

"Depends on how far they force the issue," Gavin replied. "If I could get by with just eliminating the Councilors forcing the issue, I'd leave it at that, but if it comes to it, I'll go as far as I have to go to see you leave Qar'Zhosk alive and safe. That's what it means to be under my protection."

"You as the Archmagister?" Natan asked.

Gavin shook his head. "No. I would have done that long before Bellos convinced me to accept that particular albatross. When I offer someone my personal protection, that person is protected by *Kirloth*."

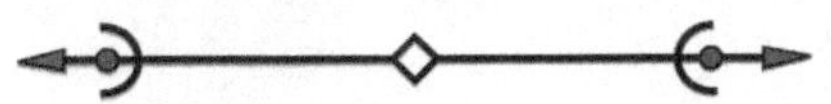

CHAPTER 11

Gavin led his party into the cupola that served as the Council of Clans' meeting space. Terris, Natan, Paul, Kiri, and Lillian clustered behind him. The councilors recognized Paul in short order, and they inferred Natan's identity from the family resemblance. Their reaction was not kind. Several councilors surged to their feet, baring teeth far too similar to dragons' teeth and flexing their clawed hands.

Gavin stepped forward to stand between the Council of Clans and his people. He squared his shoulders as if preparing for a fight before he spoke.

"If you would harm them, you must first face me."

That simple statement, delivered in a tone far closer to 'Kirloth' than Kiri or Lillian had heard in a while, set the councilors back. They all focused on him.

"You would defend those...humans?" one of the councilors asked, and Gavin suspected it was an act of will to refer to Natan and his son by species instead of epithet.

"I defend *any* who have accepted my protection," Gavin replied. "I *told* the lot of you what happened between Natan and myself was *our* business and no one else's. You chose to stick your snouts where they neither belonged, nor were needed, and we have come to settle this amicably...before the lot of you do something even more stupid than withdrawing from the world. Are we going to act like civilized beings, or will you force my hand and perpetuate Qar'Zhosk requiring a new Council?"

Xask was the first to speak. "We should talk."

Soon, the rest capitulated.

Gavin made eye contact with the Councilor from the Qar'Kirloth Clan and nodded his thanks.

"What would you have us do?" one of the councilors asked. "We've already made the proclamation regarding Claymark's conduct."

"Revoke it," Gavin replied, without missing a beat. "I'm not aware of anyone walking the face of this world who is infallible. You made a mistake. Admit it. Apologize to Terris and Natan and move on."

"Apology is a sign of weakness," the same councilor said, "and humans are weaker than dracons."

"I've never believed that nonsense," Gavin countered. "Apology is *not* a sign of weakness, and humans aren't as weak as you think. Dracons surpass humans in some regards, of course; it cannot be denied. But at the end of the day, each of us need the others. None of us are as strong as all of us."

"Claymark should not have done what he did," another councilor hissed. "It was an affront to all we hold dear."

"You people really need to adopt the concept of jurisdiction," Gavin said, sighing. "First, you have no authority in Vushaar, and if you try to push your values and beliefs on others, you will be stopped."

The most recent speaker seemed to sneer. "And just who will stop us?"

Gavin looked the dracon right in the eyes and held his gaze in silence for several moments before he spoke with utter certainty. "I will, and if you don't believe I can do it, you're a bigger fool than you seem."

The dracon seemed to realize where he stood and whom he faced, and he stepped back.

Gavin kept his eyes locked on the councilor for several more moments before he shifted his attention to the others. "You might want to keep an eye on him and his clan. He seems a bit more militant, and perhaps expansionist, than is good for your people. But back to the matter at hand.

"Second, Natan Claymark has every right to decide who visits his property, and to be quite honest, banning me from it matters less to me than the average annual rainfall of Vas Edrûn. It doesn't threaten me or anyone under my protection. It certainly didn't keep me from achieving my goal of returning Kiri home.

"Third, I understand your view of the matter; you feel your entire people owe my family a debt that you cannot hope to repay. Don't bother denying it; it's utterly apparent in every 'tradition' you've established regarding how your people interact with me or my family. There's just one thing none of you seem to understand. My mentor— the man you call the Liberator—didn't count debts. Debts, especially debts of this type you're trying to force on us, simply did not exist to him. I'm not exactly wild about your near-slavish reverence for me, either. People shouldn't be thanked or revered for doing what's right. That says such conduct is far too rare, and I don't like that. I would rather it was the rule than the exception. Now, I'm finished talking for a while. Get your scaly butts over here and work this out with Terris and Natan. No one's leaving until and unless we part as friends."

Gavin turned away and moved off to one side of the space, conjured a rather comfortable-looking chair, and flopped into it.

* * *

IT WAS SOMETIME LATER when Lillian drifted over to where Gavin was lounging, watching the two groups.

"You were a little rough with them," she said by way of greeting.

Gavin shrugged. "I didn't want to be, but they were quickly

approaching the point where I might have done something far less palatable. At least this way, they're talking, and no one's drawn blood yet."

"'None of us is as strong as all of us.' You really believe that?" Lillian asked.

"Yes, I do," Gavin replied, adding a nod for emphasis. "I believe it with every fiber of my being. I don't care what your motivations are. I don't care what you want out of life. As long as we can find some common ground—even one little thing we agree on—we can work together to build something better than what we currently have. It's when people—no matter their species—try forcing their views and beliefs on others, or deciding some people don't matter, that you start having problems."

Gavin shifted in his chair just enough to look directly at Lillian. He continued, "Take my situation, for example. Anyone who says returning to Tel is going to be all smiles and roses and cheers and happiness is delusional. And let's be honest, I'm going to turn what has been 'normal' on its ear. There are going to be countless people who hate what I'm going to do, and honestly, that's fine with me. I don't mind people not agreeing with me. I do mind people fighting me instead of working with me, instead of presenting their side of it to see what would work better for both of us. I don't like binary thinking, Lillian. The world is not black and white, us or them. I just have to figure out how to *show* everyone that."

"It's times like this, right now, where I'm not sure we deserve you," Lillian said, her voice so small and quiet Gavin almost didn't hear her.

Gavin chuckled and shook his head. "That's utter horseshit, too, Lillian. Don't you dare start thinking I'm perfect or anything like that. I can't do what needs doing alone, and I have no doubt there will be days I won't want to do any of it. I'll be relying heavily on my friends, those days. You, Kiri, Mariana, Braden, Wynn, Declan, and so many others are why I accepted Bellos's offer. I didn't want this job, but I didn't want anyone else to have to face it, either."

"Kirloth making the hard choices, so no one else has to?"

Gavin's eyes drifted to the other group and focused on Kiri specifically as he said, "Yeah, something like that."

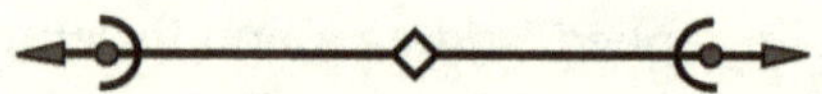

CHAPTER 12

With the dracons assisting, the rebels in the former siege camp soon had nowhere to go. Recognizing their situation, they surrendered en masse when Terris promised fair treatment and no executions. It soon became a matter of moving through the horde of people with Divination of Truth to identify those who had brutalized others. Gavin, his apprentices, and his friends made quick work of that. It took little more than two weeks.

* * *

TERRIS FOUND Gavin standing in the small garden his wife had loved tending. A slight breeze ruffled the leaves and flowers. Gavin turned when he heard someone walking across the gravel behind him.

"I'm not sure what's left for me to do here, Terris," Gavin said, almost sighing. "The rebellion is broken. Kiri is home where she belongs. The slave marks are no more."

Terris answered with a nod. "You're a good man, Gavin. I will never forget everything you've done for us. You should visit Kiri before you go."

"Yes, I suppose I should," Gavin replied and turned to go. He stopped. "Terris, if you should ever find yourself in a situation where you don't know who to trust, look for people with runic tattoos on the inside of their left wrists, just behind the joint. I think you'll recognize the glyph at the tattoo's center."

By the time Terris had processed what Gavin had told him, the new Archmagister was gone. The dominant thought in Terris's mind was that he'd seen Declan with a tattoo on his left wrist.

* * *

THE DOOR swung open moments after Gavin knocked. Several emotions flitted across Kiri's expression as she held the door to her suite with her left hand.

"So, it's that time, then?" she finally asked.

Gavin nodded. "I'm not sure what else there's left for me to do here, and as much as I'd rather not, I should probably get back to Tel Mivar. I did agree to do a job there."

Kiri's eyes roamed across the gold robe Gavin now wore. "Yes, I suppose you did."

Just then, a woman dressed as a maid and carrying a laundry basket came up behind Kiri.

"This is Lilly," Kiri said as she gestured for Gavin to step inside and clear the doorway. "She's one of my personal maids."

"It's nice to meet you, Lilly," Gavin said, noticing how the maid took extra effort to show Gavin the tattoo on her left wrist. He leaned close as she passed, and he whispered, "If any harm ever comes to her, you and your associates had better be dead."

"Of course, Milord," Lilly replied, also in a whisper, before going on her way.

Gavin closed the door behind him and turned to find Kiri eyeing him.

"What was that?" she asked.

"She's one of several people scattered throughout the palace like Declan," Gavin answered.

Kiri's eyes shot wide. "You mean—"

Gavin nodded. "Yes. I told your father to look for their tattoo if he ever finds himself not knowing who to trust. The same goes for you. If you ever need me, and I mean *right now*, tell one of them." Gavin took a deep breath and released it as a sigh. "Well, I'd better go. Take care of yourself, Kiri."

Gavin turned and reached for the door, but before he grasped the latch handle, Kiri took two quick steps and wrapped her arms around him. Gavin returned the embrace and held Kiri tightly for several moments. Then, he pulled away and was gone.

* * *

GAVIN ARRIVED in the palace courtyard, the bottomless semi-sentient satchel hanging from his left shoulder by its padded strap. Roth, Q'Orval, and Terris stood with his friends and apprentices. When Gavin approached, Roth stepped up and extended his right hand.

"Thank you for being such a friend to Vushaar," Roth said as Gavin accepted the handshake.

Gavin nodded. "You're welcome, Roth. Take care of Kiri, and help Terris as much as he'll let you."

Roth grinned. "I see you've figured out how it works around here."

Gavin returned Roth's grin with one of his own, and the Cavalier released Gavin's hand and stepped back. Gavin approached Terris, who held out his hand, and Gavin accepted it and gave a firm handshake.

"Gavin, I will be forever grateful for everything you've done," Terris said.

Gavin nodded. "You're welcome, Terris. I'm glad I was able to help."

Movement at Gavin's right drew their attention. Gavin saw Declan standing a couple feet away, lute in one hand and a packed duffle bag over his other shoulder.

"And it seems I'll be taking a bard off your hands," Gavin remarked.

Declan grinned. "You're the first Archmagister in six hundred years, Gavin. Do you honestly think I'd let you return to Tel without me there to record it?"

Gavin chuckled. "No, I suppose not." He turned back to Terris. "Take care of yourself. I'll be here if you need me."

"As will I," Terris replied.

Terris stepped back. Gavin approached his friends and three apprentices, Declan still at his side.

"Well, I think we've done as much damage as we can do here," Gavin said, his eyes sweeping across his friends. "Are you ready to go?"

Each one nodded. Lillian said, "We are."

Gavin regarded his apprentices. "Are you sure you want to go also?"

Xythe, Holly Walsh, and Fallon's nephew Jasper each nodded. Gavin knew that Jasper and Xythe had taken Holly under their wing, so to speak, helping the young girl get used to being away from home. Gavin made a mental note to speak with them and make sure they knew he appreciated it.

"Very well. In that case, I think it's time."

Grooms from the palace stables brought the mounts that had carried them from Tel, and Gavin took a moment to rub Jasmine's nose and neck when she pressed against Gavin's chest.

"I know. I've missed you too, girl," Gavin said, "but we're going home."

Mariana shook her head, still in disbelief over Gavin's relationship with Jasmine.

Once Gavin finished giving Jasmine some attention, he turned to an open area of the palace courtyard. He focused his mind on his memories of the College gate and invoked the Word, "*Paedryx.*"

The resonance of Gavin's power washed over every wizard present as a sapphire archway of crackling energy rose out of the paving stones. It was easily wide enough to drive a wagon through. When the archway rose higher than two horses standing atop each other, it flashed, creating a gateway to Tel Mivar.

Gavin turned and nodded once more to Terris and said, "Farewell, my friend. I'll be in touch."

Terris lifted his hand in reply as Gavin led his friends and apprentices into the central market of Tel Mivar.

CHAPTER 13

The last Grand Moot had occurred roughly six hundred years ago, when the dracons voted to withdraw from the world. Now? The Council of Clans for Qar'Zhosk had been face-to-face with the new Archmagister, and what's more, he was of the Liberator's House. An arcanist of House Kirloth occupied the office of Archmagister for the first time since the Founding. Faced with that new development, the councilors in Qar'Zhosk saw no other option than to call another Grand Moot. It would be the third in their entire history.

THE ANCIENT COUNCILOR from Qar'Zhosk stood to address the assembled councilors, and all chatter in the hall stilled.

"We called this Grand Moot to convey a startling revelation," he said. "Last week, Gavin Cross, the Scion of the Liberator who helped us fix our skies, returned to Qar'Zhosk. He returned wearing the gold robes of the Archmagister. We have since prayed to Bellos, and Bellos verified that Gavin Cross did indeed accept the position of Archmagister of Tel. Bellos further informed our clerics that He chose not to name another Archmagister following Bellock Vanlon's death, because Valthon counseled Him to wait. The naturals never offended the gods."

There were graveyards louder than the assembled councilors, as they processed Bellos's information. If that was indeed true—and no one would dare call Bellos a liar—it was the *dracons*, not the naturals, who had given offense. That was not so pleasant for them to contemplate.

The silence in the hall became awkward. One dracon stood, and the ancient councilor recognized her. "This offense *must* be corrected. It cannot be allowed to stand. Did Bellos provide any guidance on how we should do so?"

"Not that I am aware," the ancient councilor answered. "Should we interview the mystics who conversed with Bellos?"

Another councilor stood, the ancient recognizing him before he spoke. "It is not the gods' place to tell us how to correct our mistakes. My opinion is that we should reverse our decision to withdraw from the world and ask the assistance of this new Archmagister for insight on the best way or ways to correct our mistakes."

Councilors around the hall nodded as that councilor resumed his seat. Another stood, soon recognized by the ancient. "I petition the Grand Moot to vote. The petition is to repeal our decision to withdraw from the world and, afterward, seek the Archmagister's guidance in making right our error."

The councilor returned to his seat, and the ancient intoned, "The Grand Moot has been petitioned. Cast your vote in favor or against."

A podium stood in front of each councilor. The head of the podium had two inset stones: one white and one black. In all formal votes, touching the white stone indicated a vote in favor; touching the black voted against. The dracons had five cities that sent thirteen councilors each to the Grand Moot for a grand total of sixty-five voting attendees. In order for a petition to be binding across all dracon society, three out of four councilors in the assembly had to vote in favor of the petition, and no one could abstain. When the final vote was made, fifty-five councilors voted in favor.

The dracons would rejoin the world.

* * *

Many leagues north of Qar'Zhosk, another council met. The Necromancer of Skullkeep looked across the table at each of his lieutenants, though 'barely competent lackeys' might be a better description. The current speaker, rather vehemently, was advocating an outlandish idea.

"I'm telling you, Master," the mage insisted, "this is the perfect time to act! The new Archmagister hasn't presented him- or herself yet, and when they do, there will be all kinds of learning to do. Whoever it is will be unbalanced and not ready. We should attack Tel Mivar *now*! Taking Tel Mivar puts us that much closer to our goal."

"And just how well did that idea work out for Master's pawn and his friend Sivas?" another lieutenant—this one supposedly a wizard—asked, practically sneering. "By the gods, man, the current Kirloth was trained by the man who dueled Milthas. Do you honestly think any of us here, except Master, can stand against him? Especially if he rallies the Great Houses? You might yearn to commit suicide, but I do not."

"You're a coward," the mage replied. "It's common knowledge that Kirloth and his apprentices are in Vushaar. They left almost a year ago now."

"You are correct," the Necromancer said, entering the discussion and neglecting to add *for once*. "I have received word that Ivarson now resides in the king's dungeon and his army is broken. Our campaign to secure Vushaar has failed, and that failure rests on the shoulders of Kirloth."

Silence descended on the room as the lieutenants looked at one another.

A mage at the far end of the table ended the silence. "Master, how can we prepare to war against Lornithar now? Doesn't this mean our cause is in jeopardy?"

Silence stretched before the Necromancer answered, "The situation is no longer as clear as it once was. For now, we will consider what our next steps should be. Have your thoughts or recommendations ready for the next meeting in two weeks."

CHAPTER 14

Gavin blinked and then smiled at the hint of salt on the air as he stood in the courtyard of the College of the Arcane. It seemed like such a long time since they'd started their journey to Vushaar. Looking around, memories of his first few days here flitted through Gavin's mind. The place didn't *quite* feel like home, but it was far closer than any other place Gavin could think of.

"All right," Gavin said. "Let's get our mounts to the stables, then we'll see about getting Xythe, Holly, and Jasper settled in some rooms."

Lillian reached out to touch Gavin's upper arm, before pointing up in the sky and saying, "Gavin, look up there!"

Gavin stopped and looked where she was pointing. A massive castle hovered above Tel Mivar, easily hundreds of feet in the air. It was built on a piece of earth with the underside rounded and it gleamed in the sunlight. Gavin realized it was the other intense node of power he'd felt through his *skathos* during the time he'd been in Tel Mivar.

"That's the Citadel," Mariana gasped. "It hasn't been seen since the death of Bellock Vanlon, the last Archmagister."

Gavin merely nodded and turned toward the stables, leading

Jasmine by her reins. It took little time to reach the large collection of structures set slightly apart from the main grounds by a simple fence. Master Robillard stepped from the main structure as Gavin and his people approached.

"So, the rumors are true, then," Robillard remarked. "Bellos finally named an Archmagister."

Gavin nodded. "Yes, he somehow roped me into accepting."

Robillard laughed. "Oh, I daresay you'll do a better job about it than most, and no one can say you came up through the ranks and carry any intra-Society feuds or rivalries with you."

"There is that," Gavin replied.

Robillard nodded, saying, "Well, I won't keep you out here yammering on. Leave your horses with me, and I'll see that they receive the best care."

"By any chance," Gavin asked, "do you happen to have some leather cordage? Like something one would use to make a necklace?"

"I do believe I do."

"I'd like to buy two pieces from you," Gavin said.

Robillard shook his head. "I'd never dream of charging the Archmagister."

Gavin now shook his own head. "Nope. If you're not willing to sell it to me, I'll get it somewhere else. I'll not have anyone giving me stuff just because I'm the Archmagister, when they would've sold it to me as Kirloth."

The stable-master sighed. "So be it. Two coppers a piece, then."

Gavin produced his coin pouch and retrieved four copper pieces. When Robillard returned with the cordage and a few stable hands, Gavin traded him the coins for the cordage. The stable hands waited while Gavin and the others collected anything from their saddlebags they didn't want stored with the tack. For Gavin, that meant he moved the ward-stones he'd used when setting camp from Jasmine's saddle-bags to the bottomless satchel where the rest of his belongings had spent the trip. Leaving the stables, Gavin scooped up three small stones, each about the right size to make a pendant.

As he led the group to the Tower, Gavin said, "Lillian, would you mind asking your grandfather if he'd be so kind as to host a Conclave of the Great Houses for me?"

"Of course, Gavin," Lillian replied.

"If it's at all possible, I'd like the Conclave to happen before the midday bell," Gavin continued. "Before I get my apprentices situated in my old suite, I'm going to stop by Valera's office and ask her to arrange a meeting with the Council of Magisters this afternoon. I would like to have visited the Conclave before then."

"If you don't need me before the Conclave, I'll go right now," Lillian said.

Gavin nodded, saying, "That's fine."

"What should the rest of us do?" Braden asked.

Gavin stopped and turned to regard his friends. "You're free to do as you will...well, within the confines of the Arcanists' Code. You're no longer my apprentices, so from here on out, it's up to you. But that doesn't mean I wouldn't mind seeing you from time to time. I consider all of you my friends."

"Why don't you come with me?" Lillian interjected. "We can discuss what we want to do."

The others nodded or vocalized their agreement, saying their farewells to Xythe, Jasper, and Holly before leaving with Lillian.

* * *

SERA, Valera's long-time assistant, looked up as the outer door opened and promptly gaped, her jaw dropping. Gavin led a dracon, a young girl, and a young man into the office and stopped at her desk.

"Hello, Sera," Gavin said. "Would you please tell Valera I need to speak with her?"

Sera stared at Gavin, her mouth still open, which continued until the silence became a bit awkward. Gavin looked at Sera's desk and saw a small dish of berries. He retrieved one from the dish and tossed it into Sera's mouth. The moment the berry hit her tongue, reflex caused her to close her mouth with an audible *click* of her teeth, and seemed to jerk her out of her reverie. She practically leapt to her feet and scrambled to the door of Valera's office, skittering inside without even knocking.

VALERA LOOKED up when the door opened and watched her assistant dash inside. Sera closed the door and hurried to stand at the edge of the desk.

"He's here," she hissed, her semi-whisper urgent.

Valera waited a heartbeat or so before asking, "Who's here?"

"Kirloth," Sera answered. "I mean, the Archmagister."

Valera blinked. "Gavin's back? Or the Archmagister is waiting? I'm not sure I understand, dear."

Sera shook her head. "No, no, no...Gavin *is* the Archmagister, and he's outside with a little girl, a young man...and—and a dracon."

Valera leaned back against her seat. "Well, now. I never imagined that *Gavin* would become the next Archmagister. 'You shall know their victory by the golden flame' indeed. And you say there's a dracon with him? Are you certain?"

Sera nodded with sufficient force that Valera feared for her neck.

"Then you should probably show them in," Valera replied. "And do try to relax, dear. Gavin never wanted you to fear him when he was just Kirloth; I doubt that's changed now that he's the Archmagister."

Sera reopened the door enough to squeeze through, leaving Valera alone for a moment or two.

GAVIN LOOKED up as the door to Valera's private office opened and Sera returned.

"The—the Magister will see you now," Sera said, pointing to the door.

Gavin tried not to smile as he led his apprentices around the desk before saying, "Thank you, Sera."

Gavin opened the door and led his apprentices inside. A cursory glance around the room showed him the office hadn't changed much while he was in Vushaar. He saw Valera starting to rise.

"If you're going to kneel," Gavin said, "please don't. I'm already very tired of people kneeling to me."

Valera smiled. "As you wish, but I assume you're going to introduce your associates?"

"Indeed," Gavin replied. "This is Holly Walsh from Thartan Province in Vushaar, Jasper who is the nephew of Terris Muran's Court Wizard, and Xythe of Qar'Zhosk. They are my apprentices. Apprentices, this is Valera Muran. She serves as both the Magister of Divination and Collegiate Justice."

Valera moved to shake hands with Holly. "Welcome to the College of the Arcane. I hope your time here is enjoyable and instructive."

"Your family name is Muran?" Holly asked. "Are you related to King Terris? He introduced my father to Gavin."

Valera smiled. "Yes, I am his grandfather's youngest sister." Valera's eyes flicked to Gavin. "I received a letter not too long before the sconces in the halls re-lit. It seems the King of Vushaar somehow saw an unedited copy of the Muran Genealogy and felt it incumbent upon himself to reinstate me into the family history and records. Did you meddle, Gavin?"

Gavin grinned. "I meddled all over Vushaar, Valera. Why should you be exempt?"

"Fair point," Valera replied, moving to Xythe. "It is both a pleasure and honor to meet you, Xythe. Welcome to the College of the Arcane. This is the first time I've ever met a dracon, and I hope your people will soon return from their seclusion. The world is less with their absence."

"Only time will tell, Magister," Xythe responded. "I do know the Council of Clans in Qar'Zhosk called for a Grand Moot after Gavin visited them a short time ago, but I do not know if it has happened yet or what the outcome will be. I thank you for your welcome."

Valera moved to Jasper, shook his hand, and offered him warm words of welcome as well.

"Please, be seated," Valera said as she returned to her side of the desk.

Gavin sat in the chair to Valera's right, and Xythe settled in the other, lifting Holly onto her lap. Jasper stood behind them, clasping his hands at his waist.

"How can I help you, Gavin?" Valera asked.

"Can you arrange for a meeting with the Council of Magisters this afternoon? Perhaps scheduled for the first afternoon bell? I should probably introduce myself as the new Archmagister. I also hope to have a Conclave of the Great Houses before the midday bell."

Valera nodded. "I can easily arrange that."

"Thank you," Gavin replied. "I'm going to put my apprentices in my old suite. I should probably get used to the idea of being in the Citadel now."

"Yes, that is the Archmagister's residence. Most would look forward to it."

Gavin sighed. "I don't like that it's so removed from Tel Mivar. I mean, it's floating up there, showing everyone in Tel Mivar how the Archmagister is above them. I'm not above them. I'm...just me."

Valera gave Gavin a soft, partial smile. "Perhaps, that is part of the reason Bellos chose you for the post. Can you imagine what things would be like if Tauron was the Archmagister?"

"He wouldn't have lasted," Gavin countered. "Marcus would've killed him."

Valera snorted a laugh. "Yes, you might be right."

"Very well," Gavin said, nodding once and slapping his knees. "Thank you for your time and hospitality. I need to get them settled and then see about that Conclave. I'll check back to confirm that we're on for the Council meeting."

"Gavin," Valera replied, her tone almost chiding, "You're the Archmagister. Of course, we're on for the Council meeting."

Gavin nodded and shrugged, before leading his apprentices out of the office.

* * *

THE MIVAR ESTATE didn't look like it had changed while Gavin was in Vushaar, either, so he decided to test something as he approached the manor wall. Instead of reaching for the bell rope, Gavin walked right up to the manor wall's gate. As it would for Lillian or her grandfather, the latch clicked open, and the gate swung wide. Gavin went ahead and rung the bell once, so they'd know someone was approaching the house, before walking through.

Gavin approached the steps up to the manor's portico and the door. Adelaide Mivar stepped outside. Her eyes widened at seeing Gavin's gold robe, and she started to move into what Gavin feared would end with her kneeling.

"Please, don't kneel to me," he said. "Especially in your own home."

"The whole city is all abuzz with whispers ever since the street-lamps and braziers atop the city walls re-lit," Adelaide replied. "Torval told Lilly there was a new Archmagister that no one had seen yet, and she just grinned and didn't say a word."

"It happened while we were in Vushaar," Gavin said. "Bellos talked me into it after I destroyed the slave marks."

Adelaide nodded. "You did a good thing, there, Gavin. Those slave marks were a blight on the world. Please, be welcome in our home. The others are already in the Conclave room."

"Thank you," Gavin answered and stepped into the manor.

Eight heads turned as Gavin opened the door to the meeting room for the Conclave. Torval, Sypara, Carth, and Lyssa all displayed signs of shock or surprise. Lyssa's surprise quickly shifted into a triumphant—almost maniacal—smile, and she pumped her fist in the air.

"Yes!" Lyssa cheered. "Those sorry wastes of space on the Council are in trouble now!"

Gavin sighed as he walked to the chair set aside for Kirloth and said, "It's nice to see you, too, Lyssa."

"Now, we know why no one has seen the new Archmagister," Carth remarked.

Gavin nodded. "Thank you for not kneeling to me. I teleported straight to the gate outside because I'm so very tired of telling people to stand up."

Torval coughed into his fist. "Yes, well, we probably should have kneeled, but I for one was too surprised."

"Let's take our seats and begin," Gavin responded. "I don't know that this needs to be a formal Conclave. I just wanted to meet with you, basically to give a fair warning that a lot of things are going to be changing in Tel over the coming months. Everyone and anyone appointed to any kind of civil administration post by the late, unlamented king will find themselves out of a job. You will once more resume full and complete authority over your respective provinces as was set down in the Constitution of Tel, as well as resume your position as advisors to...well...me. One of the first things we need to do is examine as many of the laws and tax codes as we can and strip out anything the Royal Family instituted that is truly unjust. Start discussing this among yourselves and come up with a few ideas to bring to me. Any questions?"

The dukes and duchesses around the table all looked to one another before turning back to Gavin and shaking their heads.

Gavin nodded once. "Very well. Mariana, do you mind tracking down the head of the Battle-mages and sending him to find me? I'll be in either my suite or the Citadel.

"Right, then. If you'll excuse me, I have a suite to move out of and a floating castle to move into. I'll send a messenger once I have a vague idea of a proposed meeting schedule."

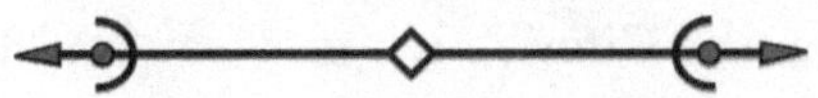

CHAPTER 15

The Citadel was both the residence of the Archmagister and —technically—the Kirloth Estate in Tel. Every doorframe contained the Glyph of Kirloth centered in the lintel, as did the keystone of every archway in every corridor or hallway. Paintings and tapestries lined the walls, and exquisite rugs and carpets lined the floors.

The moment Gavin entered the Citadel, a phantom—much like the College's Master of the Field—faded into view a few feet in front of him.

"Good day to you, Milord," the phantom said. "I am Hartley. I serve as both the head of the Citadel's staff as well as your personal assistant. Part of my duties is to liaise between you and those who serve and maintain the Citadel. If I may say so, Milord, it is good to see that Bellos has named an Archmagister after all these years and especially gratifying that a wizard of House Kirloth was named. My belated condolences for the loss of your kinsman."

Gavin nodded. "It's good to meet you, Hartley. I'm Gavin Cross. Please, feel free to call me Gavin."

"I understand, Milord," Hartley replied, a hint of a smile flicking across his ghostly features.

"It's going to be one of those, then," Gavin remarked, returning the specter's smile. "I'm going to have the head of the Battle-mages looking for me at some point. Is it possible for one of the Citadel's staff to meet him when he enters College grounds and bring him to me?"

"Of course, Milord."

"In that case, Hartley," Gavin said, "why don't you give me a quick tour? I don't even know enough to ask intelligent questions about the Citadel at this point."

The specter nodded once. "Of course, Milord. If you would, please walk with me."

* * *

GAVIN WAS GETTING all of Marcus's trunks settled in a corner of the Citadel's library when a specter faded into view.

"Milord," the specter said, "please forgive the interruption, but Hartley said you wanted to know when the head of the Battle-mages was available. He is in the sitting room on the main floor."

Gavin looked up from the trunk in front of him. "The sitting room on the main floor...right. I have no idea where that is."

"If you like, Milord," the specter replied, "I shall guide you there."

"Perfect. Let's go."

THE MAIN FLOOR turned out to be where Gavin first arrived in the Citadel. The specter led Gavin to an arched doorway a short distance from the entry portal. Gavin stepped through the archway and found an older man waiting for him, who stood the moment Gavin entered the room. Of average height, Gavin's guest had a bulky, muscular build. The mantle he wore over his red robe was burgundy, the color for the Battle-mages of Tel. The sleeves of his red robe bore silver runes that proclaimed him both a specialist in Evocation and a *Magus* within the Society. He kept his silver-flecked, dark hair cropped close, and the intelligence in his hazel eyes belied the man's somewhat brutish appearance.

"I'm Gavin Cross, Head of House Kirloth and the new Archmagister," Gavin said, approaching the man and extending his right hand. "Thank you for coming on such short notice."

The man grinned. "When the new Archmagister summons you, you don't send a note asking where and when. I'm Garris Roshan, Commander of the Battle-mages of Tel."

Gavin blinked. "It's a pleasure to meet you at last, and I want to thank you again for loaning me some of the Battle-mages to assist with sorting out the fallout of the Rite of Holsgyng."

"You're welcome, Milord," Garris replied, "and it is a pleasure to meet the young man who has done so much to turn both the Society and Tel on its ear."

Gavin shrugged. "I'm just me. I can't help it if doing the right thing means I'm creating waves. Let's sit. Would you like refreshment?"

"Some tea would be nice if you have it," Garris answered.

"Hartley," Gavin said, and the specter came into view. For a brief moment, Garris looked like he was going to jump out of his skin.

"Yes, Milord?"

"Garris and I would like tea while we discuss some matters. Could you see about arranging that?"

The specter nodded once. "Of course, Milord. It will just be a moment."

"Well, that was different," Garris remarked, once Hartley had vanished. "Is he really gone?"

Gavin shrugged. "I would assume so, but the staff of any place like the Citadel always knows what's going on anyway. If he wants to keep an ear on my conversations, I'm not too worried about it as long as he keeps what he hears to himself. But...on to business."

"Of course, sir," Garris agreed. "Forgive me."

Gavin replied with a dismissive wave. "Don't worry about it. I want you—well, everyone really—to feel comfortable discussing or saying anything with me. I don't want anyone feeling like he or she can't say what needs said.

"I asked Mariana to communicate my interest in speaking with you for a couple of reasons. First of all, I'd like to borrow some Battle-mages again. I'm going to disband the Royal Guard. While I feel very confident that there are not enough of them to pose a threat, I'd rather have them leave the palace compound without violence. If it comes down to violence, I'll wipe them out, but quite frankly, I have enough of a personal body count as it is."

Garris nodded. "That's easily arranged. Do you have an idea of how many you'll need?"

"Not at this time," Gavin replied. "I should have that information soon. The other matter I wanted to discuss is that I'd like for you to be part of my advisory council. You'd share the table with the Conclave of the Great Houses right now and possibly Ovir Thatcher-son, if he agrees when I ask him. Valera Muran would probably be a good person to ask, too."

Garris twitched. "Did you say Valera *Muran*? The Magister of Divination is a daughter of Vushaar's royal line?"

"Yes," Gavin replied, smiling. "Her father disagreed with her decision to stay in Tel and pursue her studies in the Society and decided to eliminate her from the family's records and history. I made the current king aware of that, and apparently, he chose to re-instate her. Didn't you ever look up the glyph in her wizard's medallion?"

"No," Garris answered, shaking his head. "In all truth, the idea never occurred to me."

Just then, Hartley returned with a full tea service on a chair-height wheeled cart.

"Apologies for taking so long, Milord," Hartley said as he placed the cart at an equidistant position between the two men. "I made the unfortunate discovery that the Citadel's larder is rather bare and had to send to the College's dining hall for the tea. We have a selection of sugar, cream, and honey for the tea and pastries to choose from, as well."

"Thank you, Hartley," Gavin replied. "Don't worry about the larder. That's easily rectified."

"Indeed, sir. Said rectification is already underway," Hartley responded. "Will there be anything else, Milord?"

Gavin directed a questioning glance at Garris, who shook his head 'no' while reaching for what appeared to be an apple pastry. Turning back to Hartley, Gavin answered, "No, thank you, Hartley. I appreciate your assistance."

"Of course, Milord." The specter faded from view as he left the room.

Gavin helped himself to some tea, deciding he liked it without any additives. He selected an apple pastry for himself as well. Both he and Garris sat in a companionable silence while they enjoyed their refreshments.

"There is one other thing," Gavin said after refilling his cup. "I'd like for you to devote some time to consider things that need changing here in Tel. I have the Conclave resuming their traditional authority over the provinces and preparing a review of Tel's laws and tax code. In some ways, I still feel very much the outsider to Tel, and I'm not sure what all needs fixed. The former Royal Guard, obviously, is one...but what else is sitting out there?"

"You make an excellent point, Milord," Garris responded. "I'll give it some thought."

Gavin glanced at the lower shelf of the cart and smiled at seeing containers for both the tea and the pastries.

"I greatly appreciate you taking time out of your day to speak with me," Gavin said. "I hate to chat and run, but today is very hectic with it being my first day back in Tel. But Hartley was thoughtful enough to supply a small jug and sack. Please, take the tea and pastries with you if you like."

"Oh, I couldn't," Garris began.

Gavin shrugged. "I can't swear that they won't go to waste if you don't. Don't feel like you *have* to take them, but if you're even slightly interested, you're welcome to them."

Garris glanced at the tray of pastries again and, after a moment, nodded. "Thank you, Milord. My officers will enjoy them when I call on the command conference to discuss your request for troops."

It was a simple matter to transfer the tea and pastries, and Hartley arrived to escort Garris out when they stepped into the hall.

* * *

GAVIN ENTERED the suite that had been his home and, in some ways, still was. A part of him still expected to see Marcus sitting in the left-hand armchair by the hearth. Xythe stepped out of the room Gavin had shared with Kiri and nodded a greeting, just as Jasper stepped out of what had been Marcus's room.

"Hi," Gavin said. "I just wanted to see how you're settling in."

"I believe we are well," Xythe replied. "With your permission, we would like to visit a tailor soon. While I don't need clothes as such, Holly left Vushaar with just what she was wearing."

Gavin nodded. "Yes, if you can wait until after I meet with the Council of Magisters, I'll take you both to the tailor Marcus used for Kiri and me."

"May I ask when you are planning to start lessons?" Xythe asked.

"That's an excellent question," Gavin remarked. "Right off the top of my head, I'm thinking tomorrow. If not tomorrow, then definitely the day after that. I have to sort through some matters dealing with my return to Tel, as well as being the Archmagister, but I'm hoping that won't be too involved. Is that good?"

Xythe nodded. "Of course."

"Okay. The dining hall opens for lunch at the midday bell, but they also keep a selection of finger foods available throughout the day. The dining hall is on the main floor. Just turn right when you reach the bottom of the Grand Stair and it'll be on your right about two or three doors down."

"Thank you," Xythe replied.

"I'll check back in with you after I meet with the Council."

Gavin turned and left the suite.

* * *

The Council of Magisters occupied their seats around the horseshoe-shaped table. Several of them whispered among themselves about the Archmagister's identity, as Valera had chosen not to share it when she called the meeting. More than one of her associates came close to glaring at her over it.

Moments after the first bell after midday echoed through the Tower, the door of the Archmagister's private entrance opened and closed, and the magisters heard footsteps. But the Archmagister's seat and dais blocked their view. Everyone watched the space around the dais intently, and soon, a gold-robed figure stepped into view. Valera kept her expression neutral, but the rest of the magisters gaped at the new Archmagister in silence.

Well...all but one.

Tauron's voice carried throughout the chamber when he said, "Oh, shit..."

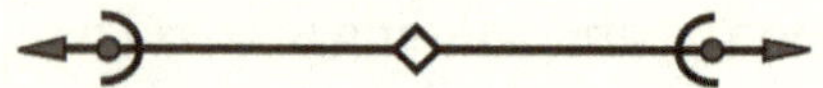

CHAPTER 16

Gavin sighed as he stepped through the entrance to the Citadel. The meeting with the Council of Magisters hadn't been too arduous, and to be quite honest, Gavin rather enjoyed how Tauron never quite got beyond an expression that reminded Gavin of a poleaxed cow. The entire meeting, it seemed like Tauron had problems keeping up; he never once objected or raged over anything.

The meeting with the Council was a formality for the most part, a mere introduction to identify himself as Archmagister. Gavin didn't have any significant changes to the College or the Society as yet, but a small voice in the back of his mind whispered that it would only be a matter of time.

Gavin was so tired that Hartley resolving into view beside him didn't provoke surprise at all.

"Good afternoon, Milord," Hartley said. "Did the meeting with the Council go well?"

"It went," Gavin replied, adding a shrug. "I'll leave it up to someone else to define it as 'well' or something else."

Hartley nodded. "I see, Milord. We have yet to discuss a comprehensive agenda and itinerary. What do you need to focus on next?"

Gavin turned that question over in his mind a couple times before he nodded. "I should probably speak with Nathrac, Hartley. Can you arrange that?"

"Of course, Milord. When would you like to do so?"

"I have no idea, because I don't know what his schedule is like. I would like for it to happen sooner rather than later. It's been a long day, and I'm looking forward to sleep."

Hartley nodded again. "I shall ask about a fairly immediate meeting, then. In terms of sleep, I have taken the liberty of having the bed linens replaced in the master suite, Milord. I spoke with the tailor Marcus used, and—"

Hartley stopped speaking when Gavin growled and whacked the closest wall with a fist, though not hard enough to do himself any harm.

"May I ask what is wrong, Milord?"

Gavin sighed. "I was supposed to take my apprentices to that very tailor after the Council meeting. Do you know how long the tailor is still open today?"

"The tailor—like almost all businesses in the city—is open until the evening bell. You have at least three bells until then, Milord... plenty of time."

"Okay," Gavin said. "I'm going to take my apprentices to the tailor. Track down Nathrac and ask him if he'd be available to speak with me once I return."

"Of course, Milord."

Gavin pivoted on his heel and returned to the entry portal, stepping through it and vanishing from the Citadel.

* * *

GAVIN ARRIVED in the hallway outside his suite and saw Lillian as she stepped out of her family's suite further down the hall. He smiled.

"Hi, Lillian."

"Hello, Milord," Lillian replied, and Gavin fought the urge to cringe. "I was just retrieving some items I'd left in the suite before our trip to Vushaar. How are Xythe, Holly, and Jasper settling in?"

Gavin nodded. "Well, I think. Say...would you mind helping me with something?"

"Not at all. What do you need?"

"I'm taking them to the tailor Marcus used, but I don't know what a young girl like Holly would need in terms of clothes. And...well..."

Lillian smiled. "You'd like me to go along and help?"

"If you have the time," Gavin replied.

"Of course, I have the time. If you don't mind, I'll carry these things with me and head to the estate once we finish at the tailor."

Gavin nodded again. "That will be just fine."

GAVIN, Lillian, Xythe, Jasper, and Holly went to the tailor shop Marcus had taken Gavin and Kiri to all those months ago. As they traveled, a couple people surreptitiously made themselves known to Gavin by showing their wrist tattoos, and he couldn't keep from smiling. He suspected he was getting the iceberg treatment, certain the Wraiths he identified were—at best—ten percent of the total number around them.

When they arrived at the tailor, the middle-aged elf fawned all over Gavin being the new Archmagister. Gavin bore up as long as he could but soon redirected the tailor's attention to his apprentices, explaining he was just seeing to their introduction and covering all expenses. That declaration made, he found a comfy seat and let the tailor whisk everyone else into the back to work her brand of magic.

* * *

GAVIN AGAIN ENTERED THE CITADEL, and he felt like sighing. He'd just left his apprentices in his old suite, thrilled with their purchases from the tailor. Well, Holly was. Xythe only got some brown initiate robes, and Jasper—like most guys Gavin knew—seemed largely indifferent to his clothes. Gavin shrugged; he had never seen dracons with an overabundance of clothing, so maybe it was racial.

Hartley faded into view, saying, "Excellent timing, Milord. Nathrac just arrived and is waiting for you in the sitting room where you met with Commander Roshan."

"Thank you, Hartley."

Gavin walked the short distance to the sitting room and saw a figure in a purple robe standing by the hearth. The figure turned, revealing fiery-red eyes with vertical slits for pupils inside otherwise impenetrable shadow.

"Thank you for seeing me, Nathrac," Gavin said. "Please, be seated."

"You're welcome," Nathrac replied, "and congratulations on your new title."

As before, Nathrac's voice was so deep and powerful that it seemed to resonate against Gavin's bones.

"I'm not totally certain congratulations are in order, but thank you," Gavin remarked. "It's only my first day back in Tel, and I'm so tired I've wanted to sleep since midday."

Nathrac nodded. "That has seemed to be the case with those who have held the position in the past. They often remarked about not having enough hours."

"Well, at least I'm off to a good start, then. I wanted to speak with you about some changes I want to make to the Constitution of Tel. Specifically, the sections regarding what happens if there's never an Archmagister. As it is written right now, civil authority passes to the royal family with authority over the Society passing to the Council of Magisters. I would like to change it so that you become the interim Archmagister until such time as Bellos names a new one. Are you agreeable to that?"

"The constitution certainly needs to be changed, given that the royal family is no more," Nathrac remarked. After a few moments' silence, he added, "Yes, it is agreeable. In any instance where there is no Archmagister or the current Archmagister is unavailable, I will step in and oversee the Kingdom and the Society until Bellos names a replacement or the Archmagister returns."

Gavin smiled. "Thank you. That is a weight off my shoulders. I'll publish the change along with the notification that the Royal Guard is disbanded."

"May I ask what you'll use the palace complex for?"

Gavin shrugged. "Honestly, I was thinking of turning it into a kind of Embassy Row, if I can repair all the damage the royal family did to our relations with other countries. It'll probably require extensive remodeling to achieve that, but nothing worthwhile is ever easy."

Nathrac nodded. "I would not be surprised if the other races or countries are rather quick to re-establish diplomatic relations. You are, after all, the last of the Divine Emissaries. I cannot imagine anyone risking Bellos's displeasure if they snub you. Personally, I feel Bellos would be indifferent to anyone snubbing you, as it's your situation to handle, but most mortals wouldn't think that way."

"Well, I'll take whatever advantage I can get," Gavin replied, grinning.

"Is there anything else?" Nathrac asked. "I have time for anything you need, but I don't want to keep you from your rest."

Gavin turned the question over in his head for a couple moments before shaking his head. "No...I think we've covered everything I wanted to discuss."

"Then, I shall bid you farewell," Nathrac said, as he stood. "Should you have need of me, merely call out my name."

A column of flame that neither burned nor radiated heat enveloped Nathrac from the floor up, and when it disappeared, he was gone.

CHAPTER 17

The morning of his second day back in Tel, Gavin met two companies of Battle-mages outside the palace complex. The officer in command was a woman who introduced herself as Major Ilona Saveen. If anyone had asked him before that morning how Battle-mages deployed for action, Gavin would have guessed that they wore robes just like any other arcanist...and he would've been incredibly wrong.

The Battle-mages in front of him stood in two rectangular formations of ten across and twenty-five ranks deep. They wore chainmail shirts and coifs and carried everything from single-bladed war axes to double-headed war hammers. The only consistency appeared to be they all wielded one-handed weapons. Belted tabards hung over their armor, colored to show their personal philosophy toward the Art, and the tabards were trimmed in a colored band that represented their specialization within the Art, if any.

"Didn't expect us to be in armor with weapons, did you, Milord?" Major Saveen asked, clearly to enjoy Gavin's surprise.

"No...no, I really didn't," Gavin said, his eyes still roaming over the assembled troops.

Saveen smiled. "We get that a lot from people who've never seen us in training or on deployment. If I may ask, what's the situation? Commander Roshan just said to bring two companies and meet you at the palace complex this morning."

"We're disbanding the Royal Guard," Gavin replied. "I'm hoping your presence will convince them to go peacefully. I could go it alone, but I fear they would try to fight a single person, which would force me to eliminate them. I'd rather not add to my personal body count today; it's already high enough as it is."

Saveen nodded. "I can see that. Very well, Milord. Lead the way; we'll have your back."

GAVIN APPROACHED the gates of the palace complex and found two Royal Guardsmen standing just inside.

"Open the gate," Gavin said. "I'm here to speak with everyone in the former Royal Guard."

"What do you mean 'former?' We're still here," one of the guardsmen said.

Gavin looked the man right in the eyes. "Are you or your friend going to open the gate or not? I'm not going to discuss my reason for being here until I'm in front of the entire group. I will not repeat myself."

The two guardsmen looked to one another and actually shrugged. Gavin felt like sighing and shaking his head. In the end, though, they opened the gate.

"Major, if you would, please leave four here to secure the gate," Gavin said as he entered the palace complex for the second time in his life. He heard the order repeated through the ranks behind him as he followed the guardsmen.

The guardsmen led Gavin and the Battle-mages not to the barracks but to the former throne room. That was the first surprise. The second was that the guardsmen had turned the throne room into a dining hall. Tables and benches lined the space, and the man Gavin expected was the head of the Royal Guard occupied the throne. The third—well, it wasn't really a surprise at this point when one of guardsmen addressed the man on the throne as 'Your Majesty.'

"Yer Majesty," one of guardsmen leading Gavin began, "he approached the gate and demanded to see you. He said he had something to say he wasn't going to repeat."

The man on the throne waved the two guardsmen away and said, "It is considered wise to request an audience with one's king."

Gavin couldn't help it. He laughed, finally saying, "Are you really certain that's how you want this conversation to go? I don't do take-backs or forgiveness."

"And just who are you to tell me any different? I control the palace. The kingdom's taxes come here. The town guard reports here. To me, that says I control the kingdom."

Gavin sighed. "Very well." He whispered the invocation of a Word of Transmutation that ensured both his voice and Major Saveen's would fill the hall. "I am Gavin Cross of House Kirloth and, by Bellos's choice, the Archmagister of Tel. You have no authority to crown yourself king, as the Constitution of Tel clearly specifies the Archmagister has full authority over the kingdom. Vacate that throne immediately and cease your witless posturing, or I will find you and anyone who stands with you in rebellion and guilty of treason."

If someone had dropped a pin on the flagstones at the palace gate the sound would have echoed throughout the room like a thunderclap.

"Major Saveen, under the laws of Tel, what is the penalty for treason?" Gavin asked.

"Death, Milord," Saveen answered. "The exact method has varied historically, but the end result is always death."

Gavin looked pointedly at the man sitting on Leuwyn's throne and said, "Last chance."

The man didn't budge, and Gavin's eyes narrowed, his expression hardening into a glare as he invoked the Word, "*Thraxys*."

The resonance of Gavin's power slammed into every wizard within half a city block. The would-be king's head lolled as the corpse slumped to one side. The guardsmen sitting around the tables looked from each other, to the corpse of their leader, and to Gavin...several times.

Gavin lifted his hands, producing a parchment scroll. He unrolled it and read, "By the authority vested in me as Archmagister of Tel, I—Gavin Cross—hereby decree the organization known as the Royal Guard is disbanded. This decree shall be effective immediately upon its delivery to the palace complex, the fifteenth day of Bilfar in the 6082nd year of our victory in the Godswar." Gavin lowered the scroll and regarded the former guardsmen. "How this situation ends is up to you. If you surrender your arms and armor and leave peacefully, you will have a clean slate. I give you my word I will not investigate any of you for any crimes you may have committed while a member of the former Royal Guard. If you decide to follow the corpse that's cooling on Leuwyn's throne, you'll join him in whatever afterlife you deserve."

"And just what are we supposed to do?" one of the former guardsmen asked.

Gavin shrugged. "It's not my place to answer that, but I will say this. My offer of a clean slate only applies to your *past*. If you accept my offer and walk out of here to become a bandit, thief, or commit some other crime, that's on you, and I won't save you."

Silence reigned in the hall for several more moments before one of the former guardsmen stood. He pushed his dishes to the center of the table and placed his weapons-belt—complete with sword and dagger—in the newly open space. He then removed the tabard identifying him as a member of the Royal Guard and walked toward the door Gavin and the Battle-mages had entered through.

As he neared Gavin, Gavin held out what appeared to be a blank piece of parchment. The man accepted without thinking, and the moment his hand touched it, writing appeared. The right corner, closest to Gavin, bore the Glyph of Kirloth.

"What's that?" the man asked, gaping.

"That is a note instructing the Bank of Tel to withdraw three gold pieces from my personal account one time and present it to you in whatever form you want...gold, silver, copper, whatever you want," Gavin replied, his voice still filling the hall.

The former guardsman blinked. "Why?"

"If you're wise enough to choose starting a new path and not forcing me to kill you," Gavin answered, "the least I can do is give you something to help you get on your feet. I should also point out that it will only work for you. If someone were to steal that, it would revert to a blank piece of parchment."

The man's eyes started glistening in the light, and he stumbled through a nervous, "Thank you, Milord," before leaving the hall. Moments later, the sound of weapons-belts landing on tables filled the hall, and a line formed in front of Gavin as he handed out pieces of parchment that became notes for the Bank of Tel. As the last former guardsman left the hall, Gavin cancelled the invocation that projected his and Saveen's voices throughout the hall.

Major Saveen turned to Gavin. "If I may say so, Milord, what you just did doesn't wholly match up with your reputation."

Gavin shrugged. "Oh, I certainly could have wiped the palace complex—along with everyone and everything in it—off the face of the world, but that's a very short-sighted response to me. For all we know, one of their grandchildren will be the next Declan the Dandy or an artist that sets a new standard in our culture or...there's no way to know. For that matter, one of those men might have it within them to make a lasting impact on the world, hopefully for the good. If I had just killed them all, I would be robbing the world of that potential while adding weight to my soul I don't need. This was the best outcome all the way around."

Saveen gave Gavin an appraising look. "You are both like and unlike your mentor."

"I've heard that before," Gavin replied, grinning. "Major, I appreciate your presence and assistance this morning. I will communicate to Commander Roshan that I couldn't be more pleased with the conduct and assistance of you and your people. Thank you."

"Our pleasure, Milord," Saveen responded. "We are here to serve."

"Well, I'm going to take the shortcut back. Is there anywhere I can send you?"

Saveen seemed to consider the matter a moment before saying, "Well, the Battle-mage barracks is just outside North Gate."

"I'm not sure I've been there," Gavin replied, "but I have been to North Gate. Let's step outside to the courtyard, and I'll open a gateway."

About fifteen minutes later, Gavin closed the gateway to North Gate and teleported himself back to the College.

* * *

By that evening, town criers across the Kingdom of Tel had posted Gavin's decree disbanding the Royal Guard on noticeboards and added it to the list of news they announced.

CHAPTER 18

Gavin appeared in the College's courtyard. He started for the entrance to the Tower and had only traveled maybe fifty feet when the sound of a terrified, young voice begging reached his ears. Gavin's eyes narrowed, and he turned to follow the sound.

He walked around the far corner of the Tower of the Council, the central structure for the College, and found five older students in front of a younger student. The younger student was being held against the Tower's wall several feet above the ground. The older students laughed at the young one's plight and pleading amidst sobs, and a smile that held no mirth curled Gavin's lips as his eyes settled on the silver chains of wizards' medallions hanging around the older students' necks.

Gavin focused on his *skathos*, identifying the telekinesis effect that held the young student against the wall. Gavin quickly built a picture of what he wanted in his mind and poured his entire focus into it, invoking a composite effect. "*Rhosed-Rhyskaal.*"

Gavin's intent was two-fold: first, dispel the telekinesis effect; and second, gently lower the youngster to the ground. The resonance of Gavin's power struck the immediate vicinity like a master smith's hammer upon an anvil. The tormentors cried out in pain as they clutched their midriffs and collapsed to their knees; three of them retched. Gavin watched the younger student slowly float to the ground, riding the invisible platform of force he'd created under his feet.

Gavin approached the group. The young student who had just landed gaped at seeing someone in gold robes, and Gavin gestured for him to keep silent and wait.

"By the gods," the lead tormentor bit out the words, still unable to stand, "do you have any idea who our parents are?"

"Do you have any idea how little I care?" Gavin asked, his voice still into the deeper, uncaring tone that represented 'Kirloth.'

"You should. They—" Whatever else the young man was going to say never came, as he lifted his eyes to see who he was threatening... and then promptly wet himself as he gaped.

Gavin turned to the youngster. "Would you please go to the Collegiate Justice and tell her that Gavin Cross needs her here now?"

The boy jerked a couple swift nods before shooting off as fast as his legs would carry him.

None of the other tormentors had accidents like their so-called leader, but terror swept through all four of them. By the time Valera arrived, the tormentors were on their feet, though unsteady.

Gavin said, "I found these five torturing the youngster who came for you. The one with wet trousers was holding him easily some thirty feet in the air with a telekinesis effect. What you felt was my composite effect that dispelled the telekinesis and lowered the youngster to the ground."

Valera shook her head, *tsk*ing as she did so. "Oh, you boys are in it now. I've told you several times that we do not condone hazing here, and Gav—the Archmagister—feels particularly strong about it. Last year, a number of upper classmen spent a week with their loincloths as wreaths of holly leaves, complete with thorns, when they tried hazing the students he was mentoring."

"How soon can you call an assembly of all students, instructors, and any magisters who are in residence?" Gavin asked.

"The easiest would be to announce it at the midday meal to take place immediately thereafter," Valera answered.

Gavin nodded. "See to it. Every student and instructor will be in the galleries of the Council's Chamber immediately after the midday meal, and I want to know anyone who misses it. I'm not as concerned about all the magisters, but any who are here at the College should attend as well. Do we have any Inquisitors here?"

"Two are stationed at the College at all times," Valera replied. "The current pair are Reyna, Mariana's friend, and Vikram Scahr."

Gavin turned to the youngster he'd saved. "Do you know where the Inquisitors are?"

He again nodded rapidly.

"Tell Reyna that Gavin Cross needs her and her associate outside the Tower, please, and bring them here."

The boy pivoted and was off like shot. He returned shortly, leading Reyna and Vikram. Both expressed their surprise and shock at seeing Gavin as the new Archmagister.

"Thank you for coming," Gavin said. "Reyna, I hope the days have treated you well. Sir, my name is Gavin Cross."

"Vikram of House Scahr, Milord," the second Inquisitor replied as he and Reyna both knelt.

"Stand, please. I do not enjoy people kneeling to me." Gavin gestured at the five students once the Inquisitors were on their feet. "I want these five sequestered and under guard until the assembly I've called after the midday meal. I caught them hazing the youngster who came for you; they were holding the boy some thirty feet in the air by telekinesis."

Reyna's expression hardened into a glare as she regarded the five students. "As you command, Milord."

Gavin watched the Inquisitors lead the students away, the set of his jaw and the hardness of his glare broadcasting his anger for all to see. When they turned the corner out of sight, Gavin shook himself and turned to Valera.

"My apologies, Valera," he said after a deep breath. "That wasn't how I wanted to say 'hello' today."

Valera smiled and shrugged. "It is what it is, Milord. You never were one to sit idly by while something you deemed an injustice occurred."

"Yeah...that's probably why Bellos offered me the job," Gavin replied.

* * *

Lillian, Mariana, Wynn, and Braden occupied one of the sitting rooms at the Mivar Estate. The ladies relaxed at opposite sides of a sofa, while Braden and Wynn each occupied an armchair facing their associates across a small, shin-height table. A full tea service—complete with a selection of cookies and pastries—occupied the table, and they each held a cup.

"Well, if no one else is going to say it," Mariana said, "I will. I'm bored. I never thought I'd be bored coming home, but I am. Who else misses the way things were when we were with Gavin?"

Wynn and Braden both broke into grins.

"It's just not the same," Braden rumbled in his deep voice. "Yes, I'm free to pursue my research into imbued items...or anything else that catches my interest, really. But you're right. There's only so much time you can spend catching up with the family."

Lillian sighed. "And it's a whole different dynamic now, too...at least for me. When we left, we were apprentices, but we came back adults and full members of the Society. I don't know about you, but it's been a little difficult figuring out what my place is now."

"So-what-do-we-do?" Wynn asked. "Form-an-adventuring-company? Hunt-bandits?"

"As much as I'm sure that would appeal to some," Mariana said, "I don't really see myself as one of those raggedy adventurers. Besides, Tel is fairly tame, for the most part. We'd have to go pretty far afield to find work."

Lillian leaned forward and refilled her cup from the teapot. "I have an idea. Why not go talk to Gavin?"

"How do we even find him?" Mariana asked. "Does anyone know how to reach the Citadel?"

The four friends looked to one another, and all shrugged.

"Maybe-Valera-knows?" Wynn asked.

"That might be the best way to find Gavin at this point," Braden agreed.

Lillian nodded. "That's not a bad idea. I bet Gavin has been speaking with her on a fairly regular basis, since she's the Collegiate Justice. Let's go."

They drained their cups and returned everything to the tray, with Mariana snagging a handful of cookies. Within minutes, the tray was back in the kitchen, and the four friends were on their way to the College.

* * *

LILLIAN LED the way into Valera's outer office, and she smiled a greeting to Sera. "Hello, Sera. We apologize for dropping by unannounced. Would Magister Valera have any time for us?"

"Let me check," Sera replied as she stood. "She just came back, so she might not have had time to get started on anything." Sera slipped into Valera's private office after knocking. Moments later, she returned. "Yes, the magister can see you now."

Lillian led her friends across the room, knocking once on the door before opening it, and they filed inside.

Valera smiled as her guests entered the office. As soon as the door closed, she said, "Welcome back to Tel. How are you settling in?"

"Well," Lillian answered, "that's kind of why we're here. Settling back into our old lives is proving difficult—"

"And boring," Mariana added.

"And boring," Lillian agreed with a smile. "We were hoping to discuss the matter with Gavin...and hoping you might have some idea of where to find him."

Valera grinned. "He's probably in the Citadel...or perhaps his old suite. We parted ways at the foot of the Grand Stair not even half an hour ago. Gavin found some Fifth Tiers terrorizing a First Tier, and... well, he was not happy."

"Molten rock and charred earth?" Braden asked.

"No, thank goodness. He wasn't *that* unhappy," Valera countered. "But he did have Reyna and her associate sequester the Fifth Tiers until a full assembly of the College later today. Matter of fact, I just sat down to arrange that when you arrived."

Lillian, Mariana, Wynn, and Braden looked to one another, and they nodded. Lillian turned back to Valera. "Thank you for your time, ma'am. One last question, if we may, what's the best way to reach the Citadel?"

"The easiest would be to speak with the specter at the last landing of the Grand Stair before the roof. He controls the public gateway to the Citadel."

"Thank you, ma'am," Lillian said.

Everyone started filing out of the office. Just as she reached the door, Lillian turned back to Valera. "If I may, ma'am, did you know what was going to happen when you counseled me not to focus on choosing a specialty?"

Valera smiled at the memory. "The specific events? No. I never see specific events, merely possibilities."

The magister opened the top, right-side drawer of her desk, removed two strips of parchment, and extended them toward Lillian. Lillian accepted the parchment and read them. Her eyes widened, and she looked to Valera.

"The top came from the first vision I'd had in twenty years," Valera explained. "It woke me in the middle of the night, and it was at most three weeks before Gavin was found. The other is from a vision I had in this very office, somewhere around the time you and the others left to deal with Sivas's mercenaries."

"So, you assigned Gavin as our mentor on purpose? And then, you asked Gavin to go to Vushaar?"

Valera shrugged. "As I said, my dear, I only see possibilities."

A shiver ran down Lillian's spine, and she returned the pieces of parchment to Valera. After giving Valera a final nod, Lillian turned and went to catch up with her friends.

* * *

GAVIN MOVED the final batch of journals to the shelf and stepped back to survey his work. Marcus's journals took up over half of a bookcase, and Gavin had arranged them in chronological order starting at the top left. Now...all he had to do was read them, as if life would deign to give him enough uninterrupted time.

"Milord," Hartley said as he appeared in the library's doorway, "the Apprentices are asking to see you."

Gavin turned to face the specter, asking, "Xythe, Holly, or Jasper?"

"Forgive me, Milord," Hartley replied. "Perhaps, I should have said Ladies Mivar and Cothos and Lords Wygoth and Roshan."

"Oh! Yes, of course. How much time do I have before the first bell after midday?"

"At least three bells, sir."

"Then, by all means, invite them in," Gavin said. "Do we have a larger sitting room than the one where I spoke with Garris?"

"Of course, sir," Hartley answered. "I shall take you there on the way to meet your guests."

MINUTES LATER, Gavin turned when Hartley announced his friends, and he smiled at seeing them. The smile lasted right up until they bowed—every single one of them—and they didn't do so out of humor.

Gavin sighed. "I get enough of that from everyone else. Please, don't you guys do it, as well...and don't start with any of that 'milord' crap, either."

"How have you been?" Lillian asked.

"I would be doing a lot better if I hadn't discovered a group of Fifth Tiers tormenting a First Tier," Gavin said, punctuating his statement with a frown. "Otherwise, I suppose it's nice to be able to effect real change. But quite frankly, I think I preferred how people treated me when I was just Kirloth. You four are the closest friends I have, and you *still* bowed. I can't go anywhere in the College without people kneeling."

"Most people would eat that up and consider it their due," Mariana remarked.

Gavin gave Mariana a flat look. "I'd like to think we've well established that I'm not most people."

"Have-you-decided-what-will-happen-to-those-Fifth-Tiers?" Wynn asked.

"You'll have to attend the assembly to find out," Gavin answered. "I wouldn't want to spoil the surprise. Oh, goodness...I'm sorry. Please, let's find seats. Hartley, if we're still going when it comes time for the Assembly, would you let us know?"

The specter nodded. "Of course, Milord."

Gavin held out his hands toward Hartley like a showman indicating a new prize. "See? Even Hartley does it."

The specter chose the better part of valor and simply faded away.

Once everyone was seated, Gavin regarded his friends for a moment or two. "As much as I would like to think you tracked me down just to say 'hi,' I have a suspicion that's not quite the case."

Lillian half-winced. "I'm afraid you're right, Mi—Gavin. We were hoping to discuss something with you."

"Oh? What's on your minds?"

"We're bored," Mariana said. "We miss doing things."

Gavin grinned. "So, the novelty of being back home has already worn off, then?" All four of his friends nodded. "What would you like to be doing?"

"Honestly, I'm not sure we've made it that far," Braden answered. "I tried using the laboratory back home to work on researching imbued items, but it just didn't grip me. It felt like...well, it felt second best."

Mariana nodded. "I tried a day back with the Battle-mages, and that got old *fast*. I ended up resigning, but Commander Roshan didn't accept. He made me the official liaison with the Conclave of the Great

Houses—basically detached duty. If he really needs me, he'll call me, but otherwise, I'm pretty much on my own."

Gavin scanned the faces of his friends and sighed. "Want me to put you to work?"

"What did you have in mind?" Lillian asked.

"Well, I do have three apprentices who need training, and I seem to remember Wynn saying he enjoyed teaching. Beyond that, I also need to start rebuilding the old alliance. The members south of us already know me, but I've never been north. There are the giants, the dwarves, and the elves north of Tel...correct?"

"The High Forest borders most of Tel to the north," Mariana answered. "But the northeast corner touches the foothills of the Godswall Mountains and forms a kind of joint border with the dwarven and giant lands, respectively; it's almost like a triple frontier. Depending on where you stand, you're either in Tel, the dwarven lands, or the giant lands."

Gavin nodded. "Lillian, I would like for you and Mariana to go on a diplomatic mission to the northern races. Introduce the 'new' Kingdom of Tel, as it were, and investigate the possibility of exchanging ambassadors. Are you interested?"

"When would you have us leave?" Lillian asked.

"How long would it take you to prepare?" Gavin asked.

Lillian looked to Mariana, who shrugged. "We could probably be ready to leave within three days, depending on the availability of supplies."

"Sold!" Gavin replied. "I'll prepare a letter of introduction and a formal grant of diplomatic authority for you. Braden, do you mind visiting our friends to the south? Specifically, the dracons, Othron, and Vushaar? I'd like to invite them to a meeting of the old alliance members, here in Tel Mivar. Othron won't need it but offer teleportation to the Vushaari and dracons' representatives."

Braden nodded. "Sounds like fun."

"Very well, then," Gavin said, nodding once. "Looks like that's sorted. Who wants the two-copper tour?"

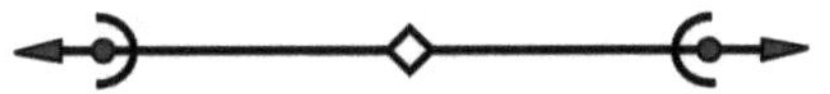

CHAPTER 19

Every instructor and student in the College occupied the galleries overlooking the Chamber of the Council. Several magisters waited in their seats at the large, horseshoe-shaped table. When the first afternoon bell rang, signaling the end of the midday meal period, a door that hadn't been regularly used in almost six hundred years opened, and whispers soon filled the hall as the new Archmagister entered the chamber. The whispers took on an excited overtone as the Archmagister stepped into view.

Gavin looked to Reyna by the door leading to the hall and nodded. "Bring them in."

Reyna and her fellow Inquisitor led the five students into the chamber and stopped them at the end of the carpet leading from the door to the recessed area where the magisters' table stood.

Gavin nodded once and lifted his eyes to the galleries. "I would have thought many of you would remember the stories of the fate that befell a group of Fifth Tier students last year who chose to haze First Tiers in my mentor group. And yet, I found these five students tormenting a young man I have since identified as a First Tier. I want each and every one of you to have a very clear understanding of this next point: few things set my blood to boiling more than bullies. I will not abide such conduct happening here.

"For those who merely participated and cheered the torment on, they are suspended for the rest of the term and forfeit all academic progress beyond the beginning of Fourth Tier. The instigator of the group—the one responsible for using the Art to torment and torture another—is hereby suspended for the rest of the term and forfeits all academic progress beyond the start of Third Tier.

"These five have used up *all* of my patience and compassion for this offense. The next time verified hazing occurs, the offender—or offenders—will receive fifteen lashes before the entire student body. The third time, those responsible will be expelled, and any knowledge they gained here will be stripped from their minds. The fourth time...well, perhaps you should pray to the gods that there is no fourth time."

Gavin shifted his attention to Reyna. "Inquisitor Reyna, please, notify the families of these individuals. On my authority, the families have one month to retrieve them from the College, or you will turn them out to the streets. See me if any of their families are sufficiently distant that one month is an unreasonable hardship. Any questions?"

Reyna answered at once. "No, Milord."

Gavin shifted his attention back to the galleries. "My rulings in this matter will be posted throughout the College by the end of the day. The normal course schedule will resume for the next closest class time. All of you are dismissed."

Gavin pivoted on his heel and strode out of the chamber.

* * *

THE MAID LED Lillian into Kiri's suite. Kiri looked up from where she sat and smiled at seeing her friend. The maid left them, and Kiri came to Lillian, pulling her into fierce hug.

"I know it's only been a few days," Kiri said, releasing Lillian, "but it feels like so much longer than that."

"I missed you, too," Lillian agreed. "How have you been?"

Kiri sighed. "Getting settled back into being the Crown Princess hasn't quite overwhelmed me, but it's been close a couple times."

Lillian nodded. "I can see that. It was tough for us to go back to Tel and not have anything to do. Well...it wasn't that we didn't have anything to do; it's just that we were on our own. We could do whatever we wanted. It didn't take long at all for that to be boring, as Mariana likes to say."

"Oh, my...what are you going to do?" Kiri asked as she led Lillian over to the sitting area, where they settled.

"We talked it over with Gavin, and he gave us jobs. Wynn's back to teaching Gavin's apprentices. Braden will be visiting the dracons, Othron, and your father about setting up some kind of meeting of the old alliance."

Kiri smiled. "So, that's two of you. What did Gavin have for you and Mariana?"

"We're putting together a diplomatic expedition to the giants, dwarves, and elves," Lillian replied. "Gavin wants us to make the initial efforts toward repairing the damage done by the royal family. They weren't especially kind to non-humans."

"I've never understood people who act like that," Kiri said. "So... uhm...how's Gavin? Is he settling in as Archmagister?"

Lillian inhaled and released it very slowly. "You know, I'm not sure. I know he doesn't like—no, I'm pretty sure he *loathes* people bowing and scraping to him. He disbanded the Royal Guard and only had to kill one person in the process, so that was good. When we spoke with him today, well, part of me wants to say he was putting on a happy face for us. I'm not really sure how happy he is."

"I wish I was there for him," Kiri remarked. "I worry about him."

* * *

THE NECROMANCER STRODE into his suite at the very top of the fortress's central keep. He pulled off the wizard's medallion as well as the robe whose runes proclaimed him a magister and almost threw them into the armoire. Withdrawing one of his black robes that bore no runes, he settled it in place and walked to the window overlooking the mountains to the south.

The mountain vista normally helped to calm him, but not at this moment. He ground his teeth together as he considered all that had happened over the past couple days. Not only was there a new Archmagister, but it was none other than that reckless upstart Marcus had trained.

How was he supposed to create a force capable of resisting Lornithar's hordes if he was defeated and opposed at every turn?

Even an infant should be able to understand that the old alliance was little more than a corpse, clutching at life like some kind of terminally ill beggar. That much had been apparent even a thousand years ago, and the solution seemed so clear: infiltrate the governments making up the old alliance, suborn them utterly, and then announce victory. Then, all that remained would be to start assembling the forces necessary to march east through Hope's Pass and put an end to the threat of Lornithar's minions once and for all.

But no. His former mentor, Emperor Xartham, hadn't seen the plan as being achievable, and their argument over the disagreement was so fierce he hadn't spoken to Xartham since, a thousand years later. And Othron, the one who had taught Xartham how to cheat death, had no interest in supporting his plans. The old lich had made that plain enough the one time they'd talked.

It had taken over five hundred years to gather the artifacts and devise the rituals and spells that allowed him to maintain the undead army that had captured Skullkeep, and it had seemed like everything was falling into place, just like it should. Until Gavin Cross.

A cautious knock pulled the Necromancer out his musings. He turned, wanting to glare at the door but couldn't bring himself to do it.

"Enter," he called, his voice *not quite* a growl.

The lieutenant who often served as his liaison entered the room.

"Master, please forgive the interruption," the young man said.

"Word just arrived of the Archmagister's identity. It is Gavin Cross of House Kirloth."

The Necromancer's thoughts flitted back to his seat in the Chamber of the Council of Magisters for just a moment before he said, "I already know."

CHAPTER 20

The sun shone down from a cloudless sky, and hints of salt and the harbor drifted on the breeze. Gavin stood with Lillian, Mariana, Wynn, and Braden in the College's courtyard. Lillian and Mariana held the reins of horses outfitted for long travel, and Braden stood with them.

"Do you have everything you need?" Gavin asked.

Mariana nodded. "We have what we *know* we need, and we can both teleport back if we run into something serious."

"Very well," Gavin replied. He reached inside his robe and withdrew two small discs that looked to be made of sandstone or something similar. Both surfaces held a number of runes etched in them, and the Glyph of Kirloth occupied the center. "Each of you take one of these. If you need help and can't teleport back here, snap one in half; I'll be there. Braden, here's one for you, too, just in case."

Braden nodded as he and his friends accepted the discs.

"I'll open a gateway to home," Mariana said. "That will bring us much closer to the border and cut a few days off our travel time."

Gavin nodded. "Give my regards to your mother, please."

"I will."

Mariana turned, prompting Lillian to do so as well. She lifted her free hand and invoked the Word of Transmutation. "*Paedryx*."

Gavin felt the resonance of her power as an archway of burgundy-colored, crackling energy rose from the courtyard's cobblestones. When the archway was tall enough to accommodate the horses, the center flashed and became a portal to another place. Lillian led Mariana through the gateway, which vanished after Mariana's transit.

"Well, I guess that's my cue," Braden said in his deep, rumbling voice. "I'll visit Vushaar first, then Othron, and finally the dracons. I thought to save the dracons for last, since they have the least distance to travel."

"That works," Gavin replied. "Be safe, and don't forget that disc if you need me."

"Thanks," Braden said. "I can't imagine I'd be more than a week, but if my progress is slower than I anticipate, I'll send word."

With that, Braden turned, invoking the same Word as Mariana. Unlike Gavin or Mariana, the energy of his gateway was a deep, deep green. Seconds later, Gavin and Wynn stood alone.

As Gavin turned toward the Tower, Wynn said, "I wanted to ask your thoughts on enrolling Holly, at least, in some of the basic classes here at the College. She's just about the right age to start regular school, at least here in Tel. Does Vushaar offer general schooling to their people?"

Gavin noticed Wynn was speaking slower than he normally did and almost asked him about it. Then, he realized it was probably an effect of teaching the apprentices. Teaching would be very difficult if the learner couldn't keep up with the instructor.

"I have no idea, Wynn," Gavin answered. "That's something that never came up. I see no reason not to enroll Holly, and we should show the class list to Xythe and Jasper to see if there are any classes they'd like to take that won't be covered by the apprenticeships. Let's go talk with Valera."

.   .   .

Gavin and Wynn entered the reception office for the Collegiate Justice. Sera looked up from her desk as the door opened and visibly forced her expression to remain neutral. She stood and bowed once as she said, "I'll inform the magister that you're here, Milord."

Sera stepped into Valera's private office and returned almost immediately. "The magister can see you now."

Gavin nodded. "Thank you, Sera."

Leading Wynn around Sera's desk, Gavin opened the door and stepped inside. As he entered, Valera smiled and stood, offering a deep bow.

"What can I do for you, Gavin?" Valera asked as she shook Gavin's hand and then Wynn's. She gestured to the two chairs and, once Gavin eased into one, resumed her seat.

"Wynn has been handling the training of my apprentices," Gavin began, "and he brought me an excellent idea. One of my apprentices is a young girl by the name of Holly Walsh, and she's young enough that I'm not sure what kind of general schooling she's had. I know the College makes a provision for that in the curriculum, and the only class I'm completely opposed to her taking is the one dealing with the history of Tel. You and I both know quite a bit of it is utterly wrong, especially about certain aspects of the Founding."

Valera nodded. "Yes. You're not the first to broach the topic of our history curriculum. How would you like it changed?"

Gavin blinked. "I'm sorry? How would I like it changed?"

"Yes, of course. As the Archmagister, you have final authority over the College's entire curriculum and faculty roster. Previous Archmagisters have left the day-to-day administration of the College to the Council of Magisters, but there's absolutely no reason you can't exercise your office's traditional authority."

"In that case, the history curriculum—at least the course material surrounding the Godswar and the Founding—should be based on Mivar's Histories," Gavin replied. "I have it on very reliable authority that they are the most accurate accounts, and the textbook that makes no mention of Mivar, Bellos, and Kirloth devising the system of spells mages use should be removed from printing. That's merely the most egregious of its inaccuracies."

Valera nodded and made a note before picking up a bell on the corner of the desk and ringing it twice. Within moments, Sera entered.

"Yes, ma'am?" Sera asked.

"Sera," Valera replied, "would you please retrieve...oh, say, five copies of the class list for the upcoming term?"

Sera nodded once and closed the door behind her. Moments later, she returned with the requested class lists, handing them to Wynn and leaving once more.

"Once you know what classes your apprentices will be joining, let me know, and I'll see that they're registered," Valera said. "Now...as long as I have you here, do you have a moment for a slightly related topic?"

Gavin grinned. "Of course, Valera, and thank you for the class lists."

"What are your thoughts on establishing a curriculum specific to wizards?"

"The idea bears merit," Gavin replied and turned to Wynn. "Ever given any thought to becoming a full-time instructor here?"

"I have not," Wynn answered, "but I'm certainly not opposed."

Valera almost gaped at Wynn. "Forgive me, Wynn, but I think that's the slowest I've ever heard you speak."

Wynn's cheeks and ears took on a redder hue. "Yes...well, I learned in Vushaar that Gavin's apprentices were having difficulty following what I was saying, so I practiced slowing down and speaking with what I hope is greater clarity."

"If I may say so, you're doing a fine job. I'm proud of you," Valera said, making Wynn's blush deepen.

Gavin smiled. "What do we need to do to start this wizard-specific curriculum?"

"Personally, I would love to have you both teaching," Valera replied, "but I realize the demands of being Archmagister might prevent you from doing so, Gavin. If you like, I will work with Wynn to get the curriculum ready for your review."

"That's probably best," Gavin agreed, nodding. "If you have the time for preliminary discussions right now and if Wynn is available, I can leave you to it while I pursue other items on my list."

Wynn nodded. "Today's a practice day for Holly and the others, so I have time."

"Well then, thank you both for your time, and find me if you need me." Gavin stood, prompting Valera and Wynn to do so as well, and left.

* * *

GAVIN APPROACHED the Grand Stair just as Declan was placing his right foot on the first step. The bard looked over his shoulder and smiled upon seeing Gavin.

"Ah, there you are, Milord," Declan said, turning to Gavin. "I was hoping you might have some time."

"Of course, Declan," Gavin replied and pointed to the Grand Stair. "You want to take the quick way or the long way?"

One of Declan's eyebrows quirked. "Uhm, the quick way?"

"*Paedryx*," Gavin invoked, causing a sapphire archway of crackling energy to rise up from the floor. It became a doorway to a hallway in short order, and Gavin gestured for Declan to lead the way.

"I wasn't aware it was possible to teleport to the Citadel," Declan remarked as the archway disappeared after their transit.

Gavin shrugged. "It isn't, unless you happen to be the Archmagister."

They walked a short distance down the hallway, and Gavin turned into the sitting room where he'd hosted Garris Roshan, gesturing for Declan to pick his seat. Before they even had a chance to begin, Hartley arrived.

"May I offer you refreshment, Milord?" the specter asked.

Gavin looked to Declan, giving him a questioning expression.

"No, thank you," Declan replied.

Now, Gavin nodded once. "I'm good for now as well, Hartley. Thank you."

"Of course, sir."

Once the specter faded away, Gavin shifted his attention back to Declan, saying, "So, what's on your mind?"

"I just wanted to inform you that my associates have spread the word throughout our respective chapter-houses to be aware of Lillian and Mariana. We have no reason to believe there are any specific threats to them lurking out there, but it never hurts to be vigilant—especially when you're traveling."

"Thank you for that," Gavin said. "How has everything else been going?"

Declan smiled. "Quite well. I've been working on my various projects, one of which chronicles the rise of a new Kirloth."

Gavin fought the urge to roll his eyes. "I'm not sure I'm worthy of a chronicle, Declan."

"Let's see..." Declan lifted a hand and raised fingers, counting. "First, you're the first new member of House Kirloth known to exist in six thousand years. Second, you ended slavery across the known world. Third, you are the first Archmagister since Bellock Vanlon. Hmm...I do believe you are worthy of *at least* one chronicle, Gavin, possibly more."

"You're not going to let this go, are you?"

Declan grinned, his expression totally unrepentant. "Of course not. I'm a bard! Your exploits are the stuff the greatest chronicles are made of."

"Okay," Gavin said, heaving a sigh. "I won't fight you about it on the condition you never make me listen to it. I'm sure it will be a masterwork, but it would just be too embarrassing to sit through a performance or reading of a chronicle based on my life. Deal?"

"Of course, Gavin. We can agree on that much. Is there anything else I can do for you?"

Gavin nodded. "I'd like you to speak with our mutual associates to arrange a comprehensive report on the state of Tel. Torval and the others are already preparing reports for me, but they might not know all the necessary information I need. Besides, there's always the chance they'll filter what they tell me based on what they think I want to know."

"That won't be a problem, but honestly, I don't see the dukes and duchesses filtering information about their provinces," Declan said. "They need you far more than you need them, but I suppose it will be a good way to verify they're as truthful as we expect them to be."

"I'm also putting together a governance council for Tel. What are your thoughts on one of your associates attending that council?"

Declan shook his head. "I don't think that will work. My associates strive to reduce the attention directed their way, and attending a governance council is pretty much the opposite of no attention. Whichever poor soul attended would be visible to everyone else on the council and would be questioned mercilessly about the sources of the information they presented. It's far better to keep them away from prying eyes."

Gavin nodded. "Very well. If you'll see to the report, I'd appreciate it."

"What's next for you?" Declan asked.

"I'm supposed to stop in and visit with Wynn and my apprentices," Gavin replied and chuckled, shaking his head. "As often as it's Wynn training them instead of me, they should probably be Wynn's apprentices."

Declan shrugged. "Will you teach them anything he wouldn't or couldn't?"

"I don't know. There's some stuff that Marcus told me, mainly about what it means to be Kirloth, but none of them are Kirloth. I know I didn't hold anything back in training Wynn and the others, so maybe it would be just as well to make them Wynn's apprentices."

"You're forgetting one thing," Declan countered. "There will be a certain amount of prestige attached to being Kirloth's apprentices, let alone the Archmagister's apprentices. That could make things better, or worse, depending on who they're dealing with."

Gavin frowned. "You're saying someone might try to use them to get to me."

"It's always a possibility. It has happened before."

"Well, that's nine kinds of special," Gavin remarked, a mixture of a sigh and growl.

"I wouldn't worry too much about it," Declan replied. "We make sure they're well covered if they leave the College grounds, and the protections Marcus and the others built into the College should be more than sufficient to keep anyone with ill intent from entering."

"Then, how did those Guild of Shadows people get through? They certainly bore me ill will—to start with anyway."

Declan blinked, and his expression turned thoughtful. "No idea, honestly. I can only guess someone invited them into the College."

"That makes sense, I suppose," Gavin remarked. "Anyway, that's all I had for you, so unless you need me for something else, I'll let you get back to your day."

Declan smiled as he stood, Gavin standing also. "I think I'm good. I'll find you if I need you."

Hartley appeared to show the bard out. Gavin and Declan shook hands, and Declan left.

CHAPTER 21

Unique among her fellow province capitals, Tel Cothos occupied a massive island in a lake from which the kingdom's two greatest rivers flowed. The Vischaene flowed south to the Inner Sea, and the Cothori flowed west to the ocean through Wygoth Province. Strong breezes were common in and around the city, as the water of the lake leached the heat out of the air and the warmer air from the land rushed in to fill the 'void.'

The Cothos Estate occupied a promontory near the island's edge, with a translucent balcony that extended out over the lake and a large, prominent railing to help any visitors from experiencing vertigo. Lillian and Mariana stood in the estate's courtyard, a happy smile curling Lillian's lips as she closed her eyes and basked in the warm sun and light breeze.

"It is so beautiful here, Mari," Lillian said, her voice soft. "I don't see how you ever get any work done."

Mariana laughed. "I suppose I'm immune to it by now. It never seemed anything more than home to me."

Lillian opened her eyes to regard her friend. "Yes, I can see that. Goodness knows, I don't see anything special about Tel Mivar."

Movement drew Lillian's attention, and she saw Mariana's mother approaching them. A groom followed and accepted the reins of their horses and led them back to the stables.

"Starting the mission to the giants, dwarves, and elves?" Lyssa asked.

"Yes, ma'am," Lillian replied.

Mariana turned and met her mother, pulling her into a tight hug as she said, "I thought we'd visit on our way north, Mother."

Lyssa smiled. "That's fine, dear. You know I always enjoy seeing you. How long can you stay?"

"We were thinking of leaving tomorrow," Mariana replied. "Has there been any response yet to Gavin's new proclamations?"

"Not really," Lyssa said, leading them into the manor. "It's only been a few days. I doubt we'll see much reaction for at least a week. When we finally overhaul the tax laws and implement *those* changes, I think people will start taking much more notice of Gavin's reforms."

Lillian and Mariana both chuckled. They hadn't really discussed Gavin's long-term plans too much with him, but they were aware that Gavin wanted to rework Tel's tax laws to better distribute the tax burden across the various socio-economic levels of the populace. The challenging part of the plan was the phased roll-out over a period of time; the changes Gavin wanted were too different from the existing tax laws and might break the entire economy if he switched them all at once.

"How loud do you think the screaming will be?" Mariana asked, her expression almost smirking.

Lyssa shrugged. "There's no way to tell, really, but I do think Gavin's reforms will be more popular with the middle and lower classes. Once everything has a chance to take hold, I think everyone will see improvement in their finances...as long as they manage their money well. But that's enough work chat for the moment. Let's get you girls settled."

* * *

THE PALACE GATES in the capital city of Vushaar hadn't changed since Braden had last seen them. Several Cavaliers milled about the courtyard and waved upon seeing Braden arrive. Braden greeted those he passed as he crossed the courtyard to the palace complex's main entrance. A short time and some exploration were all Braden needed to find Varne, the Royal Herald.

"Braden!" Varne smiled upon seeing his visitor. "I didn't expect to see you again so soon. What brings you back to Vushaar?"

"The Archmagister has sent me with an invitation for Vushaar to send a representative to Tel Mivar for a meeting of the old alliance," Braden said. "Is today one of the days His Majesty holds court?"

"It is," Varne replied, "but I'm afraid you're already too late. Court is over for the day. Still, I'm sure His Majesty would consent to a private audience, especially for one of the Apprentices. I'll just go ask him about it."

Braden grinned. "Thank you, Varne. I appreciate your time."

"You're welcome, Braden." Varne led Braden out of his office. "As far as I'm concerned, Vushaar has a long way to go in repaying the debt we incurred to the Archmagister and the Apprentices. The five of you quite possibly saved Vushaar, and that's certainly not something to take lightly."

"I don't know that I'd characterize it that way," Braden said.

"Well, I certainly would, and I'm not the only one, either."

Varne and Braden continued chatting as they moved through the halls of the palace complex. Before Braden realized it, they were at the door to Terris's private study.

"Give me just a moment," Varne said. "I'll see if His Majesty has time for you." Varne knocked twice and stepped inside. Moments later, he emerged, smiling. "His Majesty is happy to see you now, Braden. Please, enter."

Stepping inside the study, Braden saw that it hadn't changed since the one time he'd visited after reconstituting the section of the outer wall. Terris sat at the desk and immediately stood, crossing the room to greet Braden with a respectful handshake. Varne quietly withdrew from the study.

"Thank you for receiving me on such short notice, Your Majesty," Braden said. "I greatly appreciate it."

Terris waved the matter away. "You're welcome. But please, think nothing of it. Also, I thought you were one of the six people permitted to address me by name." One of the king's eyebrows quirked upward.

Braden took a deep breath and nodded. "Of course...Terris. It's not easy, though."

"Do you address Gavin as 'Milord'?"

"Oh, no," Braden answered, shaking his head. "It didn't take us long to see what he thought of his friends addressing him as the Archmagister, no matter what official protocol decreed."

Terris smiled. "Well, if it helps, consider me the same as Gavin. Please, have a seat. Make yourself comfortable."

"Thank you."

Terris returned to the chair by the desk, and Braden sat on one end of the nearest sofa.

"So," Terris began, "what brings you back to Vushaar so soon?"

"Gavin asked me to visit you, Othron, and the dracons to deliver invitations to send a representative to Tel Mivar. He wants to start rebuilding the old alliance. Lillian and Mariana left just before I did on a mission to visit the giants, dwarves, and elves."

Both of Terris's eyebrows shot up, showing his surprise. "Gavin certainly doesn't wait around, does he?"

"Not at all," Braden agreed. "He's already disbanded the Royal Guard, and despite what a lot of us expected, that went fairly well. From what I understand, Gavin only had to kill the head of the Royal Guard who was trying to stylize himself as the next King of Tel."

Terris chuckled. "Yes, I'm sure that didn't go over well with Gavin, especially considering his feelings toward the previous King of Tel."

Braden nodded. "It's a bit morbid to say this, perhaps, but it's probably for the best that the former royal family of Tel died during Gavin's purge of anyone who used the slave brands. Gavin probably would've arrested them for the various crimes they'd committed and had to execute them anyway."

"Yes, a nasty situation all the way around, that. I agree it was better for Gavin to indirectly dodge it." Terris leaned back in his seat. "As for the reason of your visit, Vushaar is quite happy to send a representative to Tel. When does Gavin want to hold the meeting?"

Braden blinked. "You know, he didn't say. That's a bit of a glaring oversight, isn't it?"

"He probably has so much going on that it just slipped his mind," Terris remarked. He swiveled his chair and grasped the nearby bell-pull, pulling twice. Moments later, the study door opened, and a servant entered.

"You rang, Your Majesty?" the servant asked.

"I did indeed," Terris answered. "Thank you for such prompt response. Would you please ask Q'Orval and Roth Thatcherson if they have time for me?"

The servant bowed deeply at the waist once more. "Of course, Your Majesty."

"Thank you."

The servant backed out of the study, and it wasn't long at all before Q'Orval and Roth arrived. Both gentlemen looked a bit surprised to see Braden sitting in the king's study.

"You sent for us, Your Majesty?" Q'Orval asked.

Terris nodded. "Thank you for coming so quickly. Lord Wygoth brings a message from the Archmagister of Tel. It seems our friend is already working toward strengthening the old alliance and has invited us to send a representative to Tel Mivar. I'm thinking of sending Roth, and Q'Orval, I wanted your thoughts on the choice of delegate."

"I couldn't think of a better representative, Your Majesty," Q'Orval replied. "The Archmagister already knows him and has a good working relationship with him, at least as far as I know."

Terris turned his attention to Roth. "Your thoughts, Roth?"

"I'm happy to serve however you need, Your Majesty," Roth answered. "I don't know that I really have much of a working relation-ship with the Archmagister, but Q'Orval is correct that we do know each other."

Terris nodded again. "Thank you. The precise timing of the meeting, conference, or what have you is a bit unclear at this time, but I trust you and Lord Wygoth will be able to sort it out. Keep me apprised, please, and expect that I'll want a full report of each meeting."

Roth nodded once, snapped to attention, and saluted Terris. "Yes, Your Majesty."

"Very well, gentlemen," Terris said. "Thank you."

Q'Orval and Roth turned to leave, and Braden took that opportunity to stand.

"Your Majesty, with your permission, I'll go with Roth to discuss potential days for the meeting before moving on to the next on my list."

"Of course," Terris replied, nodding once. "Safe travels, and thank you for bringing the Archmagister's request. Are you sure I can't offer you our hospitality for the night? I'm sure Kiri would appreciate hearing how her friends fare."

Braden weighed the options in his mind and decided that he might as well accept Terris's offer. He'd told Gavin that he was planning on taking a few days with this, so spending a night in Vushaar wouldn't be a bad thing.

"Thank you, Your Majesty," Braden agreed. "I would be happy to accept your hospitality for the night."

"You're welcome. Q'Orval, would you mind letting Kiri know that Lord Wygoth is visiting from Tel?"

"Not at all, sire," the aged majordomo replied. "I'm happy to do so."

With that, all three of Terris's guests filed out of his study.

CHAPTER 22

The next morning, Lillian and Mariana set out from Tel Cothos. A ferry delivered them to the northern shore of the lake, where the ages-old trade route would take them to their ultimate destinations. In the years since the royal family took over the civil administration of Tel, trade between the members of the old alliance gradually waned, much like the diplomatic relationships. As such, the old trade route was little more than a forgotten track the farther they traveled from Tel Cothos.

"Do you think Gavin will be able to rebuild the old alliance?" Lillian asked as their horses *clip-clopped* along the road that had weeds growing up between the paving stones.

Mariana shrugged. "This probably sounds like I'm avoiding the question, but if anyone can, it's Gavin. He has a lot of work ahead of him, though. Most of these problems are six hundred years in the making."

Lillian sighed. "I don't understand how the royal family could let things get so bad."

"It's not really that difficult to understand, Lillian," Mariana countered. "Bigotry, indifference, and greed. I, personally, am a little confused about how the bigotry developed, but the king was offering a bounty on elf ears. Just how sick is that?"

"I'm glad that part of our history is over. I know we still have to clean up the consequences of it, but at least, we're not perpetuating anymore."

Mariana shook her head. "Don't kid yourself; I'm sure there are quite a few people out in the hinterlands still advocating the king's policies toward non-humans. That kind of social change takes decades, if not centuries. And to be fair, not all Archmagisters have been beacons of enlightenment and fairness. Like the tides, their moral character has been both high and low."

Lillian smiled, her expression regretful. "It would be nice if we could make more progress than we lose, though."

"It would indeed."

* * *

BRADEN STOOD outside the ruined gatehouse of Othron's keep. His eyes roamed over the ancient script carved into the stone, and he wondered about the people who had built it. Oh, he was sure he could find information about them in the archives of the Vushaari capital, but there was still something about seeing such a massive artifact of a civilization that no longer existed. Shaking his head and reminding himself of his purpose here, Braden walked through the gatehouse and approached the keep.

The moment he passed through the gatehouse, Braden felt a Conjuration effect wash over the courtyard, and Othron's voice surrounded him. "Ah...Young Wygoth! How nice of you to return. Please, be welcome. I am in my study."

Braden smiled as the Conjuration faded and entered the keep. The hidden staircase was where Sarres had found it, and Othron had either triggered the hidden door or it had been open since they'd first visited. A short walk down the stairs delivered Braden to the underground residence of one of the greatest arcanists to ever live.

"Good day to you, Othron," Braden said, approaching the ancient lich.

Othron nodded once. "Good day to you as well, Young Wygoth. How can an old skeleton be of service?"

"Oh, you're more than just an old skeleton," Braden countered. "Gavin asked me to visit you and deliver an invitation to attend a council of the old alliance. Vushaar is sending Roth Thatcherson, and once we've finished, I'm going to the dracons."

"Interesting," Othron replied. "So, Gavin's rebuilding the old alliance under the auspices of the Great Houses of Tel?"

Braden shook his head. "Not quite. He's the Archmagister now."

"He is? Oh...that is priceless! For the first time since the Founding, an arcanist of House Kirloth is the Archmagister of Tel. I can only imagine the consternation and dismay Gavin is leaving in his wake."

"Well, he's already suspended a group of Fifth Tiers for bullying and tormenting a First Tier. The toadies get to start as Fourth Tiers in the new term, and the leader will be Third Tier, assuming they all come back."

"Yes," Othron agreed. "That sounds like Gavin. They should be rather happy Gavin found them and not my old friend. Amdar could be...excessive at times."

Braden frowned, but after a moment's thought, he recalled that Amdar had been Marcus's birth name. "I think, perhaps, excessive might be an understatement where he was concerned...at times."

Othron erupted into laughter, which was really odd for someone who didn't have lungs. "Oh, yes! Amdar never suffered fools well, and he did not exactly have a deep wellspring of patience. But we digress. Has Gavin determined the schedule for this meeting?"

"Not as such, no," Braden replied. "At least not that I'm aware of. You'll probably be seeing me again once he sorts that out."

"Of course, Young Wygoth. You and your associates are always welcome here."

Braden nodded. "Thank you, Othron. If you'll forgive me, I should be moving on to the dracons. I imagine I'll have my work cut out for me there, since they withdrew from the world and all."

"Yes...rather unfortunate, that. Be well, and safe journey, lad."

Braden nodded his respect once more and left.

* * *

LILLIAN AND MARIANA were not even an hour back into their journey after stopping for their midday meal, when a massive tree fell across the road no more than twenty-five yards ahead of them. Eight people —both men and women—charged out of the trees at a full sprint and soon stood in an arc around them.

"Thank ye kindly for traveling our road today," one of the men said. "It's time to pay the toll."

Mariana and Lillian shared a look. Lillian gestured for Mariana to speak.

"The toll?" Mariana scoffed. "There's never been a toll on this trade road. The only fees associated with it are included in the permits for trade caravans."

"Lookee here, boys," one of the women cheered. "We got us a lawyer!"

"No," Lillian countered. "You have Lillian Mivar and Mariana Cothos. If you have even the minimal sense the gods gave a common cur, you'll run back to your forest hideaway and pray we don't follow."

"Now, see here, missy," the original speaker began. "There's eight of us and two of you."

"If our mentor were here," Lillian replied, "he'd offer to wait while you rounded up more people. It *might* make a difference, but unlikely."

Mariana nodded. "Yes. What is Gavin's record for most people killed at one time, do you think?"

Lillian frowned, her expression thoughtful. "Oh, I'm sure I don't know. It had to have been that manor the slavers had taken over. There was something like three hundred horses with full tack for each one."

The ladies returned their attention to the would-be bandits, and

Mariana addressed them, "Look. We're not really interested in making the trade roads more safe right now. If you run away, we'll let you live."

"Step down from those horses, girls," the original speaker growled, pointing at them with his drawn sword, "and hand over your valuables."

"Left four," Lillian said.

Mariana nodded, and in unison, Lillian and Mariana invoked a Word of Interation, "*Thraxys.*"

None of the corpses even released a death rattle as they collapsed where they stood.

Mariana sighed. "Do you want the tree or the bodies?"

"I'll take the tree," Lillian replied, and she focused on the tree lying across the road and cleared her mind of all thoughts except her intent as she invoked the Word of Transmutation, "*Rhyskaal.*"

In the blink of an eye, the tree became neat stacks of firewood with associated stacks of kindling made from the branches and leaves.

Mariana considered the kindling a moment and looked back to the corpses of the would-be robbers. She nodded once and invoked the same Word, turning the kindling to coils of rope. A composite effect, invoked as "*Rhyskaal-Paedryx,*" had the corpses dangling from their necks on nearby branches, supported by the rope. One last Transmutation effect converted a couple pieces of firewood to a sign implanted below the dangling corpses, describing their crime.

Looking over their handiwork, Lillian grimaced. "Well, this was an unpleasant diversion."

"It is rather unfortunate they didn't see reason," Mariana agreed. "I would have been willing to ask Mother to pardon them if they had surrendered. I know...probably a waste of effort, but still."

The ladies nudged their horses and resumed their journey. They weren't even out of Tel yet.

* * *

BRADEN ARRIVED at the gates for the tunnel that led to Qar'Zhosk. Two dracons stood just inside, and they nodded their greeting to Braden as he approached.

"Good day to you," Braden said. "I bring a message to the Council of Clans from Gavin Cross, Head of House Kirloth and Archmagister of Tel."

"We bid thee welcome to Qar'Zhosk," one of the dracons replied as the other opened the gates.

Soon, Braden approached the massive cupola at the center of the underground city and was pleased to see the Council of Clans was meeting. They all turned to face him as he stepped between the cupola's columns. Xask nodded once in greeting.

"Welcome back to Qar'Zhosk, Young Wygoth," Xask said. "What brings you to our city?"

"I bear a message to the dracons from Gavin Cross, Head of House Kirloth and Archmagister of Tel," Braden answered. "He invites you to send a representative to Tel Mivar to attend the first alliance council in over six hundred years."

Various councilors nodded, as Xask asked, "And would he be receptive to an emissary as well?"

Braden blinked. "An emissary? Forgive me, but may I ask for clarification?"

"An ambassador," Xask replied. "The Grand Moot voted to rescind our withdrawal from the world."

"Uhm, I'm pretty sure that's bigger news than Gavin calling an alliance council," Braden remarked, his eyes wide. "I, for one, would love to see the dracons out among us again, and I feel very safe in saying Gavin and my friends think likewise. Yes, I'm confident Gavin would welcome your ambassador in Tel Mivar."

Xask nodded. "Thank you. We are sending a mission to Vushaar, the giants, and the dwarves as well."

"Not the elves?" Braden asked, before he realized that might be overstepping.

"Not at this time, Young Wygoth," the ancient councilor

answered. "We have heard whispers from the High Forest that concern us."

"Forgive me for being new to diplomacy," Braden replied, "but may I ask what those whispers are?"

"Several factions within the elven nobility are agitating for attacks on the Kingdom of Tel, and other whispers suggest Nature's Protector is behind it."

Braden took a deep breath and released it as a heavy sigh. That *was* troubling. Nature's Protector was the title the elves gave the head of their government. Not quite a monarch but not quite an elected official, each new holder of the office was traditionally chosen through agreements between the Sylvan Synod and the elven nobility.

"Thank you for sharing that," Braden said. "In regard to the alliance council, I'm afraid Gavin didn't specify a precise schedule. With your permission, I'll return once I've learned more."

The ancient councilor nodded. "Of course, Young Wygoth. You and your associates are always welcome within our lands."

"Thank you for seeing me," Braden replied, bowing and leaving the cupola. Now, all that remained was scheduling the meeting. Focusing on Tel Mivar, Braden created a gateway and went in search of Gavin.

CHAPTER 23

Gavin regarded the journal he was holding and considered returning to it. It was one of Marcus's, dated shortly before the Godswar began. He'd already read the journal that contained Marcus's accounts of finding his wife and daughter murdered, and the description of what he had done to the Temple Guardsmen responsible chilled Gavin to his very soul.

"Milord," Hartley's voice pulled Gavin's attention away from the journal, "you have a visitor. It's Young Wygoth."

Gavin smiled. "Thank you, Hartley. Please, show him in."

Moments later, Braden strode into the library and froze, taking in the sight before him. The Citadel's library was easily half the size of the College's library, at least. Catwalks connected the upper levels of the bookshelves, and rolling ladders waited on each platform.

"I know," Gavin said. "I felt rather gobsmacked, myself, when I saw it the first time."

"Is there a catalog?" Braden asked. "Do you know what all is in here?"

Gavin gestured toward a small reading table with a couple stacks of books and shrugged. "Those tomes serve as the catalog and index of the library, and someone spelled them at some point. When I put

Marcus's journals on those shelves over there, entries for them appeared, even though they were referenced as 'Journals—Amdar of House Kirloth.' It surprised me until I remembered that was his name. I never think of him as anyone other than Marcus."

"I know," Braden agreed. "Othron referred to him as Amdar, and it took me a moment to catch up."

Gavin smiled. "That is an excellent segue. Do please sit and be comfortable. How did you fare on your travels?"

They both eased into plush armchairs in the reading area of the library as Braden said, "Terris appointed Roth to serve as Vushaar's representative. Othron agreed to come, and the dracons apparently had another Grand Moot that revoked their decision to withdraw from the world. They have asked to send a formal ambassador to Tel."

"I wondered if they would call another Grand Moot after seeing me as the Archmagister," Gavin remarked. "Of course, I welcome their ambassador. I'm planning to restructure the old palace complex to serve as a kind of Embassy Row, and I'll make provisions for every government sending ambassadors. Hmmm...I wonder how many there are."

Braden held up his hand and lifted fingers as he said, "Vushaar, Xartham's lands, the High Forest, the dracons, the giants, the dwarves, the minotaurs, the halflings—that's eight right there, and I have absolutely no idea what kind of governments exist beyond the Godswall Mountains."

Gavin sighed. "Perhaps, we should find out. It's been six thousand years; I'd like to think Hope's Pass won't go to waste."

"You'll have to do something about Skullkeep, first," Braden countered. "There's no way you're getting a diplomatic mission through Hope's Pass until the old alliance controls that fortress again."

"And I have this feeling that there won't be any way to secure that fortress as long as the Necromancer lives, if you can call whatever the Necromancer is as living. He's...what...three hundred years old?"

Braden shrugged. "No one really knows. He announced himself when he took over the fortress...oh, almost four hundred years ago now. The elves swear he isn't an elf, but then, can you blame them? Given everything he's done, I'm not really fond of him being human, either."

"Do we know for certain it's the same guy? I mean, it could be a title, passed from person to person."

"I suppose that could be the case, but that would make these people scary powerful. Everyone says there's no way to control that many undead, and yet, he's doing it. If it is a title passed from person to person, each person in the chain has to have your level of power or higher. I mean, do you think you could control an army of undead?"

"I've never really thought to try," Gavin replied. "It isn't the kind of thing I've felt the need to experiment with."

Braden nodded. "I don't blame you at all. Before you accepted us as your apprentices, I wasn't looking forward to the one section of Necromancy the College requires everyone to take."

"What? The College requires a section on Necromancy?"

"From what I remember, it's more of a survey course that touches on all the branches of Interation," Braden replied. "The other Schools of Magic are rather straightforward, but I guess the Council feels all the disciplines that make up the School of Interation—like Necromancy, Mysticism, and such—warrant a course."

Gavin chuckled. "I didn't exactly follow the 'normal' course of study, so I suppose I shouldn't be surprised about classes I've never heard of."

Braden nodded. "If I may, when were you thinking of holding the alliance meeting? Everyone asked, and I didn't have an answer. Were you planning to wait for Mariana and Lillian to return?"

"No, I don't think we can afford the time," Gavin answered. He leaned his head back against the armchair and heaved a sigh before returning his attention to Braden. "There is simply so much to do; sometimes, it boggles the mind."

"In your defense, you are trying to fix almost six hundred years of mismanagement and corruption...in addition to rebuilding our relationships with everyone else. No part of any of that could be called 'easy.'"

"You're right. It isn't easy, and I keep having to hold myself back from wanting everything to happen *right now*. Rome wasn't built in a day, after all."

Braden blinked. "Uh, what? I've never heard of Rome, Gavin."

Gavin opened his mouth to explain, but the gray mists on the fringes of his consciousness swirled deeper. He closed his mouth and his eyes, fighting the urge to growl in frustration. After a couple heartbeats, he opened his eyes and said, "It must be something out of my missing memories, Braden. Sorry. Ever since Iosen Sivas, those fragments have become more common."

"Don't worry about it," Braden replied. "I can't imagine what it's like to deal with something like that."

"Heh...it's just the way things are, after this long," Gavin replied, adding a shrug. "I can't change it, so why get worked up about it? As far as the meeting, I don't have a concrete calendar of appointments yet, so I'm willing to operate on their schedules. Do you mind handling the organization of it and keeping me apprised?"

Braden shook his head. "I don't mind at all."

"Thank you."

"That's all I have," Braden remarked as he stood. "Do you need anything else, Gavin?"

Gavin shook his head, standing as well. "No, and thank you, Braden. I appreciate your help."

"You're welcome. I'm going to check on Wynn as long as I'm here, and then, I'll make the rounds again and let you know once we have a schedule."

Gavin nodded once, and Braden left.

After watching his friend leave, Gavin returned to his seat. It was so easy to feel overwhelmed. In a lot of ways, Gavin felt like he was making up 'being Archmagister' as he went along, and while he didn't exactly like that, he didn't know what other option he had. It wasn't like he could turn to his predecessor for an orientation.

Still, there were worse jobs Gavin could have. A part of him wished he could just be an instructor like Wynn; his memories of sharing what he'd learned from Marcus as they traveled to Vushaar were some of the best he had. No matter how much he might like the idea of being 'just' a teacher, Gavin couldn't shake another memory: the day Marcus told him what it meant to be Kirloth. He hadn't seen it at the time, but there were some decisions *only* Kirloth could make, or at the very least, decisions no one should have to make. Was Gavin qualified to follow in the footsteps of his mentor? He wasn't sure; he could only do his best.

* * *

TERRIS TURNED when the door of the study opened. He smiled as Kiri entered and closed the door behind her. He stood and met her half-way, pulling her into a tight hug.

"Hello, Father," Kiri said, her voice slightly muffled by the hug.

For several moments, father and daughter stood in silence. Terris offered silent prayers of thanks that Kiri had survived and come home. The first moment or two of every meeting, Terris remembered how it felt to believe his daughter had died.

"Hello, Kiri," Terris said at last, breaking the hug. "What can I do for you?"

"Nothing, really," Kiri replied. "I...well, I just wanted to see you. There have been mornings, even lately, that I woke up feeling surprised to be home."

Terris nodded. "I know exactly how you feel, and you're welcome to visit me anytime." Kiri's expression darkened for the briefest of moments, but Terris still noticed it. "What was that? Is there anything you'd like to talk about?"

Kiri sighed. "I miss waking up and seeing a stack of blankets on the floor beside the bed, too, Father."

Terris frowned, not following her thought, but understanding came to him mere heartbeats later. "You miss Gavin."

Kiri nodded and stepped back into her father's embrace. "All I wanted was to be home and somehow remove the mark, but now that I am home and no longer have the mark, I realize I miss Gavin. I know it's only been a week or so, but it feels odd not having him somewhere close."

"Want me to let you in on a little secret...that isn't so secret?" Terris asked.

"What?"

Terris leaned back far enough to make eye contact with Kiri and said, "It felt odd when your mother wasn't close, too."

Kiri worked her lower lip between her teeth as she gazed into her father's eyes. After a few moments, she looked away. "Before he left, Gavin came to see me, and I wanted to tell him that I love him."

"Did you?" Terris asked.

"No. I've never felt what I feel for Gavin before. I certainly didn't feel this way about Thaddeus; that was adolescent infatuation."

Terris chuckled. "If I may be so bold, I'm glad. Thaddeus...well, he didn't suit you."

Kiri's lips quirked into a mischievous grin. "He wasn't good enough for your little girl? Is that what you're saying, Daddy?"

"Let's just say I didn't quite see him as your spouse, especially once you are Queen of Vushaar. I never felt he had the stomach to stand at your side through tough times."

"And what of Gavin? Can you see him standing at my side?"

An image popped unbidden to the forefront of Terris' mind. Gavin standing beside the throne, while Kiri sat in the full regalia of Vushaar's monarch. His expression was hard and devoid of emotion. He held his right hand at chest level, cupped as if holding an apple. An orb of raw, seething power hovered over his palm, easily the size of a honeydew and colored gold, like the robes of his office.

"Kiri, I don't see Gavin simply standing by your side," Terris said at last. "As long as he favors you, I see all manner of threats vanishing in the dead of night, before anyone is aware they even existed."

Kiri grinned. "Yes, it is like that around him, rather often in fact. What were you working on before I interrupted you?"

"I was reading over a petition from the Merchants' Association. They're asking for improvements to the roads between the province capitals as well as improving the roads connecting the larger towns to the province capitals."

"Do we have the money for that?" Kiri asked, almost frowning.

"Perhaps across the long-term, yes, but they're asking for work to begin all at the same time. I agree that we need it, and I also agree that improving our roads will make it easier for trade to flourish. I'm just not sure what priority it deserves, especially while we're rebuilding from the civil war." Terris shifted his attention back to Kiri, his expression thoughtful. "Come to think of it, this is an excellent opportunity for you to become better acquainted with the demands of the kingdom. I'm going to hand this petition off to you, and I'll also give you the report on Vushaar's budget prepared by the Exchequer. I'd like for you to read over both and see if you can devise a way to give the Merchants' Association what they want without too much of an impact on our other priorities."

Kiri started to smart off, but she realized this was exactly something she would be facing once she inherited the throne. Gavin had said she needed to get settled back into her life before he would discuss a betrothal, so this seemed like as good a place to start as any.

CHAPTER 24

"Thank you, Hartley," Gavin said, passing the cleared dishes and utensils to the specter. The items were all that remained of a breakfast that would have put almost any gourmet to shame. "Oh, Hartley…is there a room somewhere in the Citadel for meetings of the Conclave of the Great Houses?"

The specter paused in its movement toward the kitchen and pantry, turned to face Gavin, and answered, "Of course, Milord. If you have a moment, I will be happy to conduct you there once I've settled the remains of breakfast, or, if you prefer, I can direct you there now."

Gavin smiled. "Hartley, I would never dream of depriving myself of your company. I can wait for you to deliver that to the kitchen."

A few minutes later, Gavin and Hartley were on the second floor of the Citadel, just a short distance from that floor's access to the library. Like every other doorframe he'd seen, this one bore the Glyph of Kirloth in the center of the lintel and gave no indication of which room lay beyond. Hartley opened the door for Gavin before he could stop the specter. Stepping inside, Gavin found himself in a room almost identical to the meeting room he'd used many times at the Mivar Estate.

One major difference caught Gavin's eye right away. The head of the table, where the Glyph of Kirloth was on Mivar's table, bore no glyph at all. Gavin approached and brushed his fingers across the vacant space. The moment he did so, Gavin felt a deep *THRUM* through his *skathos*, and the table etched the missing Glyph of Kirloth into its surface.

"Wow," Gavin said.

"This is the only table of its kind," Hartley explained, from Gavin's side. "Unlike the tables in the meeting halls of the estates, this table manifests the glyph of the current Archmagister's House."

"And the Archmagister has always been a wizard?" Gavin asked.

The specter nodded. "So far, that is the case, Milord."

"Interesting," Gavin remarked before he shook himself and returned to his purpose. "Can you arrange for a message to reach Torval, Sypara, Lyssa, and Carth?"

Hartley's ghostly expression looked almost indignant.

"Right, sorry. Please coordinate with them to determine a schedule for meetings. I want to start working through the tax laws— well, any laws enacted by the royal family, really. Aside from the alliance meeting, that is my current priority."

"Of course, Milord," Hartley replied at once. "I shall see to it immediately."

* * *

THE DAYS BLURRED into one meeting after another for Gavin. It wasn't long until he was spending whole afternoons in the Conclave meeting room with the Dukes and Duchesses of Tel. Even when he wasn't specifically working on the legal system, that project always seemed to swirl in the back of Gavin's mind.

"Milord?" Hartley's voice pulled Gavin out of his focus, and he looked up.

"Yes?"

"Young Wygoth asks if you have any availability," the specter replied.

Gavin smiled. "Yes, of course! Please, send him in. Oh...and ask him if he'd like any refreshments."

Hartley nodded once. "Of course, Milord."

Moments later, Hartley ushered Braden into the study Gavin had claimed as an office. Gavin stood and met his friend with a handshake, ultimately offering him a choice in seating.

"How have you been?" Gavin asked, once they were settled.

"I've been just fine," Braden replied. "I also have a proposed schedule for your alliance summit."

"Excellent! When?"

Braden smiled. "How does next week sound? All participants have cleared their schedules, and I can provide transportation to minimize the traveling they have to do."

Gavin nodded. "If the meeting extends past one day, we can either teleport them home or offer them rooms in the Citadel...and there's just one last person to ask."

"Oh?"

"Yes," Gavin answered. "I should've thought of it sooner, but I'd like Ovir to attend as well."

Braden responded with an understanding nod. "That makes sense. Besides, it'll give Ovir and Roth a chance to catch up. There's no way to know how long it's been since they were face-to-face."

"In that case, we might as well go visit Ovir now," Gavin said, pushing himself to his feet.

Braden blinked. "Uhm, do you want me to deliver your invitation?"

Gavin frowned. "Why? I've been to the Temple before."

"Gavin," Braden said, his tone very similar to a patient parent addressing a clueless child, "the Archmagister doesn't go to people. People come to the Archmagister. You're the last of the Divine Emissaries."

Heaving a sigh, Gavin grimaced. "I don't know why people keep calling me that. Bellos hasn't spoken with me since offering me the job."

"People have referred to every Archmagister after Kirloth—I mean, Marcus...uh, Amdar ...whatever—as the last of the Divine

Emissaries. During the Founding, almost all the new gods—at least those who accepted a mantle of divinity after the Godswar—named an emissary. Those emissaries worked together to rebuild the society that the war shattered. No other position among mortals is chosen by the gods anymore; the Archmagister is the only one."

"Not even the Royal Priest of Tel?"

Braden shook his head. "Not as far as anyone has said."

All of his interactions with the individual Bellos had identified as Valthon flitted through Gavin's mind. "Heh...knowing that old rascal, I bet he meddles behind the scenes."

Braden looked a little wild around the eyes when Gavin referred to Valthon as an 'old rascal.'

Gavin merely grinned. "He is certainly an old rascal, Braden. Take a moment to examine his statue in the Hall of the Gods when we get there. The old man's a mischievous imp."

"Uhm...I always thought that was just the sculptor's interpretation."

"The first time I saw it, I thought the same," Gavin said, "but Dakkor's statue looks entirely too much like the man who visited the Council meeting during that mess with the Guild of Shadows. I'm not so sure those statues were 'sculpted.'"

* * *

THE TEMPLE OF VALTHON looked just as Gavin remembered it from before his trip to Vushaar. But then again, he suspected it hadn't changed much across the thousands of years it had existed. The acolyte in training occupying the greeter post looked up as Gavin led Braden up the steps. There was a look of incredulity as his eyes opened wide, and he almost leapt from the chair to kneel before Gavin.

Gavin fought the urge to sigh. Yes, it was good for the people to respect the office of the Archmagister, but that didn't mean Gavin enjoyed everyone bowing and kneeling to him, and he sincerely hoped he never started.

"Please, return to your seat," Gavin said.

"Uhm...ah, welcome to the Temple of Valthon, Milord," the greeter stammered as he returned to the chair behind the desk. "Is this your first time visiting us?"

Gavin smiled. "Not exactly. I believe you have a standing order that Gavin Cross, Head of House Kirloth, is always to be permitted access to Ovir?"

"Yes," the young man replied. "I was informed of that during my orientation as a greeter."

"Excellent," Gavin remarked and pointed at his medallion. "I am Gavin Cross of House Kirloth."

The young man's eyes focused on Gavin's medallion and, for the second time, snapped wide. "Forgive me...uh, Milord. I didn't notice."

"It's quite all right," Gavin said. "My associate and I have business with Ovir, so I shall wish you a good day."

Without waiting for the young man to reply, Gavin led Braden past the greeter's desk and into the Temple. As they passed through the Hall of the Gods, Gavin stopped and gestured for Braden to examine the statue of Dakkor. Just as Braden approached, the statue winked, and Braden almost jumped back.

"Yeah," Gavin said, "I think there's more to all these statues scattered around than anyone realizes."

Braden turned to regard Valthon's statue before glancing around to all the others, his eyes just a bit wild. "Do you think they're all..."

Gavin shrugged. "No idea."

After giving Braden a few more moments to contemplate the possibility of the gods watching everywhere one of their statues existed, Gavin turned and headed off toward the main areas of the Temple.

It didn't take them long to find Ovir, and the old priest smiled at seeing Gavin in the gold robes of the Archmagister. He didn't say anything, though, beyond inviting Gavin and Braden up to his residence with an offer of refreshments.

"Well now," Ovir said, once they were all seated, "I do believe you've received a promotion."

Gavin scoffed. "Some days, it feels like a sentence."

"I have no doubt that it does, my boy," Ovir agreed. "So, I'm not about to suggest that the Archmagister's time isn't supremely valuable, but I am glad to see you returned from Vushaar intact. What brings you here, if I may ask?"

"Braden has been organizing a meeting of various members of the old alliance for me," Gavin answered. "Everyone has agreed to meet next week, and I realized I wanted to invite you but hadn't spoken with you about it. I'm sorry that it slipped my mind and for the short notice."

Ovir scoffed. "If something like this is all that's slipped your mind, you're doing a far sight better than I would be in your place. I'm sure you have all manner of messes to clean up, given how long the royal family had unrestricted authority over Tel. As for the meeting, I would be honored to attend. I can hand off my participation in the daily services here to one of the senior priests on any days you need me."

"Thank you, Ovir," Gavin replied. "We're planning to begin at the morning bell of the first work-day. I'm hoping it won't last the entire week, but like you said, there's no way to know for certain."

"If I may ask," Ovir began, "who else is attending?"

"Vushaar is sending your brother Roth as their representative," Gavin answered. "Othron has agreed to attend, and the dracons are sending an ambassador to Tel who I think will double as their representative."

Ovir blinked. "The *dracons* will attend?"

"Sorry," Gavin replied. "I probably should have mentioned that they apparently called another Grand Moot and revoked their decision to withdraw from the world."

Ovir stared at Gavin in silence for several moments before he closed his eyes and shook his head. When he focused on Gavin once more, he said, "I never realized we were living in such momentous times. First, Bellos names a new Archmagister, and then, the dracons return to the world. It's enough to make an old man wonder what will come next."

"Reclaiming Skullkeep," Gavin replied. "That's why I'm pushing this alliance summit so much. We all need to start building toward that goal, and once we achieve *that*, I want to send a diplomatic mission through Hope's Pass. It's long past time we investigated the possibility of opening a dialogue with the people who live beyond the Godswall Mountains."

"You certainly don't dream small," Ovir remarked. "Do you think they'll talk to us?"

Gavin shrugged. "There's no way to know until we ask. For all we know, the people over there *want* to communicate with us but have either been afraid to reach out to us or can't get past Skullkeep. The Necromancer has been a source of all kinds of unrest and threats to everyone on this side of Hope's Pass, so we need to deal with him or it or them, no matter what. But once we have, why not send a delegation through the Pass to say hello?"

"You make an excellent case, Gavin," Ovir responded. "The more I think about it, the more I feel like we should be ashamed for allowing the situation to remain as it has for so long. Valthon never intended it to be a permanent exile when He raised the mountains; that's why he created Hope's Pass in the first place."

Gavin shook his head. "There's no reason to feel ashamed, Ovir. I'm sure it was a combination of many factors, not the least of which being fear of the people who remained loyal to Lornithar and His pantheon. For that matter, I freely admit that the chance exists it will all be for naught; I just think they deserve an opportunity to prove otherwise. Even if there isn't some sort of grand reunification, I'm sure there are ways we could improve each other's lives...simply through trade and communication, if nothing else."

Ovir's expression became somber. "I remember what it was like to feel that kind of hope."

"Then, you owe it to yourself to feel it again, my friend. Hope is one of those things that makes life worth living."

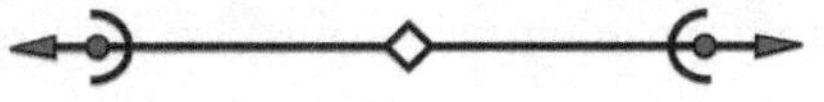

CHAPTER 25

By the time the first day of the alliance summit arrived, Gavin had added five more attendees: Torval Mivar, Sypara Wygoth, Carth Roshan, Lyssa Cothos, and Nathrac. The more he considered it, he soon decided they needed to be aware of what transpired, and besides, one never knew where the best solution to a problem might come from. The key to any meeting was to keep the group as small as possible so it actually achieved something, instead of just dissolving into a meet-and-greet.

Gavin smiled as he surveyed the room. Specters that served as part of Hartley's staff for the Citadel offered refreshments as the attendees chatted among themselves, and Gavin was glad to see everyone included the dracon ambassador. Ovir wasn't the only one who was shocked that the dracons had ended their withdrawal from the world, but at least Othron and Roth had warning ahead of time.

They occupied one of the general meeting rooms on the main floor of the Citadel, a massive circular table occupying the center of the space. Everyone—all ten of them—took up less than half the seats. No one seemed to mind, though. If anything, they enjoyed being among the first people to visit the Citadel after so long a time.

"All right, people," Gavin said. "Let's take our seats and get started."

The chatter faded as people found seats around the half of the table closest to Gavin's, with Nathrac occupying the seat directly opposite Gavin.

"I had intended this to be the first meeting of the alliance council since the death of Bellock Vanlon," Gavin began, "but with the inclusion of the Great Houses of Tel, perhaps it would be better to call it the first meeting of the war council to reclaim Skullkeep."

Of those sitting at the table, only Ovir didn't look surprised.

"Besides," Gavin continued, "Lillian Mivar and Mariana Cothos are currently carrying out a diplomatic mission on my behalf to the giants, dwarves, and elves, the other primary signatories to the old alliance. I suppose it's difficult to have an actual alliance summit meeting if three of the members aren't in attendance."

When Gavin said nothing more, the dracon ambassador did. "Reclaiming the fortress of Hope's Pass is a worthy endeavor, and on behalf of my people, I declare our full support for that goal. When were you thinking of acting?"

"That's part of what this council will determine," Gavin answered. "I can't imagine we'd be able to mobilize any time soon. I mean, Vushaar is still recovering from its recent civil war, and I'm up to my neck cleaning up Tel's government. I have proof that the Necromancer caused the Vushaari civil war; he supplied a cadre of wizards to support Ivarson. I also have proof that Leuwyn, the last King of Tel, served the Necromancer, so there's no way to know how much of Tel's situation is because of Leuwyn's mismanagement or the result of directives from his master. Reclaiming Skullkeep will not be easy, and it's something we need to be as prepared for as possible, or we'll fail and do ourselves even more harm in the long run."

"You raise excellent points," Roth Thatcherson agreed. "I can tell you that Vushaar is in no way able to mount any kind of military expedition at this point. Aside from sorting out the traitors from the loyalists in the army, Ivarson's forces and sympathizers wreaked havoc on the kingdom's infrastructure. The bright side, though, is that we'll be able to hide quite a bit of preparation under the guise of repair and improvement."

The dracon ambassador's gaze flicked between Gavin and Roth as she said, "Is any of the work needed something my people could help with? We would be happy to help with whatever is necessary to bring all of us to a state of readiness for the campaign. Training, construction, magical assistance...all this and more we could do."

Roth nodded. "I will take that to His Majesty. Ultimately, the decision is up to him, but I thank you for the offer nonetheless."

Discussions continued throughout the day, only stopping for the midday meal. By the end of the first day, they had both a framework and a schedule for future meetings established, and absent any further actionable information, they decided one day was sufficient for the first meeting.

After seeing everyone home, Gavin returned to his study, pleased with what they'd accomplished.

* * *

MARIANA SURVEYED THEIR ROAD-SIDE CAMP, or at least what was left of it after preparing to resume their journey. All the time they'd spent in Vushaar's capital had dulled the memory of just what overland travel was like.

"So," Mariana said as she swung herself into the saddle, "why aren't we teleporting back to Tel Mivar or even Tel Cothos each night to sleep in an actual, honest-to-goodness bed?"

Lillian blinked and looked over the remains of their camp. "You know, that's a good question. There shouldn't be any reason we couldn't, aside from a lack of familiarity with where we stop for the evening. Even then, I'd think we ought to be able to create a teleport beacon that we could leave on the ground somewhere."

Mariana rolled her shoulders. "I don't know about you, but my back and shoulders are not fans of sleeping on the ground. How do we go about creating a teleport beacon?"

"I don't really know, honestly. The only reason I know such a thing exists is that the foyer at the College has one. It's that massive sigil where the Grand Stair meets the main floor."

"Of course," Mariana groaned. "I want to recreate something originally made by Kirloth. That'll never happen."

"Mari, you know what Gavin would say if he heard you talking like that," Lillian said. She crouched to retrieve a stone they'd chosen not to use as part of their fire pit. It was too flat and small for that, but it could be just what they needed for a teleport beacon. Grabbing another rock, Lillian used it to scratch out a rendition of the Glyph of Mivar. It was by no means high art, but the image was recognizable at least. Then she retrieved a small knife from a sheath hanging from her belt and nicked her thumb just enough to draw a small drop of blood, which she rubbed across the stone's surface, over the glyph she'd scratched.

The final step was the most challenging. Having never created a teleport beacon before or even really knowing what one felt like through a person's *skathos*, all Lillian had to work from was her intent. She cleared her mind of all thoughts, doubts, and even stray images, focusing solely on her desire for the stone she held to resonate with her wherever it was to serve as a destination for teleportation. Once she felt her focus was sufficient, she invoked the Word of Transmutation most often used for teleporting, "*Paedryx*."

Lillian felt her power flare as the stone in her hand warmed. The stone seemed to absorb the blood she'd smeared on it, and her rough etching of the Glyph of Mivar shifted and squirmed until it was an exact duplicate of the glyph at the center of her medallion. And what's more...she felt the stone; it was almost like the resonant echo of a city's bell.

"Well, we might as well test it," Lillian said, walking around her horse to approach Mariana. "Here." She tossed the stone to her friend. "I'm going to teleport to my family estate. After I'm gone, toss the stone somewhere, and I'll try to open a gateway directly to it."

Mariana stared at the stone almost as if it were a snake that would bite her. "You realize how crazy that sounds, right? I mean, what if you're wrong?"

Lillian shrugged. "If I'm wrong, I'll just teleport back to you. If the invocation to teleport to the stone fails or doesn't feel right, I won't do it. So, are you ready?"

Mariana sighed, shrugging. "Sure, why not? It's not like you might die or anything."

"Have a little faith, Mariana," Lillian countered, a grin spreading across her face. "You'll see."

With that, the next Duchess of Mivar created a gateway to her family home and stepped through it, vanishing. Mariana wasted no time in tossing the stone a few yards farther down the road, then calmly sat atop her horse, waiting. Mere heartbeats later, an archway of crackling energy rose out of the ground, centered right on the stone she'd tossed, and as soon as it was large enough to accommodate a person, it flashed and became a gateway to another place. Lillian stepped through and allowed the gateway to vanish, then retrieved the stone.

"Well," Lillian said as she walked back to her horse, "I do believe we have a teleport beacon. Want to sleep in your room tonight?"

Mariana nodded rather emphatically. "Yes, and I wouldn't mind a bath, either. I wonder why Gavin never thought of doing something like this when we were traveling to Vushaar."

"He probably didn't realize a teleport beacon was a thing," Lillian replied. "For that matter, he could've just had Kiri focus on her memories of home and teleported us straight to the palace complex, like he did from that slaver camp he destroyed."

"But," Mariana countered, "if he had done any of that, we might never have known Kiri's grandfather needed help or that the dracons needed help with the sky, either. Beyond that, we don't know how much power it would've taken Gavin to teleport all of us to the Vushaari capital from Tel Mivar; it might have killed him. Plus, we wouldn't have met Elayna and Sarres, either."

Lillian nodded. "There is that. So, was sleeping on the ground worth it now?"

"When we were going to Vushaar? Yes. Now? Not so much. There is nothing between us and the giant capital," Mariana replied. "Absolutely nothing. Since we have the option to sleep in our beds each night, there's no reason not to take advantage of it."

Lillian swung herself up into her saddle, fighting to keep from laughing at her friend's rationalization. There was also the fact that Gavin and everyone else would have missed out on the sheer beauty of the countryside they had traveled through, but compared to helping Elayna and Sarres, the dracons, and Kiri's grandfather, beautiful countryside was a very distant fourth.

"Any thoughts on what we can expect when we reach the giants' capital?" Lillian asked as they headed out.

Mariana shrugged. "There's no way to know, really. Traditionally, the giants have been very heavily invested in the arts...music, visual art, performance art, you name it. They were also very active within the Society, too. That faded, though, as the royal family gradually shifted Tel away from welcoming non-humans. I think the giant who's a member of the Council is the only one still active in the Society anymore."

"All the damage the royal family did to Tel and our relationships with the other races is...well, both sad and infuriating," Lillian remarked. "There's no telling what we would've achieved by now if we still cooperated like we used to."

"I know," Mariana agreed, "but we're helping Gavin repair all of that. Yes, it's terrible that we've lost so much ground, as it were, but a friend told me not too long ago that I should have faith. So, I might as well have faith that things will get better, too."

Lillian returned Mariana's smirk with one of her own.

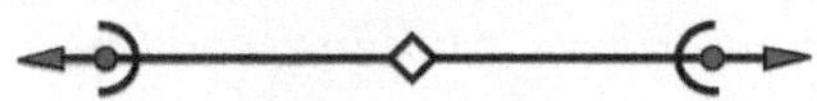

CHAPTER 26

Days passed, and Lyssa eventually stopped laughing at her daughter for teleporting back home to spend each night in a bed. Torval and Adelaide welcomed extra time with Lillian, wanting very much to get to know the woman their granddaughter had become. Granted, Lillian was only a year older—plus or minus—but sometimes a person's age is more about the sum of his or her experiences than solely a sum of years.

The giants' capital had grown out of a settlement around a quarry complex. The clay and stone of the region possessed an impressive range of pigmentation, and the giants used it in all manner of projects from pottery to sculpture. Much to the chagrin of elders who desired a more dignified ambiance for the seat of their government, the capital's citizenry refused to abandon the city's historical name.

"Welcome to Pretty Rock," Mariana read the banner arching over the city's gate. A more temporary banner hung under it, which Mariana also read: "The Spring Festival of 6082 welcomes you!"

Lillian fought the urge to grin. "I forgot that the giants' capital was named Pretty Rock. But what's this about a spring festival?"

"You know as much as I do," Mariana replied, gesturing at the two signs.

The ladies approached the gate, where a giant stood at each side of the entrance to the city. Each guard wore chainmail hauberks over padded leather armor. In addition to a blade that would've been a great sword for anyone else, they each leaned on halberds sized to fit their massive frames.

"Please, state your names and business," the giant on Lillian's left said, his tone and overall demeanor one of tired boredom. At least astride their horses, Lillian didn't have to crane her neck; Lillian and Mariana faced the gate guards at their eye-level.

"Lillian Mivar and Mariana Cothos on a diplomatic mission from the Archmagister of Tel," Lillian answered.

The guards shared a look before the one on Mariana's right said, "Are you girlies having us on? Tel doesn't have an Archmagister, hasn't for centuries."

Lillian leaned back and reached into the left saddlebag. She rummaged for a bit before producing the folio that contained the letter of introduction and remit as ambassadors empowered to exercise Gavin's full authority in his stead.

"Here," Lillian said, extending the folio to the guard closest to her.

He leaned his halberd against the stone wall that defended the city and accepted the folio. He fumbled with it a bit, but soon, it was right-side-up and looked like a small children's journal in his hand. The moment his thumb brushed the seal Gavin had stamped into the document, the lettering flashed, and a half-scale image of Gavin in the gold robe of his office appeared in front of the guard.

"Greetings," Gavin's image said, "I am Gavin Cross, Head of House Kirloth and newly named Archmagister of Tel. The ladies bearing this folio of papers—Lillian Mivar and Mariana Cothos—travel to your lands at my behest, and I certify them as ambassadors for the purpose of their visit with full authority and trust to speak in my name. I ask that you welcome them as you would welcome me and hope we can rebuild the friendship Tel once enjoyed with its fellow members of the old alliance. Thank you."

The gate guard swayed on his feet for a moment, then turned to his fellow guard. "They're legitimate. We need to pass them."

"Are you well?" the other guard asked. "Did whatever that was mess with your mind?"

"No. Here, you try it."

The guard on Mariana's right shook his head. "No, thank you. I'm just fine." The guard turned to Mariana. "The city's a bit busy, what with the festival and all. Chieftain's Seat is at the very center of town; you'll meet with Chieftain there, and your best chance for finding an inn with a room will be near the north gate. Most of the activities and events are in the southern half the city, and we have a bunch of lazy mugs running the festival this year."

"Thank you," Mariana replied. By then, Lillian had returned the folio to her saddlebag. Mariana nodded once to Lillian, and they nudged their horses to a trot almost in unison.

The gate they passed through was at the southwest corner of the city, and not thirty yards inside, the streets and thoroughfares were packed like the markets of Tel Mivar on a busy day. Tel Mivar, at least, was sized to accommodate all the traffic. Even with everything scaled up to fit its inhabitants, the throngs of people gave that area of Pretty Rock a congested, overpopulated feel.

"We should probably see about securing a room first," Lillian remarked, her expression showing dismay as she scanned the almost wall-to-wall people before them.

Mariana nodded her agreement. "I'd say we should hurry, but I don't think we can move any faster than a walk without risking trampling people."

They spent nearly an hour working their way toward the northern end of the city, but soon, they found an inn with two rooms available. They paid for two weeks, just in case, and visited their rooms. It wasn't really a surprise to find that everything was sized for giants, which meant the beds were *very* roomy for Lillian and Mariana.

Lillian draped her saddlebags over the back of the chair in her room and retrieved the folio just as someone knocked on her door. "Yes? Come in!"

The door opened to reveal Mariana, her lips curling into a smile.

"Well, I feel like I'm a child sleeping in my parents' bed again."

"You, too?" Lillian agreed. "I don't think we should do the teleport beacon when we're actually in the city. It might seem like we don't want to stay overnight here, and besides, what little I could see of the festival looked interesting."

Mariana nodded. "Oh, yes, I completely agree. Now that we're here, I certainly don't want to risk offending anyone by popping off to Tel Cothos each night."

"Are you settled in?"

"As settled as I can be, I guess. At least they had stepping blocks for us little people to get into the bed."

Lillian turned and looked toward her bed. Sure enough, there was a stepping block shaped into the form of a three-step staircase in the nook created by the nightstand and the head of the bed. "Well, that's nice of them. So, want to try scheduling a meeting with the Chieftain?"

"We probably should."

Lillian held up her left hand, brandishing the folio Gavin had given them, and they left. Locking the door was a bit interesting, but Lillian just managed it.

* * *

"MILORD," Hartley said, drawing Gavin's attention, "a Miss Holly Walsh desires to speak with you. She seems a bit distressed."

Gavin looked up from the sheaf of documents in his hand and those strewn across the desk in front of him. "Who? Oh, Holly. She's distressed?"

"It could simply be that she's nervous about being in the Citadel, Milord, but I don't think so."

"Holly is one of my apprentices," Gavin replied, "and I'm happy to see her now. I've spent so much time today with the tax laws, it feels like my eyes are starting to cross."

Hartley nodded once, saying, "Very good, sir."

Moments later, the specter led a very nervous Holly Walsh into

Gavin's office.

"Hi, Holly," Gavin said. "Would you like something to drink or eat?"

Holly shook her head as she approached Gavin.

"Okay. If you change your mind, will you tell me please?"

"Yes, thank you," Holly replied.

Gavin nodded and helped the young girl into a seat. "How can I help you?"

"I think one of the teachers at the college is in trouble," Holly answered at last. "Her name is Miss Veldin, and no one has seen her for several days."

"I see."

"I went to another teacher," Holly continued, "but they said it wasn't a matter for me to worry about. I suppose I shouldn't have bothered you with it, but Miss Veldin was very nice to me. I don't want her to be in trouble."

Gavin smiled. "Would you like me to look into it?"

Holly nodded.

"All right," Gavin said. "I'll look into it." His gaze drifted back to his parchment-strewn desk, and he smiled again. "Matter of fact, I think I'll look into it right now."

"Thank you, sir," Holly replied.

Gavin stood and offered Holly his hand as he walked with her out of the office. "How are your studies going? Are you learning a lot?"

"Oh, yes, sir! I always learn something from Mister Wynn. I don't always do so well when he gives us—independent study, I think he called it—but Xythe helps me then. Xythe's really nice, too."

"I'm glad you're doing well," Gavin responded. "I want you to feel welcome to visit me whenever you need. Whether you're having trouble with your studies or you're feeling lonely or whatever, I want you to feel welcome with me."

"Thank you, sir, but I don't want to be a bother."

"You'll have to grow some more before you're even close to being a bother, Holly," Gavin countered, smiling. "Besides, I can't help you if I don't know you need help."

After dropping Holly off at his old suite and finding Xythe almost frantic because the dracon couldn't find her, Gavin headed to Valera's office. If there was something going on with whoever Miss Veldin was, he figured she would know about it.

Sera didn't *quite* flinch at seeing Gavin enter Valera's reception space, but it looked a near thing. Gavin, though, smiled in greeting. He was fairly sure Sera was older than he was, but perhaps she was one of those people who experienced severe social anxiety. Either way, she certainly seemed unsettled anytime Gavin saw her.

"I'll inform the Magister you're here, Milord," Sera squeaked, and she almost jumped up from her seat and *not quite* dashed into Valera's private office. A moment later, she stepped back outside and gestured to the door. "The Magister said for you to come right in."

Gavin smiled and nodded once. "Thank you, Sera."

Valera stood to receive her guest as he closed the door behind him. "Hello, Gavin. How are you faring in your new role?"

Gavin shrugged. "I'm doing well enough, I suppose, but I have no idea what kind of Archmagister I am. I hope I'm not shaming Bellos too much."

Valera laughed. "Oh, I highly doubt you would ever shame anyone. Please, be seated and make yourself comfortable. So, what can I do for you?"

"Holly, one of my apprentices, told me that a Miss Veldin—who she thinks is a nice teacher—might be in some kind of trouble. She seems to like whoever it is quite a bit, so I said I'd look into it."

Valera winced. "Yes, 'some kind of trouble' might be a bit of an understatement."

Gavin blinked. "Oh? How so?"

"Well, from everything we've been able to piece together, Alanna Veldin almost outright attacked a student in one of her classes. She's always been a bit prickly, ever since her tenure as a student here, but she's never been violent. Her apparent conduct shocked quite a few of her fellow instructors."

"And let me guess," Gavin said, almost sighing, "Tauron is handling the investigation."

"Actually, no," Valera countered. "He isn't. Matter of fact, he recused himself from the whole process entirely. Reyna is the investigator of record and reports to Tauron's deputy insofar as this specific case is concerned."

"Wow. I am actually surprised...surprised and impressed. I would never have expected that level of professionalism from him."

Valera grimaced. "He's not a bad person, Gavin. He really isn't."

Gavin regarded Valera in silence, going back over all his interactions with Tauron in his mind. At last, he shrugged and shook his head. "I think we're going to have to agree to disagree on that one, Valera, but I suppose it's possible you know him better than I do. So, I need to see Reyna about the case file?"

"Yes, but are you certain—honestly certain—you want to get involved in this? Given all I'm aware of, the case seems...well, a foregone conclusion. I wouldn't think that it would be something the Archmagister would have time to investigate himself."

Gavin sighed. "On the whole, you're probably correct. All other things being equal, I probably shouldn't get involved. I'm not an investigator. I have no specific expertise in this field. As a matter of fact, I will probably make far more noise and cause more hurt feelings as I flail around in my search for a true understanding of the situation. But...this Alanna Veldin was apparently nice to my apprentice when she didn't otherwise need to be, so that makes me want to know what's happening."

Valera nodded. "I can understand that."

Gavin stood. "Thank you for your time, Valera. Where should I look for Reyna?"

"When you step outside the outer office, turn right. The offices for the Inquisitors assigned to the College are three doors down, also on the right side of the hall."

Gavin nodded his thanks again and left Valera to get back to her day.

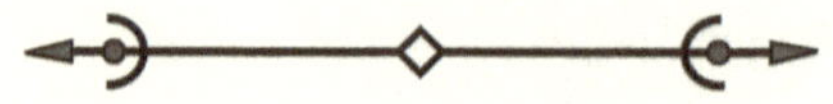

CHAPTER 27

Gavin found himself in a small reception area that led to two offices. The reception area was vacant, and both office doors were open. The Inquisitor in each office looked up when the door opened, and they both gaped at seeing the Archmagister enter. They shot to their feet and hustled to the reception area almost like hounds from Lornithar's Abyss nipped at their heels.

"Milord, it is an honor for you to visit us," the Inquisitor Gavin didn't know said as he dropped to one knee. Reyna hadn't looked like she was going to kneel, but her compatriot gave her little choice in the matter.

"I don't like people kneeling to me," Gavin said, his expression somewhat cool as he regarded the top of the Inquisitor's head. "Please, stand."

Reyna wasted no time in doing so, her associate complying with less haste. Once they were both standing, Reyna said, "How may we serve you, Milord?"

"I want to discuss a matter with you, Reyna," Gavin answered. "Do you have a moment?"

Reyna nodded. "Of course, Milord. I have no appointments this afternoon, so I am at your complete disposal. Shall we step into my office?"

"Thank you," Gavin replied and followed Mariana's friend. He supposed he should've felt bad about leaving the other Inquisitor in the reception area with no further interaction, but the man engendered a feeling very similar to the toadies and sycophants who circled Terris's court. Gavin did not like that feeling at all, especially in someone responsible for enforcing the law.

Reyna closed the door behind Gavin and quickly moved to her side of the desk, gesturing for Gavin to sit. Once Gavin did so, she followed suit.

"I am here regarding the matter of Alanna Veldin," Gavin said. "What can you tell me about it?"

Reyna winced. "That...is an unpleasant case. I've known Alanna Veldin for years. She's only three or so years older than me and Mariana.

"From what the witnesses said, one of the students went to her as class was being dismissed, and she flew into a rage and attacked him. The poor boy is still in a coma, and the healers have asked someone from the temple to attempt a healing. Most of the witnesses think they exchanged words prior to Veldin attacking him, but no one was close enough to hear what—if anything—was said or by whom.

"Alanna Veldin is currently being held in her quarters under restraint and guard, pending the outcome of the boy's situation. If he lives, it's merely aggravated assault, but if he dies, she'll be charged with killing him.

"May I ask what led to your interest in the matter?"

Gavin sighed. "Apparently, Veldin was kind to my youngest apprentice, Holly Walsh, at some point. She told me no one had seen or heard from Veldin in some time, and I told her I'd look into it. I almost regret saying that, now. I'm not usually one to interfere with investigations."

"Uhm...well, sir, you can't really interfere."

"I'm sorry for not understanding," Gavin replied, frowning. "May I ask what you mean?"

"The Archmagister holds the full power of Low, Middle, and High Justice in Tel, sir. The *only* reason Inquisitors can enforce the Arcanists' Code is that the Archmagister at the time of our founding granted us the authority to do so. It is completely within your purview to review or investigate any case you choose—everything from common street crime to something like Iosen Sivas's treason."

Gavin leaned back against his seat, hoping his expression didn't betray any of the surprise he felt. "Well, then...since you're waiting for the boy's condition to improve or worsen, I think I'll avail myself of that option. You said Veldin is being held in her quarters under guard?"

"Yes, Milord. She's in Room 355. Just look for the Inquisitors."

"Thank you, Reyna," Gavin said as he stood. "I'll keep you updated on whatever I find."

GAVIN ROUNDED the corner on the third floor of the Tower and saw a door flanked by Inquisitors. From what he could tell, Alanna Veldin's quarters were almost on the exact opposite side of the floor from his old suite. He traversed the distance with a steady gait and soon stood before the door guards.

"Hello," Gavin said. "Are you guarding Alanna Veldin's quarters?"

"Yes, sir," the Inquisitor on Gavin's right answered.

Gavin smiled. "Excellent. Open the door, please. I've come to speak with her."

"We cannot do that, sir," the Inquisitor on Gavin's left said. "We have strict instructions that no one is to speak with the prisoner."

"Oh, I see," Gavin remarked. "Well, just who gave those orders? Bellos, perhaps?"

"Of course not, sir. I doubt Bellos is even aware of this situation."

Gavin laughed. "You would be surprised what the gods are aware of, Inquisitor, but since Bellos didn't give those orders, whoever did cannot possibly outrank me. Now, are you going to open the door, or are we going to have a problem?"

For the first time, the Inquisitors seemed to realize who was speaking to them. They both paled, and the man on Gavin's right even swayed on his feet a bit. The Inquisitor on Gavin's left stammered for a moment, but ultimately, he retrieved a keyring from his belt and unlocked the door.

Gavin took one step into Veldin's quarters and froze. Alanna Veldin sat on some kind of device designed to allow the use of a chamber pot. A thick collar encircled her neck and a very thick, short chain connected the collar to a set of manacles. Unlike other sets of manacles Gavin had seen, where a chain connected the two bracelets, hers had a solid bar. Thick, heavy leg irons secured her ankles, and everything—the collar, the manacles, the leg irons, and every chain —glowed, radiating Tutation. At first, the strong aura of Tutation puzzled Gavin, but understanding suddenly clicked. They were anti-magic restraints, the weight of which also served to hobble the prisoner.

As Gavin stepped closer, Veldin lifted her head to look at her guest. For a brief moment, Gavin saw a sheer, almost animalistic panic flash through the woman's eyes before her expression settled into something of a sneer.

"So, even the Archmagister has heard of the upstart mage who deigned to strike a wizard's child?"

Gavin reached for the door, intent on closing it to afford Veldin some measure of privacy, but the moment Gavin's fingers brushed the door's handle, panic erupted in the woman's eyes once more. It was then that Gavin realized where he'd seen that reaction before: Kiri, when he'd first met her.

"I'd like to speak with you," Gavin said, "but I'd rather you not be afraid of me. I'll be right back."

Gavin turned and left, closing the door behind him.

He returned with Reyna, who he hoped Veldin would see as less of a threat and help her feel safe with him. When Gavin re-entered Veldin's quarters, he saw her tense, that same panic flitting through her eyes. Then, she saw Reyna, and it was almost like she breathed a deep sigh of relief. Her shoulders relaxed, as much as they could, and her tension seemed to vanish.

"Hello, Alanna," Reyna said, pulling a chair over to sit about seven feet away from Veldin. Gavin found his own seat, making sure Reyna was more in the foreground than he was. "Do you feel like talking with us?"

Veldin gave a jerky nod, and her eyes flitted to Gavin for a moment before she said, "I-I guess. What do you want to talk about?"

"Well, the Archmagister has taken an interest in your case, and I'm honestly hoping you'll open up a little more with him than you did with me. There are still parts of it I don't know."

"What does it matter?" Veldin replied. "They're going to execute me, no matter what. It's not like talking more will change that."

Gavin lifted an eyebrow as he looked at Veldin questioningly, saying, "You seem awfully certain of that outcome. Care to explain why you feel that way?"

"Why shouldn't I feel that way? I attacked the son and heir of a prominent wizard family. The Council will have to execute me just to keep the peace. Nothing else matters."

"Funny thing about the Council," Gavin replied, "and the Inquisitors, too, come to think of it...they work for me. Now that I'm aware of your case and have seen you sitting there like that, the only chain of events that will lead to your execution is if *I* decide that fate is appropriate. So, why don't you tell me your side of the story?"

Veldin turned to look at Reyna, her expression almost screaming the question of whether she could trust Gavin.

"Remember Rolf Sivas?" Reyna asked. "You wouldn't believe how many reports from students we had about his conduct, but it wasn't until *Gavin* caught him in the act that anything was ever resolved. I trust I don't need to recount *that* particular resolution."

Veldin shook her head, her eyes downcast toward the floor. "No. I watched it happen. I think half the College did."

"Then, please, tell me what happened," Gavin urged.

Veldin stared at the floor for what seemed like an eternity, but eventually, she spoke. "I had just dismissed the class. I was standing at the desk at the front of the classroom, gathering my papers and notes, when that little shi—I mean, when he approached me. We'd spent most of the class that day going over a test, which he almost failed, and he told me he felt his grade was inaccurate. I was tired. I-I shouldn't have reacted like I did, but I told him, 'Unlike most of your answers on the test, my grading of it was not wrong.'" Gavin turned his urge to laugh into a barely contained snort. "He sneered at me and shot back something about how his father had told him not to expect competence from me, and then, he asked me if I even knew who his father was. I didn't care at all who his father was, and I told him so. But when he told me...I-I don't know what came over me. It was like I wasn't in the classroom anymore. It wasn't a student standing in front of me, and I just lost control. I didn't realize what I was doing until Reyna pulled my hands away from his throat. I've never attacked anyone before. I'm not a violent person."

"Have they at least treated you well since your confinement?" Gavin asked.

That same raw panic flashed through Veldin's eyes, and her answer was far, far too quick. "It's fine."

Gavin heaved a sigh. "So, they haven't. Is it the Inquisitors?"

Veldin was clearly fighting to keep from cringing at the thought of the Inquisitors. She didn't succeed.

"The Inquisitors currently outside your door?"

Veldin emphatically shook her head no, but the look in her eyes screamed yes.

"Right, then," Gavin said. "Alanna, I want your word that you will not leave your quarters unless I or Reyna direct you to do so. Will you give me your word on that?"

Veldin answered with a silent nod.

"All right. Reyna, get that scrap metal off her so she can feed and clean herself. Once she's free, get that contraption out of here, too. Until further notice, no Inquisitors will guard her door, and you will be the only Inquisitor permitted to visit her. Understood?"

"Yes, sir," Reyna answered.

"How will you stop them?" Veldin asked.

Gavin grinned. "Easy. I'll ward the door. Only you, Reyna, and I will be able to cross the threshold, and if you cross without one of us, you'll be marked with a beacon."

Both Reyna and Veldin gaped. Finally, Reyna said, "That's-that's not possible, is it?"

Gavin shrugged, still grinning. "You'd be surprised what an Archmagister trained by the Kirloth who dueled Milthas can achieve when he puts his mind to it. Now, I'll deal with the Inquisitors outside while you help her clean up."

With that, Gavin stood and stepped outside, closing the door behind him.

Gavin stepped to the center of the hallway and turned to face the Inquisitors. He gave them a huge smile as he clapped his hands and rubbed them together.

"Good news, gentlemen," Gavin said. "You no longer have to worry about standing guard on a door all day. As of right now, you're dismissed to return to your regular duties."

The Inquisitors shot each other a look before turning back to Gavin.

"Uhm...we were told—" the Inquisitor on Gavin's left began.

Gavin took one step forward and all joviality and camaraderie vanished from his expression. "That is the second time you've questioned an order from the Archmagister. You have one more chance to deliver the correct response."

"What *is* the correct response...uhm, sir?" the Inquisitor on Gavin's right asked.

Gavin sighed and shook his head. "The correct response is, 'Yes, milord' or 'Yes, sir,' and you then carry out that order with all haste. As of this moment and until further notice, I am taking over this case. There will be no Inquisitors stationed at this door, and none—aside from Reyna—will enter these quarters without my expressed permission. Now, leave."

The two Inquisitors shared another glance before they stepped aside and left. Gavin was not pleased, but he had other matters requiring his attention.

He reached out and placed his hand against the door, clearing his mind of all thoughts and feelings beyond his intent. A clear picture of what he wanted formed in his mind and he invoked a Word of Tutation, "*Sykhurhos.*"

Instantly, Gavin felt the resonance of his power slam into the ambient magic, twisting reality so that it conformed to his desire. Alanna Veldin's quarters were now warded against all people or creatures. No one except Alanna Veldin, Reyna, or himself could even place a toe inside her space, and if she left without either Gavin or Reyna, Veldin would be tagged with an arcane beacon that would resonate with both Gavin and Reyna. The only outward sign of the warding were two glyphs on the door at Gavin's eye level that pulsed with light. The first was a Glyph of Tutation, and the second was the Glyph of Kirloth.

Gavin waited, leaning against the far wall in the hallway until Reyna emerged. When Reyna did emerge, Gavin righted himself and approached her.

"I want to know *everything* about that boy and his family. There's something between them and Alanna Veldin we don't know."

CHAPTER 28

Gavin entered the reception area of the Inquisitors' offices and saw Reyna's door was closed. It struck him as odd, since he and Reyna had a meeting scheduled. The other Inquisitor saw Gavin arrive and jumped to his feet, hustling to greet the Archmagister.

Before he could get his obsequiousness wound up, Gavin pointed to Reyna's door, asking, "Is everything all right? Reyna and I had an appointment."

The Inquisitor shook his head. His expression looked remorseful, but there was too much underlying glee. "Well, it seems the rising star managed to fall afoul of a superior. They've been in there quite a while."

There was always the chance he was wrong, but Gavin suspected he knew just how Reyna had fallen afoul, and quite likely who had had a hand in it. But then again, the ease with which Gavin suspected this oily sycophant of malfeasance could just be rooted in his own utter dislike of the man. Without waiting for any further comment, Gavin strode to the door and opened it wide.

"Just who—" Whatever the man was about to say vanished as he took in Gavin and his gold robe. The man's eyes widened, and his jaw worked in silence for several moments. Gavin thought he saw the man glance back out to the reception area, but that could have just been bias on his part. Stepping into the room, Gavin slammed the door closed behind him, his eyes fixed on the red-faced man in Inquisitor garb.

"And just what is happening here?" Gavin asked.

The man stammered incoherently, but Reyna was more than happy to explain, saying, "Oh, it seems I've been both demoted and fired, and possibly brought up on charges that would result in naming me a renegade. Apparently, my assertion that you had taken over the Veldin case was an obvious lie to cover up my bias in favor of the woman, and even now, I'm supposedly working on some hare-brained scheme to smuggle her out of the city. I think that's every-thing, but I might be wrong. He repeated himself quite a bit while he was ranting." The man shot her a look that seemed to accuse her of betrayal as well, but Reyna just smirked. "What? You didn't honestly expect me to be loyal to you after you've spent the entire morning in here vilifying me, did you? You're so firmly in the wrong I doubt you could even see the right with a spyglass on high ground."

The man's jaw worked some more, but before he could find his voice, Gavin said, "This is all very odd to me. It seems like the simplest of matters to verify her story. If I were indeed taking over the Veldin case, why didn't you come to me and ask? Either she's lying and you're justified, or she isn't, and you save yourself some trouble. Oh...and in case you haven't pieced together the puzzle yet, trouble is just about all you have right now. I have indeed taken over the Veldin case, and you've been browbeating a subordinate over nothing." Gavin leaned forward just enough to make eye contact with Reyna. "You have his name?"

"Oh, yes, sir," Reyna replied, smiling.

"Well then," Gavin resumed, "it's time you were on your way. Feel free to expect a summons at some point in the not-too-distant future. You've earned yourself a note on my mental corkboard, and I'll circle back around to it once we've sorted out the Veldin matter." The man looked a little wild around his eyes now, but Gavin merely smiled.

"Yes, of course; by all means, run. It won't do you any good at all, but it will occupy your time until I'm ready for you. Now—leave. You've tied up enough of our attention as it is."

Gavin shifted to one side of the office to allow the man unrestricted access to the door. He stood motionless for several moments but abruptly jerked into motion. He was out the door and gone with almost unseemly haste. Gavin saw the other Inquisitor still standing in the reception area where he'd left him, and simply raised one eyebrow questioningly. The Inquisitor flinched and hustled back to his office.

Gavin regarded the empty reception area for a moment and turned back to Reyna and asked, "Do you have everything gathered for our meeting?"

Reyna nodded. "Yes, sir. I found some…"

Reyna's voice trailed off as Gavin lifted his hand and said, "I no longer feel that these offices are the best place to conduct our business. Gather what you need and come with me."

A few minutes later, Gavin led Reyna out of a portal to the Citadel. They walked down the main hall and up one flight of stairs to the study he'd claimed as an office. Once inside, Gavin invited Reyna to spread out her materials on the desk and pick whichever seat suited her.

Reyna was just about to sit when awareness of where she was made its way into her mind. "Is…is this the Citadel?"

Gavin nodded.

Reyna almost wilted into her seat. "Yeah…this is secure all right."

Hartley chose that moment to materialize at her elbow, and Reyna almost jumped out of her seat when he said, "May I offer some refreshment, Milord?"

Gavin looked up from his perusal of the documents Reyna had laid out and thought he detected a hint of amusement on the specter's face. Ah, well…everyone needed to find their joy where they could, even specters who'd been dead for millennia.

"I wouldn't be opposed to some tea," Gavin remarked. "How about you, Reyna?"

The Inquisitor still looked a little startled, but she rallied. "I would enjoy something, thank you."

"Full service, Milord, or just the tea?" Hartley asked.

"Breakfast service, I think," Gavin replied. "I slipped out before you could sit me down for food."

"I did notice that, sir," Hartley remarked as he faded away.

Reyna looked all around, as if expecting the specter to re-appear and startle her again.

Gavin smiled. "Don't worry. The tea trolly rattles and jingles, so you'll hear him coming. Besides, it'll be a little bit, I think. They'll probably dig up a small selection of pastries and breakfast foods. So, what did you find?"

Reyna cleared her throat, stood, and went to the desk. She proceeded to take Gavin through everything she'd found about the family of the boy Veldin had attacked. The boy's father had been a Fifth Tier student at the College at the same time Veldin was enrolled, and one of the papers Reyna uncovered showed the boy's father was among a group of Fifth Tiers who had been reprimanded for their conduct toward younger students. As she was showing Gavin the report, her eyes stopped on the list of students.

"What is it?" Gavin asked, watching as Reyna stared at the parchment.

She pointed to a name on the list. "That's the Inquisitor supervisor you ran out of my office."

"Oh, my...isn't that interesting," Gavin remarked.

"This is all I've been able to find, though," Reyna said. "There's nothing in any of the archives that would connect the boy's family to Veldin beyond her current class roster."

"I've seen the reaction Veldin expressed with me before, Reyna," Gavin said, "and I fear I know the connection between the boy's family and Veldin. It's not fair, however, to voice my suspicions without proof, but there's one place we haven't searched for records. Grab that report of the father's reprimand, and come with me. Hartley!"

The specter appeared at once. "Yes, Milord?"

"Cancel the tea and breakfast, I'm afraid," Gavin answered. "Reyna and I are off to the Temple."

"Very well, Milord," the specter replied, practically frowning. "The kettle isn't quite boiling yet."

* * *

GAVIN OPENED a gateway directly to the Temple rather than deal with the crowds in the city's streets. The acolyte staffing the reception desk looked a little unsettled when Gavin and Reyna stepped through, but Gavin was past caring. Besides, it could easily be that the acolyte had never seen a magical gateway before. Without missing a beat, Gavin turned and led Reyna into the Temple, paying the acolyte no mind besides a smile and brief hello

It took them a short while, but Gavin eventually found Ovir in one of the classrooms on the third floor of the Temple. The moment Ovir saw the Archmagister and an Inquisitor standing outside the classroom, he hurriedly finished what he was saying and gave the students an assignment before dismissing the class.

"Good day, Milord," Ovir said as he approached Gavin.

Gavin lifted an eyebrow. "You've never called me 'Milord' before, Ovir."

"Yes, well, you were always alone before."

Gavin grinned. "Reyna is one of Mariana's friends. She met me before I accepted this. She hasn't quite worked herself back to Gavin yet, but we've established a truce on 'sir.'"

"Ah, well then. What do you need, Gavin?"

Turning to Reyna, Gavin asked. "What was the date on that reprimand?"

Reyna pulled the parchment from her pocket and examined it before answering, "Seventeenth of Kandilah, 6070."

"Ovir, I need to examine the sick room records for any women brought in who exhibited the symptoms of sexual assault for...oh, say, five months prior to that date."

Reyna blinked. "You think she was raped?"

"I'm almost certain of it," Gavin replied. "She acts very similar to Kiri when I first met her and Lillian the night after Sivas attacked her."

Ovir looked from Gavin to Reyna and back again. "And you believe she was brought here?"

"Or came on her own, but yes," Gavin answered.

"The sick room records are kept in the basement level below the sick rooms. I shall accompany you." When Gavin started to speak, Ovir shook his head. "The sick room records are kept sealed to all except sick room staff. You'll need me to gain access to them."

"Even the Archmagister isn't permitted to view those records?" Gavin asked, quirking an eyebrow.

Ovir shook his head. "No one who hasn't taken the Healer's Oath is even allowed on the floor, and there have been a few Royal Priests and Archmagisters who've almost come to blows over it. In all truth, I probably shouldn't even be compromising in this instance, but you have that look about you."

"'That look?' What look?"

"The headstrong knight errant charging to right a grievous injustice."

Gavin blinked and turned to Reyna. "I don't look like that, do I?"

Reyna responded with a weak grimace and a nod, saying, "Yes, sir, you kind of do. Not all the time, though, just when you're thinking of the case."

Gavin heaved a sigh. "Maybe I should get a white warhorse and some armor, then."

"The armor wouldn't suit you," Reyna countered, her expression mock serious, "but white horses are pretty."

Ovir snorted a chuckle and started toward the stairs.

* * *

THE RECORDS-KEEPERS GAVE Ovir more than one disbelieving look as he led Gavin and Reyna into their domain, and it took a bit of talking from Ovir to get them on board and not just override them. What ultimately sealed their cooperation was when Gavin stepped forward and outlined everything, even the details of the Inquisitor case that Reyna probably would not have disclosed to anyone not involved with the investigation.

The records-keepers looked to one another, and the lead for the current shift said, "Milord, the search we need to perform will take some time. Are you certain you want to wait?"

Gavin turned to Reyna, who shrugged and said, "I have nothing pressing on me, but you're the Archmagister, sir. What other necessary work will go neglected if you wait here?"

Gavin heaved another sigh. "You know, I almost miss being just Kirloth. Do you mind waiting for them to conduct the search?"

"Not at all, sir," Reyna replied. "The moment there's any news, I'll find you."

"I'll be in the Citadel," Gavin answered, "and as soon as I arrive, I'll add you to the list of people who can teleport directly there."

Reyna's eyes widened. "Sir, not even the Magisters have that authority. I don't know that it's necessary."

Gavin held back from giving her the full glare. "I don't want to wait any longer than is absolutely necessary for this information, and besides, Valera and Kantar are the only Magisters I trust to have the authority to teleport directly to the Citadel; they're already on the list. Now, please come straight there as soon as you learn anything."

Without another word, Gavin invoked the Word of Transmutation and created an archway of crackling, sapphire energy. The moment it was an actual Gateway, he vanished through it.

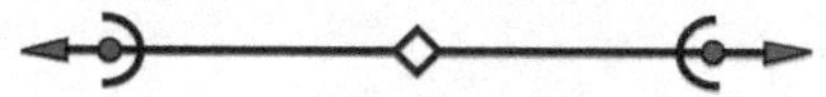

CHAPTER 29

It was something of a relief when a messenger arrived at the inn serving as Lillian's and Mariana's ersatz base of operations in Pretty Rock. Lillian and Mariana wasted no time changing into attire suitable for meeting with a head of state and followed the messenger through the crowds to Chieftain's Seat.

The building referred to as Chieftain's Seat was something of a rotunda, similar to, but not exactly like the cupola where the dracon Council of Clans met. The messenger led them to the very heart of the structure, a massive room where the leader of the giants awaited them.

Stepping into the space, Lillian and Mariana saw a giantess occupying the central seat. If she'd been human, her general looks and hair would've suggested being early middle age, but neither Lillian nor Mariana were precisely certain how giants' looks changed over time to know for certain.

"Chieftain," the messenger announced in a hall-filling voice, "I present Lillian of House Mivar and Mariana of House Cothos, accredited emissaries of the Archmagister of Tel."

"I bid thee greetings," the giantess intoned, "and offer the full welcome and hospitality of my people."

"Thank you," Lillian replied. "The people of your city and realm have been nothing but kind and welcoming."

The giantess nodded. "Well, now that the formalities are over, what can you tell me about your new Archmagister? Word hadn't reached us yet that Bellos had left His seclusion."

Lillian and Mariana smiled, Mariana answering, "The person chosen as the new Archmagister is actually a friend of ours. His name is Gavin Cross, and he is Head of House Kirloth. It also happens that Lillian and I were two of his first apprentices."

The giantess's expression betrayed her surprise. "Apprentices, you say? As was in the old ways?"

"Yes, er, how should we address you?" Lillian asked.

"The appropriate mode of address is 'Chieftain,' the giantess replied. "It is our custom that, during one's tenure as Chieftain, we set aside our identity to better act in the best interests of the people."

"Thank you, Chieftain," Lillian said, "and yes, we were his apprentices as in the old ways."

"And was he a graduate of the College?" Chieftain asked.

Mariana shook her head. "No, Chieftain. Gavin himself is a former apprentice. His mentor was the black-robe known as Marcus, who has since been identified as the Kirloth who dueled Milthas."

Complete and utter silence descended on the chamber as every giant present stared at Lillian and Mariana.

"To be clear," Chieftain said, "the Archmagister is a wizard trained not by just *a* wizard, but Kirloth, the founder of both the Kingdom of Tel *and* the Society of the Arcane? And you were in turn trained by him?"

"Yes, Chieftain," Lillian answered.

"And what does he seek in sending you to speak with me?"

"Gavin...er, the Archmagister seeks to rebuild the relationships enjoyed by the members of the old alliance," Lillian said. "There was a time in ages past when we were all close allies, trading partners, and friends. The Archmagister would see us return to that. He knows it will not be an easy journey, but he feels it is a journey all of us would be well-served to take."

Chieftain smiled. "I do think your slip speaks more of the man than the fact that Bellos chose him."

Lillian blushed, and Mariana spoke, hoping to draw the focus away from Lillian and her embarrassment, "It's true. Gavin doesn't like people kneeling to him. He doesn't approach the world as being any better than any of the rest of us. It just so happens that he's agreed to what is probably one of the most difficult jobs in the world."

"Given the conduct of Tel's royal family in recent centuries, I should say so," Chieftain agreed. "They did not act as if they had Tel's best interests at heart." Chieftain fell silent for a few moments. "I approve of the Archmagister's goal in restoring the old alliance, and I agree it would serve our people well. I invite Tel to send a formal ambassador to Pretty Rock and re-establish the long disused embassy it once had here."

"We will carry your invitation to the Archmagister," Lillian replied, her embarrassment past. "He would welcome an ambassador from the giants, as well. Before we set out on our journey, he mentioned his intention to re-purpose the royal palace, converting it to become the place where the embassies reside in Tel Mivar."

"Perhaps, one day, I will be able to see it," Chieftain remarked.

Lillian and Mariana both nodded, and Lillian said, "You would be welcome to visit anytime, Chieftain."

"I believe we have discussed diplomacy as much as we can," Chieftain said. "If I may, I would like to ask you about your apprenticeships. What was it like to learn from the man trained by Kirloth himself?"

Lillian and Mariana looked to one another, and both shrugged. Mariana was the first to answer. "I'm sure it was nothing like apprenticeships of ancient times, Chieftain. Gavin was already a friend when his apprenticeship abruptly ended with Kirloth's death, so he became a *Magus* within the Society and Head of House Kirloth in one fell swoop. Matter of fact, he probably wouldn't have been a *Magus* were it not for his elevation to Head of House Kirloth. Shortly after that, we pretty much begged him to teach us what he knew."

"Interesting," Chieftain said. "Was there any difficulty in a friend becoming an instructor?"

Both shook their heads, and Lillian said, "Even though the statutes surrounding apprenticeships did give Gavin that kind of authority, he never used it, and as far as I knew, we were all friends first."

Chieftain smiled. "When you return to Tel Mivar, would you speak with your friend and ask if we could arrange a meeting? From what little I know of him now, I would value such a conversation greatly."

* * *

"We have it," Reyna said as she entered Gavin's study.

Gavin looked up from the documents strewn across his desk and frowned. "What do we have?"

"While Alanna Veldin was a student here, and about a week before the boy's father and his friends were reprimanded, an initiate of the College was brought into the sick rooms of the Temple. She was...it was bad, Gavin. Very bad. I won't go into specifics unless you ask, but it was beyond apparent that the initiate survived one of the most brutal gang rapes I've ever heard of. The sick room orderly who admitted her wrote in the file notes that he was amazed she lived long enough to arrive in the sick rooms."

"The initiate was Veldin?" Gavin asked.

Reyna shrugged. "The initiate never gave her name to the sick room staff, but the timing fits. At the same time, Veldin left the College for a family emergency, maintaining her studies from home as best she could. She returned the following term and immediately tested into the next Tier."

"Were any complaints ever filed within the Society?"

"I checked the Inquisitor records and found nothing," Reyna answered. "Valera had been the Collegiate Justice for about two years at that point, so I asked her. She remembers Veldin writing out a full statement that named names."

"What happened to that statement?" Gavin asked.

Reyna sighed. "She told me that, as per protocol, she turned it over to the Inquisitors."

"And the Inquisitors have no record of it," Gavin remarked, his voice almost a growl. "I have a feeling I already know the answer to my next question, but I have to ask. Who was in charge of the Inquisitors at that time?"

Reyna looked at the floor and said, "Tauron. He was named Chief Inquisitor just the year before and refused to relinquish the title or position when he was named Magister of Evocation several years later."

"The people named in the statement...are they from prominent families?"

"Well, they're nowhere near the Great Houses of Tel, but yes, they're fairly prominent within the Society."

When Gavin said nothing more, Reyna risked a glance and almost gaped. Gavin was staring at the top of his desk, his expression one of barely contained fury. Then, she felt it. A crackling heat washed over her exposed skin, like a mixture of lightning and fire. The hairs on the back of her neck stood straight out. The magical sconces lighting the room began to pulse, and for the first time since meeting Gavin, she was terrified right down to the very core of her being. She was a mage, not a wizard, and his seething fury was destabilizing the ambient magic to the point that she *felt* it. That wasn't supposed to be possible. Mages didn't *feel* magic.

"How many people, Reyna?" Gavin said, and Reyna felt the blood drain from her face at the tone of his voice. "How many people has he denied their rightful justice? If he has *profited* from this, I swear by all the Gods that I will deliver a fate people will speak of in terrified whispers for a thousand years."

Gavin fell silent as he closed his eyes, and his expression softened. The sconces stopped sputtering and pulsing. After several heartbeats, Gavin regained his composure, and he was once again the pleasant and welcoming individual Reyna had greeted when she first arrived.

But for the rest of her life, Reyna would never forget what she witnessed.

While she waited for Gavin to decide the next course of action, she offered a silent prayer to Bellos that Gavin Cross never went renegade, because if he did...Reyna wasn't sure the entire corps of Inquisitors could stop him. Then again, it was doubtful the Inquisitors could've stopped his mentor, either.

"Very well," Gavin said at last, his voice once again what Reyna expected. "I don't like that we have to re-open old wounds, but the time has come to hear Veldin's story. I think I know what sparked her attack on the student, and if I'm right, I will see her exonerated."

Reyna frowned as she fell into step at Gavin's side. "What do you think happened?"

Gavin just shook his head. "Once we hear Veldin's story, I'll tell you whether or not I'm correct."

WHEN THEY ARRIVED at Veldin's quarters. Reyna stepped forward and knocked. Moments later, Veldin opened the door.

"We would like to ask you some questions," Reyna said, "and I'm afraid they won't be pleasant."

Veldin's expression filled with even more sorrow. "So, you know."

"We suspect," Reyna replied.

"Please, come in." Veldin stepped back, opening the door wide enough to allow Gavin and Reyna to enter.

As she stepped through the doorway, Reyna asked her, "Has the dining hall staff been delivering meals?"

"Yes, thank you."

"Good. I informed them the Archmagister had pulled the Inquisitors from your door and asked them to send you a tray at each meal."

Veldin nodded as she led her guests to the sitting area. "They've been taking very good care of me."

"Alanna," Gavin said, "I would not ask this if there were any other way, but I'm afraid I need to know. Tell me about the attack."

And she did. She spoke in choppy phrases at first, but soon, it all seemed to cascade. She spoke without stopping until she'd recounted the entire event, even her recuperation at home and her commitment to returning to the College the next term against her family's wishes. She named names and sobbed that nothing ever came of her statement.

"And what of the boy?" Gavin asked.

Alanna's lips pulled back in an almost feral snarl. "That little shit —h-he said that I needed to correct my mistake in grading his exam, or he would have to take me in hand like his father did. I just snapped. The next thing I knew, people were pulling me off him, my hands were covered in blood, and he was unconscious. I regret that I snapped, and I am sorry for that. I'm afraid I can't admit to feeling sorry I beat him to a bloody pulp."

"Would you consent to a Divination of Truth?" Gavin asked.

"Consent?" Alanna scoffed. "I welcome it."

Gavin nodded. "Very well. I shall take you up on that when the time is right. At this point, I would ask you to remain in your quarters for your own safety. I cannot imagine those responsible for this state of affairs are aware of where we stand, but I would not see you harmed. If you would like to leave the College for whatever reason, I will arrange protection. Alanna, I apologize that this injustice has gone unanswered for so long, but I promise you it will not go on for much longer. All that remains is to get everything ready."

Alanna nodded for a moment and then slowly brought her eyes up to meet Gavin's. "May I ask what you're going to do?"

"Something disruptive," Gavin replied with a chuckle that held no mirth.

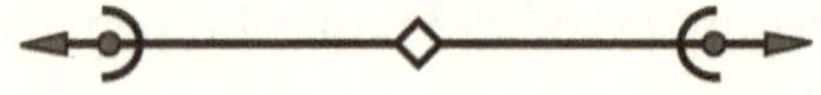

CHAPTER 30

I t was a cool, crisp morning when Lillian and Mariana bid Pretty Rock goodbye. Thin, wispy clouds traced jagged tracks across an otherwise-cloudless sky, and even as they passed through the northern gate, the music and ruckus of the festival serenaded them on the continuation of their journey. The din of the city soon faded, leaving only the sounds of nature and the mountainous countryside.

"Next step, Stonehearth," Lillian remarked as their mounts *clip-clopped* their way along the road that connected the giant and dwarven capitals. "Has there even been a human expedition to the dwarven lands lately?"

Mariana didn't quite scoff. "Define 'lately.'"

"That bad?"

Mariana shrugged. "I didn't look at the records too closely, but most of the groups passing through Cothos Province have been trading missions coming into Tel. I know the trader in Tel Mivar that Gavin likes routinely receives trade caravans from the dwarven lands; not everything in his shop comes from Tel."

"Oh, you mean Hakamri?"

Mariana snapped her fingers and pointed at Lillian. "That's the one. For some reason, I was drawing a blank on his name."

"Well, you are getting on in years, Mari," Lillian jabbed, snickering.

"Five years, Lillian. I'm just five years older than you are. That's not so different."

Lillian grinned. "What did Gavin say that one time? 'Me thinks she doth protest too much?'"

"Just wait, Lillian," Mariana said. "One day, there will be someone needling you on your age, and I sincerely hope I'm there to see it."

"How long do you think it will take us to reach Stonehearth?" Lillian asked, both out of curiosity and thinking that a change in topic might be wise.

Mariana shrugged as she swayed with her mount's motion. "The innkeeper said the dwarven trade caravans take about two weeks to reach Pretty Rock, but there's no guarantee they use the same type of mounts we do or move at the same pace."

"So, back to using the teleport beacon?" Lillian asked, grinning.

"I see no reason not to."

* * *

GAVIN LOOKED up when he felt the subtle change in the ambient magic through his *skathos*. He was just in time to see the column of fire vanish, leaving Nathrac in its wake.

"You called for me?" Nathrac asked.

"I did, and thank you for coming," Gavin replied, nodding. "I have a problem. Based on evidence I have gathered, I no longer trust the Inquisitors, and I feel it is time to institute a complete review of their entire roster. Yes, I could indeed send out a summons for all Inquisitors to report back to the College, but I feel that might permit those with open violations of the Code to run. I want to see justice done. Can the Guardians round up the Inquisitors and return them to the College?"

Nathrac nodded once and spoke in that voice that resonated against Gavin's bones, "You need only give the order, Milord."

"Before that, can the Guardians retrieve a group of arcanists if I provide their names?"

"To ensure we retrieve the correct arcanists, we would need something personal to them," Nathrac answered, "but yes, it can be done."

Gavin handed him the list of names Alanna Veldin had provided. "I want those people collected. As soon as you have them all, inform me, and I shall call a meeting of the Council of Magisters."

Nathrac regarded the list for several moments before he said, "It shall be done."

Two days passed before Nathrac reported that the Guardians had retrieved every person on the list. Then, it was a fairly simple matter to ask Valera to convene the Council in the matter of Alanna Veldin, and when the Council was ready, Gavin asked Reyna to escort Veldin to the Chamber of the Council.

Gavin led Reyna and Veldin into the Chamber and forced himself not to smile at seeing the full Council and the student Veldin had attacked waiting for them. It was good that the cleric from the Temple had been able to heal the boy; Gavin didn't want him to miss his sentencing. The moment Gavin entered, the Council members stood. Once he arrived at their horseshoe-shaped table, Gavin gestured for them to return to their seats.

"Ladies and gentlemen," Gavin began, "I asked Valera to convene the Council to discuss the matter of Alanna Veldin. As I'm sure most of you are aware, Instructor Veldin attacked this student after class one day. Upon learning of the case and listening to Inquisitor Reyna's summary, I decided to take this matter up myself and, as such, will be delivering my verdict in the matter. However, I feel it is appropriate to learn the full scope of why Alanna Veldin attacked a student, and I call her to give testimony under Divination of Truth. Reyna, please conduct the student to the gallery; we'll need him shortly."

Reyna led the young man to the gallery as Veldin moved to stand front and center before the Council.

Gavin smiled. "Valera, would you prefer to do the honors, or shall I?"

Valera stood, reciting the words for Divination of Truth in the language of magic. A gray aura appeared around Alanna Veldin, and Gavin nodded his thanks.

"State your name and title, please," Gavin said.

"Alanna Veldin, General Instructor at the College of the Arcane," Veldin answered.

The gray aura shifted to a pure, bright white.

Gavin nodded. "Lie to me, Miss Veldin."

"Uhm, I hate apples," Veldin responded, the white aura immediately shifting to a vibrant, malevolent red.

"Very well," Gavin remarked. "Now that we have confirmed the spell is working as intended, please explain the circumstances surrounding your attack on the student."

Veldin nodded and took a breath. "That day, I had just returned the most recent exam, and after class the student came to me and said that I needed to correct my mistake in grading his exam, or he would have to take me in hand like his father did. And...well, I just snapped. I don't remember attacking him. I don't remember anything, really, between what he said and the people pulling me off him."

The spell's aura shifted back to bright white the moment Alanna began speaking, and it remained so.

"And how do you feel about the attack?" Gavin asked.

Veldin sighed. "I regret attacking a student. I should have had better control of myself. However, for that particular student and what he said, I do not regret beating him bloody at all."

The aura remained white.

"And why is that, Instructor Veldin?" Gavin asked.

Veldin took a deep breath and released it before answering. "Because his father and seven of his friends beat me and gang-raped me while I was a student here. They left me lying in an alley, bleeding into the gutter and unable to walk. The dwarf merchant, Hakamri, found me and helped me to the sick rooms of the Temple of Valthon, or I probably would not be alive today."

The spell's aura was still bright white.

"Forgive me for asking you to relive that," Gavin said, "but as it directly relates to this matter, please tell us what happened. Be sure to name names."

Veldin proceeded to tell the story of how she was attacked. She went into gruesome, excruciating detail and named names. Throughout her entire recitation, the aura created by Divination of Truth remained a steady, bright white. Nothing she said was a lie.

"Did you file a complaint of the incident?" Gavin asked, when she finished.

"I did. I sat with Magister Valera and wrote out my statement and specified that I wished to file charges."

Gavin turned to the Magisters. "Magister Valera, do you remember the written statement that Instructor Veldin mentioned?"

"I do, Milord," Valera answered.

"Once it was completed," Gavin asked, "what did you do with it?"

"As is standard for all statements involving criminal acts committed by arcanists or students of the College, I turned the statement over to the Inquisitors. In this instance, specifically to Chief Inquisitor Tauron."

Gavin shifted his attention to the Magister of Evocation who still held the title of Chief Inquisitor. "This isn't the first time we've had an instance of missing statements, Tauron. What happened to Alanna Veldin's statement and its associated filings?"

Tauron glared at Gavin. "Do you seriously expect me to remember something like that? It happened over ten years ago!"

"Valera seems to remember the incident rather well, Tauron," Gavin countered. "Are you saying she's lying?"

Before Tauron could speak, Gavin invoked a Word of Divination, "*Klaepos.*"

A gray aura appeared around Tauron. The magister lifted his arms and regarded the aura before returning his glare to Gavin.

"You dare cast Divination of Truth without my consent? I challenge you to a Wizards' Duel!"

Gavin made a dismissive wave. "And I refuse. You'd be committing suicide by Kirloth. Now, answer my questions."

"You think you'll get me to say something that will allow you to dismiss me?" Tauron spat, not quite shouting. "Everything I have done has been for the betterment of the Society! How dare you question me!"

"How is hiding rape and other brutal conduct by the College's students for the betterment of the Society, Tauron?" Gavin asked. "Explain that to me."

"I refuse. I refuse to admit or accept that you have any authority over me," Tauron raged. "Do we even *know* that Bellos named you to be Archmagister? I didn't witness it. For all I know, you're nothing but a fraud."

A blinding flash of gold-colored light heralded the arrival of Bellos. Gavin regarded the God of Magic for a moment and leaned back to look at the pedestal that supported the statue of Bellos, only to find it vacant; it held no statue.

"You challenge *my* authority, Tauron?" Bellos asked.

Tauron gaped at Bellos, his jaw moving but without sound.

"I do not appreciate my choice being questioned," Bellos remarked. "I would have thought the sconces within the College and the streetlamps and braziers atop the walls of the province capitals to be plenty of proof that I made my choice. Apparently, I was mistaken."

Bellos paused for a moment and closed his eyes. When he opened them again, every person present felt a raw power filling the room.

"People of Tel," Bellos said, his voice now possessing an eerie resonance, "as some have already dared question my choice of Archmagister, I speak to you all now to verify and affirm that I have chosen Gavin Cross of House Kirloth to assume the office that has been vacant for so long. That is all."

Bellos closed his eyes once more and took a deep breath. The raw power filling the hall faded, and when he opened his eyes again, Bellos looked straight at Gavin.

"I know far more about Tauron and his transgressions than I would like, and I do not feel he is fit to hold any office or position of responsibility. That being said, I shall trust your judgment in this and all matters, as you have earned. Thank you once again, Gavin, for your sacrifice. They need you more than they know."

Another bright flash of gold-colored light filled the Chamber. When it faded, Bellos was gone, and the pedestal supported a statue once more.

Gavin turned back to the Council of Magisters, his eyes focusing on Tauron. "Well, will you confess at least? I would prefer that your associates on the Council understand why I've decided what I have."

"Do what you will, Kirloth," Tauron growled. "I have no interest in participating in your circus any longer."

Gavin sighed. "So be it. As of this moment, you are hereby stripped of all rank and authority within the Society of the Arcane." Gavin focused his mind on his intent, then invoked a composite effect, "*Zaenos-Zyrhaek.*"

Those wizards present felt the resonance of Gavin's power slam the ambient magic as Tauron screamed and clutched at his head. He collapsed back into his seat, and when he pulled his hands away from his head, everyone present could see blood trickling from his nostrils and ears.

"Any and all knowledge of the Art has just been ripped from your mind," Gavin said. "You will never be able to re-learn what you have lost. Your days as an arcanist are over. Reyna, per the authority vested in me as Archmagister of Tel, I hereby confer upon you the title and authority of Chief Inquisitor. Do you accept the position I have offered?"

Reyna gaped at Gavin for several moments before nodding. "Yes, Milord. I-I do not have the words for how much I value and appreciate your trust in me. I will strive to prove your trust each and every day."

"In that case," Gavin replied, "your first order of business is to work with the Guardians in conducting a full review of all Inquisitors. Bring any to me who do not exemplify the ideals all Inquisitors should uphold. Nathrac!"

A column of fire erupted from the floor not six feet from Gavin, delivering the Chief of the Guard.

"You called, Milord?"

"Thank you, Nathrac. Please deliver those eight people I asked you to collect."

Nathrac snapped his fingers, and eight additional columns of fire delivered those who had attacked Alanna Veldin all those years ago.

"Chief Inquisitor," Gavin began, "would you be so kind as to bring that young man to stand by his father? I'll pass judgment on them both at the same time." Reyna almost jumped to her feet and nearly dragged the student to stand by his father. "The eight of you committed a rather heinous crime against this woman while all of you were students. It is a gross miscarriage of justice that nothing was ever done, but I will now correct that." Gavin produced a piece of parchment from inside his robe and read the names of seven of the eight adults. "For your participation in the attack on Alanna Veldin, I hereby revoke your status in the Society of the Arcane and seize any assets you have amassed since that time. *Zaenos-Zyrhaek.*" The seven men screamed and collapsed to the floor, clutching their heads before ultimately falling unconscious. "Never again shall you wield the Art."

Gavin turned to the man standing beside his son. "You, sir, were the ringleader of the group, and you perpetuated the mindset that such conduct was acceptable to your son. I do not have the words for how much I want to burn the both of you to ash where you stand. I feel very strongly that your son has already internalized this mindset to such a degree that he is irredeemable. But while I am many things, I am no killer of children, even when they probably deserve it. Your family hereby forfeits all worldly possessions and wealth. The both of you forfeit any and all standing in the Society of the Arcane, both now and in perpetuity. *Zaenos-Zyrhaek-Uhnrys.*"

Both the father and the son fell to the ground, screaming and clutching at their heads. They, too, soon fell unconscious.

Gavin turned to Reyna. "Remove the lot of them from College grounds. Go to the student's room and secure any personal possessions; those are forfeit as well. You will see to it that all forfeitures declared here today pass to Alanna Veldin as reparations for their crimes." Gavin turned to Veldin. "Alanna Veldin, you attacked a student, someone entrusted to your care, but I find that you did so as the result of significant provocation that surpassed anything one could reasonably expect an instructor to face. Still, I would not want our instructors thinking that they can attack students wholesale, and so, I fine you one month of your instructor's pay. Please, inform Magister Valera when you feel ready to resume your class schedule."

Alanna Veldin gaped at Gavin as he turned to face the Council.

"Valera, please make whatever notifications are appropriate that the selection of a new Magister of Evocation is to begin." Gavin's eyes fell on Tauron who was now slumped in the seat of his former position, looking comatose. "Reyna, see that Tauron is removed from the College as well, and delegate someone to box up his personal effects and leave them with him...wherever you decide he should be put."

"Yes, Milord," Reyna responded.

Gavin scanned the faces practically staring at him in silence. "Right then. I do believe our work here is finished. Session adjourned."

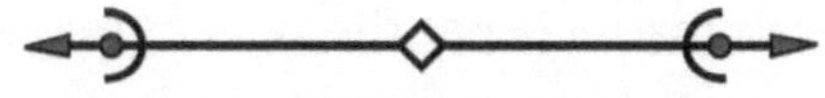

CHAPTER 31

In the days that followed their departure from Pretty Rock, Lillian and Mariana headed north to Stonehearth, the dwarven capital. The dwarves divided their society into two clans with convoluted family structures branching out from there. Clan Stone devoted their efforts to mastering the material of stone in all its types and forms; carving, masonry, and any other endeavor involving working with stone was their domain. As one might expect, Clan Metal pursued similar mastery over metals.

The dwarves were also unique of the races of the old alliance in that the position of king—or queen—alternated between the two clans. It was a life appointment, but the monarch could choose to retire at any time. No matter what the reason might be for needing a new monarch, the heads of each family within the clan would gather and decide who would serve from their clan. Ideally, they always chose the best person, but politics and family feuds did often play a role.

Clan Metal currently held the monarchy.

* * *

Lillian and Mariana approached the massive entrance to Stonehearth. A slight breeze carried the chill of mountain air and the faint scent of forges and charcoal delivered by the smokestacks jutting up through the mountainside. The entrance was a pair of massive stone doors under a portico, and a squad of dwarven soldiers conducted searches of any wagons or travelers they deemed suspect.

"Welcome to Stonehearth," said a grizzled dwarf with stringy, silver hair and beard. "Please, state your names and reason of travel."

"I am Lillian of House Mivar, and my associate is Mariana of House Cothos. We seek entry to Stonehearth and an audience with the king as credentialed ambassadors of Gavin Cross of House Kirloth, the Archmagister of Tel."

The dwarf stopped scribbling on his parchment and looked up at Lillian, giving her the squint eye. "Did you say Archmagister of Tel? You'll have to do better than that, girlie. Tel hasn't had an Archmagister since my grandfather's time."

"May I get our papers from my saddlebag?" Lillian asked.

"Oh, aye. I'm very interested to see whatever papers you have."

Lillian leaned back just far enough to access the left saddlebag and withdrew the folio containing the documents proving their status. Folio in hand, she dismounted and offered it to the dwarf. The dwarf accepted the folio and opened it, taking the time to read through everything contained therein. After several moments, he closed the folio and offered it back to Lillian.

"My apologies," the dwarf said. "News that Bellos has named a new Archmagister hasn't reached us as yet, at least not me." He pulled out a blank sheet of parchment and jotted a message, before stamping the document with his seal and offering it to Lillian. "That will get you through Monarch Gate, and you'll be able to speak with someone there about scheduling an audience."

"Thank you, sir," Lillian replied, inserting the document into the folio before returning it to her saddlebag.

Lillian and Mariana merged into the traffic flow as they entered Stonehearth. Cobblestones paved the streets, and carts and wagons drawn by rock wolves, or possibly a distant cousin, creaked and clattered along on their journeys. The city overall was dark, the streets lit by pitch lamps. Even though the space occupied by the city was cavernous, the dark and gloom contributed to a closed-in feel that weighed upon them as they traveled deeper into the city.

"I think I'm glad we saved the High Forest for last," Mariana whispered.

Lillian grinned. "There's a reason not many non-dwarves visit Stonehearth. It certainly isn't for everyone."

"Qar'Zhosk wasn't bad," Mariana responded, "but this is just oppressive."

"Qar'Zhosk had a different feel to it, especially after we fixed their sky," Lillian countered. "This is altogether different."

They fell into a companionable silence as they made their way through the city to the gate that protected the government buildings. An arched stone sign above the gate read 'Monarch Gate' in dwarven script, and the guards here had much more ornate equipment.

"State your business," a dwarf growled when Lillian and Mariana stopped at the gate.

Lillian withdrew the folio from her saddlebag and said, "I am Lillian of House Mivar, and my associate is Mariana of House Cothos. We are accredited ambassadors from Gavin Cross of House Kirloth, who is now the Archmagister of Tel. This folio contains our papers and a pass provided by the guard at the entrance to the city."

Lillian stepped down from her horse and offered the folio to the dwarf. He accepted it and read through its documents, finally settling on the note provided by the entrance guard. After reading through everything, he nodded.

"Very well," the dwarf said. "You'll want to present yourselves to the king. I don't know what the schedule is like, but he may just grant your audience when you present yourselves. Go through the gate, and a groom will see to your mounts. Anyone in Government House can direct you to the king."

Lillian accepted the folio from the guard and decided to lead her horse instead of re-mounting. Mariana stepped down to lead her horse as well, and soon, they handed off the reins to an eager young dwarf who said he'd take them to the stables and see to their care.

LILLIAN AND MARIANA entered Government House, and the well-lit, functional ambiance struck them as a sharp contrast to the oppressive, closed-in feeling the city as a whole gave them. Dwarves moved hither and yon on various tasks, and it wasn't long before they encountered a middle-aged dwarf who gave them directions to reach the king.

Lillian and Mariana finally found themselves standing in an outer office where several dwarves carried out their tasks with silent efficiency. As they entered, one looked up and smiled.

"Oh, hello," the dwarf said, the voice sounding female. "I'm Agara. How can we help you?"

Lillian presented the folio and once more introduced herself and Mariana.

Agara blinked. "Archmagister? Really? Oh, my...Gildar will want to meet you right away."

Lillian and Mariana shared a look before Lillian asked, "Gildar? Who's that?"

"Why, he's the king; you two are so precious. Is this your first time in Stonehearth, dears?"

"You address the king by name?" Mariana asked.

Agara grinned. "Well, of course, I do. He's my brother, and I'm not about to let him be taking on airs. Every time he gets even a little uppity with me, I remind him and anyone in hearing that I changed his diapers. That always brings him back to ground. He's an excellent king, though. Done a lot of good for us, he has, and I'm not just saying that because he's my brother."

Lillian and Mariana shared a look as they fought to keep a straight face.

"Now then, come along," Agara continued. "I'll introduce you to him."

Agara stood from her desk and led Lillian and Mariana through a door and into an office almost the size of the Conclave meeting room back home. A massive desk dominated the room, behind which sat a dwarf who looked to be not quite middle-aged. He looked up when the door opened and quirked an eyebrow at the two humans Agara was leading into his office.

"Gildar, these ladies come from Tel Mivar; the new Archmagister sent them," Agara said before she turned and left, closing the door on her way out.

The dwarf rose from his seat and stumped around the desk, extending his hand. "Pleasure to meet ye. I am Gildar, King of Stonehearth."

"Lillian Mivar," Lillian said as Gildar shook her hand.

"Mariana Cothos," Mariana said when Gildar turned to shake her hand.

Pleasantries concluded, Gildar gestured to a couple chairs before returning to his own. Once everyone was seated, he smiled and said, "So, the new Archmagister sent ye? And just how is Gavin these days?"

Both Lillian and Mariana gaped, Mariana overcoming the shock first to say, "You know Gavin?"

Gildar shrugged. "Well, I can't say as I've ever laid eyes on him meself, but I do know of him."

"Hakamri," Lillian said.

Gildar nodded once. "Aye. He's my...well, let's say uncle. Humans seem to get lost a bit when they try to sort out our family relationships. He's had quite a few things to say about the boy."

Mariana's lips quirked. "He isn't exactly a boy, Your Majesty."

"Call me Gildar," he replied, waving off the honorific, "and lass, I'm a hundred and thirty years old. All of ye are boys or girls to me. So, what brings ye to Stonehearth?"

"Well," Lillian began, "Gavin asked us to visit the giants, you, and the elves to start the process of rebuilding the friendships our peoples once enjoyed. I can say the giants were very receptive and will be sending an ambassador to Tel Mivar."

"That's an excellent idea," Gildar remarked. "I've been wondering when he would get around to the diplomatic side of things ever since Hakamri sent word about seeing Gavin in gold robes. I have two major areas of concern at present: Skullkeep, which shouldn't surprise anyone, and the High Forest."

Mariana nodded. "We've heard all might not be well among the elves. They are our next stop after we conclude our visit here."

"Well, be careful," Gildar replied. "They haven't completely cut off relations with us, but they're not the friendly neighbors they once were. I've heard whispers that the dark elves may be meddling, but no two whispers match or stand up to much scrutiny. Regardless, they may not be happy to see ye. But as for us, tell your boy that I'm inviting him to send an ambassador here. I like what Hakamri has told me, and I think he'll do good things for the old alliance."

Lillian smiled. "Thank you, Gildar. Gavin would welcome an ambassador from you as well."

Gildar grinned. "I'll send word to Hakamri that he's getting a promotion. He's been playing at business too long, anyway."

* * *

KIRI SIGHED as she entered her suite. It had been a long day of meetings and negotiations between various groups, and it seemed like everyone wanted a piece of the efforts to rebuild the kingdom after the civil war. It was incredibly tiring. All she wanted now was to soak for a while in a nice, hot bath.

Kiri entered her bedroom and frowned at the empty room. Usually her personal maid was waiting to help with the removal and laundering of her court clothes. Either way, she wanted out of the suffocating attire and walked to her wardrobe.

As she reached for the dress's ties, a voice said, "Good evening, Princess."

Kiri spun, her left hand drawing a stiletto from her right sleeve.

A man stood in the corner of her bedroom. He wore dark leather armor that was well-maintained. A thin mustache adorned his upper lip. He regarded Kiri with an almost sardonic grin. Kiri couldn't shake the feeling she'd seen him somewhere before.

"Oh, you won't be needing that, I don't think," the man said, eyeing Kiri's stiletto. "I'm not here to hurt you at all. Besides, I'd rather my Guild not have to suffer Gavin's retribution if I did harm you. I wager his treatment of them would make what Kirloth did to those Temple Guardsmen look rather tame."

"Dakkor?" Kiri asked.

"Aye."

Kiri returned the stiletto to its sheath and frowned. "I don't want to seem unwelcoming, but what are you doing here?"

"I had a question for you," Dakkor replied. "How badly do you want to reconcile with Gavin?"

Dakkor's question hit Kiri like a punch to the gut. "I—how did you know about that?"

"Girlie, I'm the God of Thieves. My followers aren't as adept as the Wraiths, but they do the job—mostly."

Kiri took a deep breath and tried to steady her nerves. "I would give anything to take back what I said. I miss Gavin terribly."

Dakkor nodded. "Well, if you want to have any hope of doing that, you should find a way to get to Tel Mivar, sooner rather than later. You don't have as much time as you think."

"What do you mean?"

"I've heard whispers, that's all. But several revolve around an attack on Tel Mivar. None of us knows how coming events will play out, but we do see possibilities. One possibility those whispers show me is Gavin's death."

"How—how much time do I have?" Kiri asked.

Dakkor shrugged. "Could be days, could be months. I cannot say. But I owe it to Gavin to see that you have the chance. I doubt your current attire is well suited for travel, so I took the liberty of laying out some things you might find more comfortable."

Dakkor gestured toward the bed and Kiri turned, blinking at the sight. When she entered her bedroom, the bed was devoid of anything beyond the comforter and bed linens. The leather armor and blades Declan had obtained for her in Tel Mivar, along with traveling clothes to wear under the armor, spread across the bed. Kiri noticed immediately that the leather armor had been modified—or perhaps repaired—to cover her shoulders.

Kiri gaped for a heartbeat, but when she turned back to thank Dakkor, he was gone.

* * *

ONCE THEY LEFT STONEHEARTH, the days passed with little incident, and now, Lillian and Mariana sat astride their horses at the edge of the High Forest. The sun was just visible over the tops of the tall trees that cast long shadows toward them. It wouldn't be long before night truly fell.

"What do you think?" Lillian asked. "Stop for the night and resume in the morning? Or should we press on for a couple more hours?"

Mariana looked up, her gaze intent on the horizon created by the treetops. "Both the giants and the dwarves have warned us that all is not right with elves just now. Where we stand is far closer to Arundel than if we were traveling from Tel, and I think we could reach it within a day. Let's stop for the evening and start fresh in the morning. If things are truly as bad as the giants or dwarves fear, I have no wish to travel the High Forest at night. All of nature could be their weapon."

Lillian nodded and leaned back to wrangle the teleport beacon out of her saddlebag. She tossed it into the weeds while Mariana created a gateway to Tel Cothos.

"Want to spend the night?" Mariana asked. "We have plenty of guest rooms."

"I appreciate it," Lillian replied, "but I've gotten used to seeing Grandpa and Grandma each evening. I wouldn't want them to worry."

That said, Lillian created her own gateway, and the ladies soon vanished from the roadside.

·　·　·

THE NEXT MORNING, Lillian bade her father and grandparents goodbye and teleported to Tel Cothos. She opened the gateway to her beacon after meeting up with Mariana, as had been their practice for the entire journey. The resonance of the beacon was so familiar to her that she no longer bothered scrying it beforehand, but when they stepped through the gateway, they found themselves facing several dozen elves all with blades or bows at the ready.

"Good morning, ladies," an unctuous voice almost purred, and the throng parted to reveal an urbane elf dressed in exquisite finery. "Allow me to introduce myself. My name is Nirrock, and it is my extreme joy to hold the position of Nature's Protector. Surrender, and you won't come to any...immediate harm."

"Why are you doing this?" Lillian asked. "We have always been allies."

Nirrock's expression shifted into a smile that held far more malice than mirth. "You lot have never been allies of mine. I—plus those you see around you and many I have placed throughout the elven government—are dark elves."

CHAPTER 32

The days following the resolution of the Alanna Veldin case had become grueling weeks. Between Reyna's review of the Inquisitors, the search for a new Magister of Evocation, and working with the Conclave to identify—and then fix—the more egregious abuses of the laws and tax code, Gavin was going to bed mentally—and most days, physically—drained and often waking up feeling like he hadn't rested at all. More than once he'd caught himself thinking it was less arduous to travel to another country and sleep on the ground, but all of it and so much more needed to be done to right the wrongs inflicted upon Tel by the generations of rule by the royal family.

No part of it was fun, but then, Gavin didn't really expect it to be fun, either.

* * *

GAVIN STEPPED through the portal to the Grand Stair from the Citadel so intent on his upcoming meeting with Reyna that he didn't realize someone was in front of him until the force of their collision focused his mind. His quick reflexes allowed him to catch Sera before his momentum sent her bouncing back down the stone stairs, and he held her until she restored her balance.

"I am so sorry, Sera," Gavin said. "Are you okay?"

Long exposure to Gavin had taught her that particular odd term among the many he used, and Sera nodded. "Yes, Milord, but I wouldn't have been if you hadn't caught me."

"It's the least I could do after bumping into you in the first place," Gavin replied as he released her and stepped back. "If you'll forgive me—"

"Magister Valera could use your help, sir," Sera said, surprising Gavin that she had the wherewithal to interrupt him. "The parents of the Fifth Tier you suspended and reduced to Third Tier are in her office, and they are very irate. At least, the father is. I could hear him raging at the magister through the walls and door."

Gavin's eyes narrowed as his expression hardened. "Well, I see where the son got his bullying tendencies. Would you mind dashing off to Reyna's office and telling her I'll be late for our meeting? Oh... and ask her to ready some Inquisitors as well. If he refuses to see reason, I'll have need of them."

Sera blinked. "You will?"

"It's either that or burn them to ash where they stand, and I'd rather not make a mess in Valera's office."

Sera paled just enough to notice. "Uhm—yes, Milord. I'll go to the Chief Inquisitor straight away."

Despite being near the very top of the Tower, it took Gavin little time to reach Valera's office. Just as Sera had said, Gavin heard a man shouting inside Valera's private office, and he made a mental note to bring a healer to check Valera's ears for physical harm after so much loud noise. Gavin didn't slow his stride as he crossed the reception area and opened the door. He saw a rather large man—both in height and bulk—looming over Valera's desk, his right hand clenched in a fist, except for the index finger extended rigidly toward the Magister of Divination. Someone sat at the small table beyond the man, but his bulk prevented Gavin from a good view of whoever it was. Gavin assumed it was the man's wife.

"How dare you intrude—" the man raged until he saw who was entering Valera's office. He blinked and his jaw hung open as his voice cut off mid-tirade.

Gavin looked to Valera first, asking, "Are you okay?"

Valera nodded. "I am well."

"And you are?" Gavin asked, directing his attention to the man looming over Valera's desk.

"I am the father of the young man you shamed," the bear of a man almost growled. "Do you not recognize me? Did you not recognize our House Glyph?"

"Nope," Gavin replied, adding an indifferent shrug, which seemed to only enrage the man more. "I have far more important things to do than memorize every glyph in the House Registry, and besides, your son shamed himself."

"How dare you!" the man, who still hadn't introduced himself, growled even more loudly. "I will not stand for this disrespect. Do you hear me? I will not stand for it!"

Gavin looked the man right in the eye and invoked a Word of Conjuration, "*Nythraex.*" The full resonance of his power slammed into every wizard within fifty yards—at least—and he couldn't resist taking a small measure of pleasure at the man's momentary stagger. The effect of Gavin's invocation appeared at the man's side before he finished swaying on his feet: a simple wooden chair without arms and cross-bracing between the legs, sized to fit the man.

"There," Gavin said, gesturing at the chair that he had just conjured. "If you won't stand for it, have a seat."

The red flush in the man's neck and face slowly shifted toward purple, and out of the corner of his eye, Gavin thought he saw Valera stifling a smile. The man ground his teeth together with such force that Gavin was a bit surprised he couldn't hear them squeaking, and his hands clenched into white-knuckled fists.

"You really have only two choices here," Gavin continued. "One, shut your damned mouth and accept my judgment on your son before I decide you are more responsible for his actions and attitudes than he is, or two, do something stupid and give me justification to disband your House and seize all its assets. I don't really know anything about your son's victim, but I imagine that boy's family could do with a sudden influx of wealth. I suppose there is a third option; you challenge me to a Wizards' Duel, but you strike me as a bully. In my experience, bullies are—as a whole—physical cowards who are incapable of taking what they dish out, so I can't really see you deciding to commit 'suicide by Kirloth.' Hmmm. The more I think about it, disbanding your House and seizing your assets might just be the best outcome overall. I'm sure you've made quite a few enemies, and I must confess a certain interest in seeing their response to you finding yourself without power or wealth. What do you think? How long do you think it would be before someone took their vengeance out of your hide?"

By now, all trace of anger and rage had vanished from the man's visage. In fact, it seemed to Gavin that he looked rather pale. Gavin hoped the man was considering his words and looking back over his life, but Gavin was no mind reader and, in all truth, had bigger worries to care about.

"Now," Gavin said, "you are going to apologize to Valera for your conduct in her office. Then, you will collect your son, and the lot of you will vacate the College at once. I highly suggest you spend the rest of the term and the off-season adjusting yours and your son's attitudes, because if he chooses to return next term and bullies even one more person, I'll cast your entire family out of the Society and rip all arcane knowledge and power from your very souls...after I seize your assets and split them between yours and your son's victims. Do you understand me?"

The man nodded jerkily.

Gavin's eyes narrowed into a glare. "I didn't hear you."

"I understand," the man almost growled.

"Good. Now, I believe Magister Valera is waiting for your apology, and I'd better be impressed."

The man held Gavin's eyes for several heartbeats, as if he wanted to stare Gavin down. In the end, he turned to face Valera and said, "Magister Valera, I apologize for my rude and abusive conduct in your office. It was disrespectful and unworthy of all you do to support both the Society and the students here."

"Thank you," Valera replied.

The man turned back to Gavin, who noticed the man's hands were still clenched, but the apology had seemed honest enough.

"Very well," Gavin remarked, and with the invocation of a Word of Tutation, the conjured chair vanished into nothingness. "Do you know where your son's room in the dormitories is?"

"Yes, sir," the man answered.

Gavin nodded once. "Excellent. Collect him and his personal effects and be gone. I trust I do not need to state what will happen if you are not the soul of courtesy and compassion during your remaining time on College grounds."

That said, Gavin stepped away from the door and nodded toward it. The man stepped to the door, opened it, and froze, startled. Gavin leaned forward far enough to look through the doorway and saw Reyna and five of her Inquisitors standing in the reception office.

"Thank you for your swift response, Chief Inquisitor," Gavin said, silently enjoying the man's flinch at the use of Reyna's new position, "but I'm pleased to report all is well here. I would appreciate it, though, if you would detail two of your excellent people to escort Valera's visitors to collect their son. I'd hate for them to get lost."

Reyna's smile was outright predatory. "Of course, Milord, it would be my pleasure."

The man and the woman Gavin assumed to be his wife left Valera's office and disappeared with two Inquisitors. Reyna dismissed the rest and turned to Gavin, saying, "I'll be ready for our meeting whenever you are, sir."

Gavin nodded once, and Reyna left as well.

Turning back to Valera, Gavin said, "So, are you really okay?"

Valera nodded and smiled. "Yes, Gavin, I'm fine. How did you know they were here?"

"Sera came for me," Gavin answered.

"Ah," Valera remarked. "While I appreciate her initiative, I'm not sure it was worth disturbing you."

Gavin shook his head. "I'm glad she came for me. I protect my people, Valera, which you should certainly remember."

"Oh, yes," Valera replied. "I remember, and I thank you for considering me one of your people."

"I value every arcanist who strives to create a better world and would do the same as I just did for you, but you...well, I consider you to be a personal friend."

Valera smiled. "Thank you, Gavin. I consider you a friend as well."

Gavin nodded once. "Well, if you'll excuse me, I'm due for a report on the review of the Inquisitors, but please, find me if you need me."

Valera gave Gavin her own nod, and he headed for his original destination of Reyna's office.

* * *

A knock on his chamber door drew his attention, and the Necromancer looked up from the tome he was reading.

"Enter!"

The lieutenant who always seemed to be the one chosen to report to him entered the room, and for once, he didn't look terrified.

"Master, the preparations continue to go well. The host should be ready to march on Tel Mivar within a few days."

"Excellent," the Necromancer replied. He still wasn't sure attacking the new Archmagister was the wisest course, but all of his arcanist lieutenants counseled him to do so. At worst, the plan would rid him of the idiots among them. "Are the arcanists ready to raise the ritual gate?"

"They are finalizing their preparations but assure me they will be ready by the time the host can march, if not before."

"Thank you," the Necromancer replied.

The lieutenant snapped a quick salute and vacated the chamber.

The ritual gate was a massive version of the teleportation gateway most arcanists could conjure. It was necessary to move the massive horde of undead the Necromancer commanded, and it was how he had overwhelmed what little garrison had remained at Skullkeep all those centuries ago. It would be interesting to see how the young upstart pup Bellos had chosen for Archmagister would respond to hundreds of undead rampaging through Tel Mivar.

* * *

GAVIN SIGHED as he sat on the edge of the planter designed to serve as a bench. The College's gardens existed not only to supply reagents to the alchemy classes but also served as a place of peace and relaxation. The largest tree in the entire garden shaded the planter Gavin chose for his seat. Supposedly, it dated back to the early days of the College, planted by the druids of the High Forest who helped design and tend the garden for many decades during the Founding. No matter the tree's source or age, the massive arbor's multi-colored leaves swaying in the faint breeze lifted Gavin's spirits like little else at the College could, these days. For some reason, the tree reminded Gavin of home, even though he had no memories of home to tell him why.

As he was enjoying the simplicity of nature around him, a strange sight caught his eye. A point on the tree's bark began swirling like a whirlpool and slowly expanded until it occupied the entire side of the tree facing Gavin. Oddly, Gavin sensed nothing through his *skathos*.

Gavin almost couldn't believe his eyes when the whirlpool in the tree's bark seemed to draw inward for the briefest moment before three people stepped out into the shade afforded by the mighty tree. The moment all three people had fully exited the tree, the whirlpool effect in the tree's bark vanished as if it had never been. And Gavin knew them.

"Telanna? Elayna? Sarres?" He tried not to gape at seeing his friends step out of a tree.

"Really, Gavin?" Telanna said, quirking one eyebrow upward. "You bend reality to your will as a matter of course and yet gating through plants astonishes you?"

"Oh," Gavin said. "Is that what you call it?"

Telanna nodded. "All druids who have a sufficient rapport with Nature can do it, and this tree was planted during the Founding to provide us easy access to the College...with Kirloth's full under-standing and permission, of course."

"Wow, okay." Gavin smiled as he regarded his friends. "As much as I'm glad to see you, I can't help but think you've come with a purpose."

"You are more correct than you know," Elayna replied. "Nirrock, the dark elf who controls the government of the High Forest, has taken Lillian and Mariana prisoner."

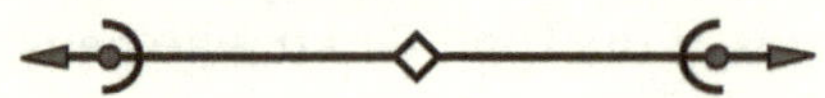

CHAPTER 33

Gavin ushered Telanna, Elayna, and Sarres into the Citadel's meeting room for the Conclave and conjured three chairs for them. Then, without missing a beat, he activated the mechanism in the meeting room that would summon the Conclave of the Great Houses. While he waited, Gavin looked at the tabletop, saw its surface decorated with the Glyph of Kirloth, and he couldn't help but wonder how all the Archmagisters down through the centuries felt about using this table when Kirloth was supposedly long dead. *Heh, if they had only known the truth.*

Torval Mivar was the first to appear. Then, Lyssa. Sypara and Carth arrived at almost the exact same moment. As soon as Carth and Sypara vacated their beacons, Wynn and Braden arrived. They scanned the room, and their eyes soon spied the three elves sitting off to one side.

Lyssa spoke first, cutting through all the pleasantries as she said, "What has happened?"

"I've just been informed that Nirrock has taken Lillian and Mariana prisoner," Gavin answered.

"And that's not all," Telanna announced. "Nirrock and a sizable portion of the elven government are dark elves."

The new arrivals all stared at Telanna in silence, shocked by that revelation.

"How?" Torval asked at last. "How did that happen?"

Telanna offered a very human shrug. "It is assumed that Nirrock was the first and slowly moved others into positions of power. As you know, dark elves are physically indistinguishable from those of us who do not follow Milthas. It has only been in the past day and a half —perhaps, two days—that everyone has shown their true allegiance. If a government official follows Nirrock without question, especially in his capture of two Heirs to the Great Houses, it is fairly safe to assume they are dark elves as well. The bulk of the populace is frankly horrified at what he has done, and they are now calling for us to resume our traditional authority."

"Us?" Gavin asked. "Perhaps you should explain that. I, for one, have no idea who you are referring to."

Telanna gave a small smile. "Some of you may be aware that I am a druid—essentially a priestess of nature. What you may not know is that all elven druids are members of the Sylvan Synod, much like arcanists are members of the Society. In ages past, the Sylvan Synod served as the government of the elves, but over time, the Synod invested more and more civil authority in Nature's Protector. We have already determined that Nirrock will be the last Nature's Protector once this situation is resolved, and the Synod will resume its tradi-tional authority in full. The key now is to resolve this situation without fracturing elven society any more than it already is."

"Why come to us?" Sypara asked.

The elves each looked to one another before Telanna gave an almost apologetic half-smile. "Forgive me, and please do not take offense, but we did not come to the Conclave of the Great Houses. We did not even come to the Archmagister. We came to Gavin."

Elayna looked at Gavin, and her lips quirked in what might have been a smile if allowed to mature. "I'm afraid I was not wholly honest with you when we first met, Gavin."

Gavin frowned as he searched his memory for that meeting.

"Yes, you had just saved our lives," Elayna continued, "but when you asked why we were traveling through Tel, I told a slight false-hood. I said we were on our way south to our embassy in Vushaar. We *were* on our way south, but we were seeking you. Grandmother told us that we would find the man to help rid us of the dark elves in Vushaar. Before we had the opportunity to plead our case to you, Bellos asked you to take on the mantle of Archmagister."

Gavin chuckled. "Yeah...that certainly complicated things."

"Wait...so, you're saying Xanta sent you to Vushaar to look for Gavin?" Carth asked.

Elayna and Sarres both nodded.

"You're taking this rather in stride," Lyssa remarked, looking at Gavin.

Gavin shrugged. "Both Valthon *and* Bellos have meddled in my life already, even before Bellos dropped the gold robes on me. Why not Xanta, too?" He turned to Telanna. "So, how are we going to get my friends back?"

"We feel the first step is returning to Arundel with us," the druid replied. "Once you're there, you can better evaluate the situation and determine a course of action."

"It's all on me, huh?" Gavin asked, his lips quirking into an almost sardonic grin.

The elves looked to one another again and shared slightly uncomfortable expressions.

Now, Gavin grinned fully. "Well, I'm afraid it'll have to be more than just me. Despite what you may think, my success is built—in part—by the people around me. Wynn, Braden—I'd like you to accompany me. I'll send for Declan as well. Besides wanting to chronicle this for posterity, I'm sure he'll have some valuable insights. I would take Xythe, but Holly has become rather enamored of her."

"Jasper could watch her," Wynn said. "He and Xythe have become surrogate siblings—if not parents—for her."

Gavin nodded, struck by how well Wynn knew his apprentices. Turning back to Telanna, he asked, "Is that large a group feasible?"

"It is possible, though I would caution trying to bring too many more."

"I honestly can't think of anyone else I'd want to bring," Gavin remarked, "but once I'm in Arundel, I can teleport back and forth if there's someone else I need." A thought occurred to him, and Gavin called out, "Nathrac!"

A column of fire that neither burned nor radiated heat erupted from the floor, delivering the Chief of the Citadel Guard.

"You called, Milord?" Nathrac asked, his deep voice resonating against everyone's bones.

"Yes, thank you," Gavin replied. "Nature's Protector in the High Forest has taken Lillian and Mariana prisoner. I'm going to sort that out, and as long as I'm outside of Tel, you are responsible for carrying out the duties and authority of the Archmagister in my absence."

"Of course, Milord. Such is as we already agreed."

Gavin grinned. "I know. I just wanted to reiterate it before these witnesses so there would be less reason to question you."

"Milord, I am a dragon over seven thousand years old. Do you really think anyone will go searching for reasons to question me?"

Now, Gavin laughed. "Perhaps not, but I try to head off trouble where I can."

"When will you be leaving?"

Gavin looked to Telanna but got no answer from her, so he shrugged. "I'd assume within the hour."

"Very well. I shall be ready."

With that, another column of flame consumed Nathrac, and he vanished from the meeting room.

"Okay, that's done," Gavin remarked. "Wynn, would you collect Xythe while you and Braden get what you need for the journey? I'll take care of rounding up Declan."

Wynn nodded as he and Braden stood. They each invoked the Word of Transmutation to create a gateway, as each had different destinations, and vanished from the meeting room.

Gavin looked at his remaining associates. "Thank you for coming. I felt you needed to know the current situation, and I'll do everything I can to bring them home safely."

"None of us doubt that last part, Gavin," Torval replied. "You've more than demonstrated that you always take care of your friends."

"Right, then. If you'll excuse me, I need to find a bard."

Gavin strode through the door, the elves following in his wake as the Heads of the Great Houses teleported home.

* * *

ARUNDEL WAS A STRIKING SIGHT. While Tel Mivar and the other province capitals were a testament to the power and foresight of Kirloth and the Apprentices, the elven capital was a study in crystal architecture. Gavin grinned like a child looking at a mountain of presents as he saw how the city's structures acted like massive prisms for the sunlight, separating it out into its component colors.

"This is beautiful," Gavin said. "How do you ever get anything accomplished? I'd want to sit around looking at all the light rays."

The three elves shared a look before turning back to Gavin. Telanna offered a very human shrug as she answered, "I guess we're accustomed to it. Yes, of course, it's beautiful...but we also grew up around it."

"Right, then," Gavin remarked, forcing himself to turn away from the optical splendor. "What's next?"

"The Sylvan Synod would like to discuss the situation and how you want to handle it," Telanna answered.

Gavin grinned. "I don't know what they have in mind, but how I want to handle Nirrock capturing two of my people is very simple. He can return them to me unharmed, or I'm prepared to re-enact Kirloth's duel with Milthas."

Elayna and Sarres directed looks at Telanna as if to say, 'Told you,' while Telanna worked her jaw, clearly at a loss for words.

Braden gave an awkward cough and said, "Gavin, Kirloth's duel with Milthas leveled half the city before it was over."

Gavin turned to look at his former apprentice, his face devoid of any expression as he replied, "So?"

Telanna's eyes widened just a bit, and her expression became one of barely contained terror, as if she wanted to ask what she'd gotten her people into but was too polite to say it.

Gavin turned to Telanna and shrugged. "Look...I don't blame the Synod or the elves in general for the conduct of Nirrock and his faction. I'm not about to exact retribution on the entire elven people, but if I have to lay waste to a section of the city to get my people back safely, it's not even a question for me. In truth, I shouldn't be Arch-magister because I'm Kirloth, the guy who's supposed to serve as the silent threat to make everyone behave. You and I both know exactly what my mentor was, and you should have some idea of just how he would've handled this situation. I guarantee you...it wouldn't have been pretty or restrained. Let's go greet your Synod so I can shake their hands and make nice for a little bit, before I visit Nirrock and see how he wants to play this."

Telanna looked to Elayna, her non-expression finally slipping. Elayna simply grinned.

"I tried to tell you how he'd react, sister," Elayna said, still grinning. "Sarres and I saw it when the slavers took Kiri in Vushaar. He's already made one object lesson for anyone who contemplates threatening anyone under his protection, and I'm thinking he's considering making another one, since word obviously never reached Nirrock."

"So, Telanna, where's this Synod we're supposed to meet?" Gavin asked.

"I...I think that it might be best if we show you where to find Nirrock," Telanna replied.

Gavin shrugged again. "Fair enough. Let's go."

Telanna, Elayna, and Sarres led Gavin, Wynn, Braden, Declan, and Xythe through the streets of Arundel, drawing more than the occasional look. Eventually, they arrived at the charred and ruined Temple of Milthas that the elves had left undisturbed since Kirloth's duel during the Godswar.

"Several years ago, Nirrock decided to start operating out of the ruined temple," Telanna said while they walked down the wide boulevard that led to the massive structure.

"And no one considered that might mean something?" Gavin asked.

The elves shared a look between them, and Elayna said, "At the time, he had what sounded like good reasons for doing so."

Gavin and Declan shared their own look, and Gavin managed to hold his tongue on any number of replies he could've made.

The elves stopped a hundred yards from the temple.

Telanna turned to Gavin. "We will go to ready the Sentinels of Nature. No one believes Nirrock will peacefully relinquish power. When the battle is joined, create a gateway, and we will assist you."

"Keep Elayna or Sarres close," Gavin responded. "I don't know that I'm familiar enough with you for the gateway to work, but they traveled with me for several weeks."

They nodded and left Gavin and his friends standing in the thoroughfare.

"Well," Gavin said, pausing for a heavy sigh, "let's go deal with this idiot."

CHAPTER 34

Gavin led his friends into the ruined Temple of Milthas. The charred structure had long since aired out and no longer smelled of burned material or death, but the visual artifacts of Kirloth's duel with Milthas still spoke to the raw energy and exigency of the battle.

"Where do you think we'll find this guy?" Braden rumbled from his position off Gavin's right shoulder.

Gavin scanned the corridor ahead of them, clicked his tongue once, and then a second time. "The primary shrine or sanctuary. That's where he is."

"What makes you say that?" Wynn asked.

"It's where Marcus confronted Milthas," Gavin replied. "I read that in his journal."

"Marcus, is it?" Declan asked, and when Gavin turned, the bard regarded Gavin with a slight quirk of his lips that might become a smile.

Gavin shrugged. "It's still difficult to think of him as Kirloth, sometimes. Besides, according to the old ways, I am now Kirloth, so it seems to me that it could get a bit confusing if I referred to him as Kirloth as well."

Declan chuckled. "I think he'd prefer you think of him as Marcus more than anything else."

The group fell into a companionable silence as they traversed the long corridor to the temple's shrine. The layout of the temple made Gavin think it was designed to place Milthas at the center of attention and ensure he was at the forefront of everyone's mind. It wasn't long before they strode through the doors of the shrine, and Gavin wasn't really that surprised to see that the statue and altar to Milthas had been restored and was well maintained, striking a sharp contrast against the rest of the ruined structure.

A gallery looked down on the shrine from the floor above, and an elf attired in finely tailored clothing stood at the center of the altar. Ten more elves stood along each wall that curved back toward the entrance, totaling twenty. As Gavin and his friends approached, the elf at the altar smiled and clapped.

"Hail and well met, I am Nirrock, Nature's Protector and High Priest of Milthas. It seems the world truly has come full circle. Kirloth and his Apprentices walk upon the earth once more, and now, you face the wrath of the one, true God of Magic."

Nirrock snapped his fingers, and the doors to the shrine swung closed, the *clicks* of the locks echoing throughout the space.

"If you beg for mercy," Nirrock said, "I may choose to grant it. After all, you cannot escape us now."

Gavin scanned the elves arrayed against him and his friends, and a smile slowly curled one side of his lips. "Nirrock, there's something you seem not to have fully considered."

"Oh? And just what is that, Kirloth?"

"You are correct; we are locked in here with you," Gavin replied. "But that also means you are locked in here *with us*. If you return Lillian and Mariana to me unharmed, I will settle for turning you and your associates over to the Sylvan Synod."

Nirrock sneered. "The primacy of you and your old alliance is over. I have come to restore my people to the worship of their rightful god. We outnumber you four to one, and there is no one coming to save you. Surrender, Kirloth, and declare before everyone that Milthas is the one true God of Magic, and I may spare your lives."

"Four to one? You really should've brought more friends," Gavin remarked. Closing his eyes, Gavin reached out into the ambient magic with his *skathos*, seeking Lillian's and Mariana's resonances. It was a gamble, yes, but it paid off. They were above him and to his right. Focusing on their resonance, Gavin cleared his mind of everything but his new intent. He would bring Lillian and Mariana with their clothes but not any restraints and simultaneously open gateways for the Sentinels. He didn't think it would be as brutal as teleporting nearly five hundred people to the courtyard of the Vushaari palace, but...well...needs must.

"Well, Kirloth? Have you decided?" Nirrock demanded.

"I have," Gavin replied and, taking a deep breath, invoked the composite effect. "*Paedryx-Paedryx.*"

Lillian and Mariana appeared next to Gavin, their expressions full of bewilderment, as two massive arches of crackling sapphire energy appeared behind Gavin and his friends. Telanna, Elayna, and Sarres led twenty Sentinels into the shrine, all carrying readied weapons.

"Damn you," Nirrock snarled. "Kill them all!"

More elves wearing Milthas's colors streamed into the shrine through doors behind Nirrock, and both the Sentinels and Xythe erupted into action. Archers stepped to the edge of the gallery and readied their bows.

"Archers," Gavin said.

Before any of his friends could react, Gavin formed his intent in his mind. He closed his eyes and took a deep breath, releasing it to invoke a composite effect, "*Stynohs-Thraxys.*"

Before the archers could even ready their bows, they and several of their compatriots died. The Divination Gavin paired with the Interation identified all those on the upper floors who could serve as reinforcements, including them as targets of the Interation as well. Gavin felt a little unsteady in the wake of the invocation, but it was nothing he couldn't handle.

Gavin turned to his former apprentices. "Stay close. We're not fighters, so we'll cover the galleries and watch for other archers or arcanists."

Lillian, Mariana, Wynn, and Braden gave sharp nods and shifted their positions to watch the quarters of the shrine and gallery railing.

Gavin wasn't sure whether the Synod wanted Nirrock alive or not, and he watched the elf for any sign he was about to bolt or cast. Nirrock's expression grew increasingly desperate as the Sentinels and Xythe cut down more of his people, and he threw up his hand, crying out, "Milthas, the time of your revenge is at hand! Your children need you!"

The shrine rumbled, and Gavin felt *something* through his *skathos*, unlike anything he'd ever felt before. Within moments, the rumbling was so fierce that the melee in the shrine all but stopped, and Gavin couldn't quite believe his eyes when the statue of Milthas took a ponderous step off its pedestal.

"*YOU HAVE SERVED ME FAITHFULLY, CHILD. YOU CALLED, AND I AM COME. RISE UP, AND WE SHALL SMITE THE UNBE-LIEVERS TOGETHER.*"

"Well, shit," Mariana hissed. "How are we supposed to fight a statue animated by a god?"

Gavin's mind went back to what Bellos had told him on the side of the Tel Roshan road, not far from the remains of Baron Kalinor's estate. The members of Lornithar's pantheon weren't the same as Bellos or Xanta or any of those who accepted the mantle of divinity after the Godswar. Valthon had granted them power in their own right, but Lornithar made his pantheon mere extensions of *his* power.

Focusing on his *skathos*, Gavin concentrated all of his senses on the statue lumbering past the altar. Yes, there was a power inhabiting it, but there was also a thread that disappeared into the vast sea that was all ambient magic. A thread that seemed to lead to the east. A thread that felt oddly similar in some ways to Gavin's own seed of power that made him a wizard.

"Huh," Gavin grunted. "I wonder if it would work."

"Wonder if what would work?" Lillian asked.

Gavin opened his eyes and walked toward the statue, while everyone around him stared at it.

"Milthas, is it?" Gavin asked. The statue turned to focus on Gavin. "I'm not sure if you know me, but I am Gavin Cross. What will matter most to you is that I am Head of House Kirloth, and I was trained by the man who spanked you like an unruly child."

The statue roared and drew back a fist. Before it could complete its unwieldy motion and reduce Gavin to a splotch of red-hued, semi-liquid goo, Gavin focused on his intent and invoked a Word of Tutation, "*Rhyskaal.*"

The concussion of Gavin's power struck reality like a massive tsunami crashing against an unprotected shore. Gavin's intent was—by far—the most powerful invocation he'd ever produced, and he collapsed to his knees and screamed as the power burned and raged through him.

But Gavin wasn't the only one screaming. Instead of striking Gavin with its massive stone fist, the statue of Milthas clutched its head and fell backward, vocalizing a level of agony far beyond anything those present had ever witnessed before. Everyone who watched expected the statue to destroy the far wall of the shrine when it struck, but instead, the statue itself shattered into small pieces of stone, its scream cutting off with such abruptness that everyone's ears rang for several moments afterward.

Nirrock collapsed to his knees like a puppet whose strings had been cut, and for several moments, everyone looked around and waited to see what came next. Gavin was on his hands and knees on the floor, his chest heaving as he gasped for air and blood freely flowing from his nostrils and ears.

"What did you do?" Nirrock raged, shattering the silence dominating the shrine. "WHAT DID YOU DO?"

Gavin lifted his head and tried to stand. He would've fallen back to the floor if Braden and Declan hadn't caught him and helped him up.

"I wondered if Lornithar's empowerment of his pantheon was

similar to a wizard's power," Gavin said, his voice weary. "It seems I was right."

Nirrock now clawed at the altar, his speech almost incoherent.

"What does that mean, Gavin?" Elayna asked, approaching him.

Gavin lifted his head and made eye contact with the elven priestess, and it looked like the effort was almost more than he could manage. "I ripped away the connection to Lornithar's power. Milthas isn't a god anymore."

Elayna's jaw wasn't the only one that dropped.

"Is—is that possible?" Telanna asked, her voice little more than a whisper.

"It must be," Gavin replied. "I just did it."

"And damned near killed yourself doing it, too," Declan growled. "Did you even consider what might have happened if you'd been wrong?"

Before anyone else could speak, a column of fire that neither burned nor radiated heat delivered one of Nathrac's Guardians to the shrine. It oriented on Gavin immediately.

"Milord, you must return to Tel Mivar at once. The Necromancer has invaded the city."

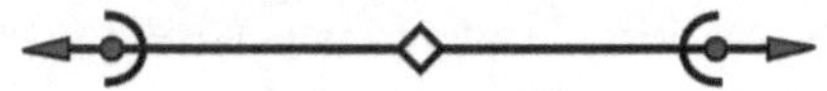

CHAPTER 35

Kiri strode through the halls and corridors of the palace complex. Unlike her normal public attire, she didn't look very 'Crown Princess' at the moment. She wore the black, studded leather armor Declan had obtained for her all those months ago, and just like when she'd ridden with Gavin to deal with the mercenary camp, she was absolutely festooned with blades of all different shapes and sizes. She felt confident she didn't *quite* have Declan's blade count when he was 'working,' but she was sure it was a near thing.

The usual occupants and guests of the palace gaped at Kiri as she passed, and the Cavaliers who saw her remembered the whispers about when she'd actually drawn a blade on two of her protection detail while Gavin was unconscious after removing the slave marks. But if Kiri was aware of the looks, expressions, or whispers that followed in her wake, she didn't show it.

Without pausing to knock or ask permission, Kiri entered her father's private study. The king turned toward the open door, and his shocked expression soon matched all the others at seeing the Crown Princess decked out like a professional assassin.

"Kiri? What—" Terris began.

"I'm going to Tel Mivar, Father," Kiri answered, interrupting him. "I can't handle being estranged from Gavin anymore, and I'm not leaving until he hears me and we work it out."

A soft smile curled Terris's lips, and he said, "Yes, well...I suppose it's only appropriate. Did I ever tell you that your mother asked me out and ultimately proposed to me?"

All thoughts of Tel Mivar vanished from Kiri's mind. "She did? I mean, isn't that—"

"Not how it's usually done?" Terris responded. "Yes, but that was your mother. When there was something—or in my case, someone— she wanted, she could be a bit relentless. That's probably part of the reason why she was available when I met her; I imagine she intimidated most men."

Now, it was Kiri who developed a soft smile. "I wish I could've known her better."

"Me, too," Terris replied. "She'd be so proud of you, and don't worry about me or the kingdom. You do what you need to do. We'll be here when you're ready to come back."

Kiri almost leapt into her father's arms, hugging him tight as she whispered in his ear. "Thank you, Daddy; I love you."

* * *

Kiri's next stop on her crusade was Fallon, the Court Wizard. She didn't have weeks to make the journey to Birsha and then cross the Inner Sea to Tel Mivar, even if she could bring herself to board another boat. She hoped he would be able to teleport her straight to her destination.

Entering the reception area of Fallon's laboratory and quarters, the sight of him sitting in an armchair with a book in his hand surprised her, though not nearly as much as the sight of the Crown Princess decked out like a traveling blades merchant surprised him.

"Y-Your Highness?" Fallon asked. "Is everything all right?"

"Yes, for the most part, it is," Kiri replied. "Fallon, can you teleport me to Tel Mivar? I need to be there, and I don't have time for a regular journey."

"Uhm, well, I didn't prepare the spell this morning," Fallon answered. As a mage, he had to prepare spells each day, and the more difficult and challenging the spell—like Teleport—required greater preparation times. "But I always keep a number of scrolls hidden around, just for situations like this. I'm afraid the best I can do is the Tower of the Council at the College. It's fairly central in Tel Mivar, so reaching your actual destination won't be too difficult."

Kiri smiled. "The Tower is perfect, Fallon."

The Court Wizard set aside his book and stood, crossing the room to a tapestry that depicted one of the ancient queens of Vushaar. He reached behind it and withdrew a scroll secured by an amber-colored ribbon. Removing the ribbon with a flourish, Fallon unrolled the parchment and proceeded to cast. In moments, a gateway made of crackling, sapphire-hued energy appeared...except it opened to the plaza right outside the College grounds.

"That's odd," Fallon remarked.

"What?" Kiri asked.

"The gateway should've opened to the central vestibule of the Tower, right where the Grand Stair opens to the main floor. That's where the teleport beacon is. But that looks like the plaza tiles right outside the College's wall."

Kiri stepped up to Fallon and pulled him into a fast but forceful hug. "It's fine, Fallon. It's still Tel Mivar, and that's where I need to be."

Without giving the matter a further thought, Kiri stepped through the gateway, causing it to vanish.

* * *

"THIS ISN'T WISE, MILORD," Torval said.

The Heads of the Great Houses and their heirs—along with Declan, Xythe, and Ovir—stood with Gavin in the Hall of the Gods inside the Temple of Valthon.

"Isn't wise, my ass," Declan growled. "Gavin, what you're trying to do isn't just stupid. It's damned stupid. You're in no condition to face the Necromancer right now. You can barely stand!"

Gavin turned to face Declan and swayed on his feet, looking for all the world like he was about to fall, but he maintained his balance and met his friend's gaze. "And just who would you send out there, Declan? You, along with everyone here, know I'm the strongest wizard in the Society. Should Lillian or Mariana go out there to face him? I'm not bleeding out of my ears and nose anymore; Ovir saw to that. But this is a golden opportunity to deal with the threat once and for all. He's right out there, less than a hundred yards away!"

"Have you considered that it's a golden opportunity for him as well?" Mariana asked. "If he kills you—"

"Nathrac will take over administering the civil government until Bellos appoints a new Archmagister," Gavin interrupted. "I've already made that change to the constitution, so Tel will never again have to face the question of who's in charge."

Just then, a column of fire that neither burned nor radiated heat delivered Nathrac to the discussion.

"Milord," Nathrac said, "I have activated the garrison. They are pushing back the undead, but it will take time. The Army of Tel— including the Battle-mages—is on the move, but between the time to mobilize and the bottle-neck presented by North Gate, it will be some time before they can reinforce the garrison." Then, Nathrac took in the expressions of everyone around him and turned back to Gavin. "Why is everyone angry with you?"

"I'm going out there to deal with the Necromancer once and for all," Gavin said. "There will never be a better time."

"Ah," Nathrac remarked. "That would explain it. Are you aware he stands with his cadre of lieutenants? None of them wear medallions, but that doesn't mean they *aren't* wizards. The medallions are part of the Society and did not exist before the Founding."

Gavin sighed. "Yes, okay. Maybe going out there is a mistake. Yes, I freely admit that I'm not exactly feeling my best. But shouldn't we do something to keep the Necromancer and his people focused on the city? Don't we want to keep them from realizing reinforcements will be streaming through North Gate as soon as they mobilize? I can't think of anything that would work better than a confrontation with me."

"No, with *us*," Lillian said, stepping forward with her friends—the other Apprentices—following suit. Gavin turned to regard her, and Lillian continued. "If we can't talk you out of confronting him and his people, the least we can do is go out there with you. That way, their entire focus won't be on you."

Gavin slowly shook his head. "No. I don't want the four of you out there. You're the Heirs of your families, and if it all goes wrong, you'll be needed when it's time to start putting everything back together."

Lillian squared her shoulders as she asked, "And just how do you think you can stop us?"

"I consider all of you dear friends," Gavin said, "and I hope I'm around for you to hate me for this later."

Without giving anyone a chance to realize what he was doing, Gavin invoked a composite effect, "*Paedryx-Sykhurhos!*"

The moment his power touched the fabric of reality, Gavin and Nathrac both vanished...and the temple doors behind him slammed shut as the very structure of the Temple developed a vermillion aura.

"Well, that wasn't fair," Lyssa said, sighing.

"What did he do, Mother?" Mariana asked.

Lyssa scowled at the closed doors for a moment before turning to her daughter. "I might be wrong, but I'd wager all the Temple's doors are now spell-locked, with the Temple itself protected from tele-portation."

* * *

KIRI STEPPED into a world of chaos.

People ran screaming from undead creatures, the likes of which Kiri had never seen before. The town guard worked to get the people to safety, and the city's garrison was fighting to corral or contain the undead horde. Turning to the College, Kiri saw that the gate was sealed and no one was visible in the College's courtyard.

She approached a nearby member of the town guard. "What's happening?"

"Are ye daft, girl? What does it look like is happening?" the guardsman replied. "The Necromancer opened a portal in the northeast quadrant of the city. No one seems to know whether it's a full-on invasion or just a raid, but these monsters are sure making a mess of things."

"Thank you." She turned and started to push her way through the crowd, toward the northeast quarter of the city. If she knew Gavin, that's where he'd be.

"Hey! Didn't you hear me?" the town guardsman shouted behind her. "There's whole lot of undead that way!"

Kiri drew her two short swords and shouted over her shoulder, "I'll be fine. There's someone I need to find."

* * *

"Okay," Kiri said, muttering Gavin's odd word to herself. "Maybe I won't be fine."

She was almost to the northeast plaza. Rotting gore covered her torso, forearms, and lower legs, and she'd already lost her swords and three daggers. The swords had snapped during the death throes of a couple ghouls, and zombies had wandered off with the three daggers, apparently deciding that unarmed citizens would be a better meal than someone who stuck them with sharp metal. It would've been nice if they had let Kiri retrieve her daggers before shambling off, though. The wind shifted, and the foul odor of the gore that covered her hit her like a stone wall.

"Gah," Kiri said, gagging and exerting all her will not to vomit from the stench. "I think I'm going to have to burn this armor later."

The chaos around her seemed to thin, and Kiri realized she was within sight of her quarry. In the distance, she saw Gavin standing at one end of the northeast plaza. Across from him, she saw a cluster of black-robed people, but she was too far away to make out any details.

She wouldn't have known it was Gavin, but she felt safe assuming a lone figure in a gold robe was probably him.

Kiri's focus was broken when she noticed a cluster of people—actual people, not undead—shifting through the chaos surrounding the plaza. They appeared to be angling to get behind Gavin, and every one of them carried some form of blade.

"So, they think to stab Gavin in the back?" Kiri whispered, almost growled. "Not if I have anything to say about it."

Kiri drew on her many hours of training with Declan, moving through the chaos and using it to her advantage. Out of the five or six people moving to flank Gavin, Kiri killed three of them, slitting their throats before the others realized anything was wrong. Then, it became a simple matter of using her training to fight several opponents at once. But just because something was simple didn't mean it was easy...

The person closest to Kiri was a rather gruesome looking man, sporting several scars across his face and hands. He was huge for a human but moved with a cat-like grace that looked wrong for someone his size. He lunged toward Kiri, attempting a double strike with his short swords. Kiri dropped into a shoulder roll that brought her within striking distance. Before her opponent realized what she was doing, Kiri thrust her right dagger up to its small cross-guard into the man's groin, at the same time she slashed deeply into the inside of the man's right thigh with the dagger in her left hand. Blood fountained from the man's wounds as he screamed and collapsed, his short swords clattering to the street right in front of Kiri.

"Don't mind if I do," Kiri remarked, returning her daggers to their sheaths on either thigh before collecting her new short swords...well, new to her anyway.

The man's screams faded as Kiri stood to face the next attacker, the blood loss becoming too much for him. Kiri considered cutting the man's throat to give him a more merciful death, but the next attacker was closing. Besides, Kiri had faith he'd die soon enough on his own with no further attention from her.

As Kiri was standing, ready to engage the woman approaching

her with blades drawn, she saw the final attacker moving toward Gavin's unprotected back, using his associate's attack on Kiri as a distraction to give him time.

We can't have that, Kiri thought as she quickly scanned her immediate area. Her eyes landed on the remains of an animated skeleton. The skull was long gone, but the rib cage was intact. Another shoulder roll delivered Kiri to the skeleton, and she speared the ribcage with one short sword. She flicked the ribcage with all her might toward her closest attacker and darted toward the man angling toward Gavin.

The man saw Kiri's gambit and shouted a warning, but he should have kept his silence. His warning distracted his associate, and the skeleton's ribcage caught her totally unawares as it slammed into her face and chest. The shock of the impact and her excessive reaction caused her to fall backward in a clatter of bones and blades, more than the force of projectile's impact alone would have caused. Unfortunately, the man was still far enough away from Gavin that his warning to his associate hadn't attracted Gavin's attention.

"You fight like a demon, girl," the man said as Kiri reached him, positioning herself so that she stood between the man and Gavin.

Kiri allowed herself a smirk. "Sometimes, it takes a demon to kill a demon."

The man scoffed. "Where'd you learn to fight? The Shadows don't teach their assassins your level of blade-work."

"Why should I tell you?" Kiri asked. "I doubt my teacher would offer you lessons."

The man shrugged. "Fair enough. It's just that you'll give me my first challenge in a while, and I'd kind of like to know who I'm about to kill."

Behind the man, Kiri saw the woman toss the ribcage aside and begin to stand. Not wanting to allow the man any more time to allow his associate to recover, Kiri threw herself at him. Their blades soon became a symphony of death, as each sought an opening amidst the attacks and parries. Kiri's ferocity forced the man back as they danced, and she worked herself into the position she wanted, her right side partially exposed to the woman she'd hit with the ribcage. The woman on the ground was lifting her feet to begin the process of a kip-up, and Kiri drew her opponent into parrying a dual strike at his head. Before he could recover, Kiri drove a savage kick into his privates and pivoted toward the woman, using her lack of defense mid-move to slash her throat before returning her focus to the man.

Kiri saw the man's eyes were on the now-dying woman collapsing back to the ground, and she met his gaze when he shifted it to her.

"Just who in Lornithar's Abyss are you?" he growled as he pushed himself back to his feet. "I've never seen anyone fight like you."

Kiri wasn't about to betray Gavin's trust and tell whoever this guy was that she'd been trained by one of the Wraiths of Kirloth. She doubted if the guy even knew the Wraiths existed. Instead, she decided to try something else.

"I'm Kiri Muran, the Crown Princess of Vushaar," she said, adding a smirk for flavor.

The man's jaw dropped as he gaped at her, and when the tips of his short swords dropped, Kiri lunged. The short sword in her left hand slipped between the man's ribs as she drove her other short sword into the man's midriff just below his ribs and angled it up. Kiri pushed the swords with all her might, and she thought she felt the blades scrape across each other somewhere inside the man's torso. The man started to lift his own swords, but the light in his eyes faded. The blades clattered as they struck the ground. As the man's corpse collapsed to the ground, he pulled Kiri's swords with him. She released her swords until the corpse settled on its back and then had to place her foot on the left shoulder while pulling at the swords to give her the leverage she needed to break the suction and retrieve them.

Kiri wiped her blades on the corpse and turned to help Gavin. Instead, she saw him collapse to his knees, and she didn't realize the scream she heard came from her.

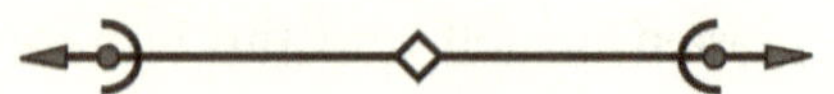

CHAPTER 36

Gavin and Nathrac appeared in an alleyway off the northeast plaza. The sounds of battle echoed all around them, a foul stench—worse than anything Gavin could remember—covered the air like a blanket.

"Do I want to know what that smell is?" Gavin asked, wrinkling his nose.

Nathrac shrugged. "Probably not, but you're not getting away from it any time soon. That is the smell of a horde of undead in various stages of decay."

Gavin turned to look at Nathrac. "So, this is what it smells like at Skullkeep all the time?"

"Yes."

Gavin sighed. "Wow. It kind of makes me feel sorry for anyone alive there." Then, Gavin shook his head to clear it and focus on the fight. "Okay. You go and oversee the defense. Do what needs done to ensure they don't establish a foothold in the city. I'm going out there to distract the Necromancer and his people. Hopefully, it will keep them from noticing the army approaching North Gate."

"I do not like leaving you alone to face them," Nathrac said. "Your friends and associates were correct; it is unwise."

"Sometimes, the best choices you have are unwise," Gavin replied, adding a shrug. "We don't have time for this, Nathrac. Go."

"Very well. I hope to see you on the other side."

The Chief of the Citadel Guard vanished in a column of flame that neither burned nor radiated heat.

Gavin squared his shoulders and walked to the plaza. He stepped out of the alleyway into the chaos, making his way to the relative calm at the center of the plaza. When he stepped out of the chaos, a black-robed figure gestured to him. A second robed figure with its back to Gavin turned, and he realized he now faced the Necromancer of Skullkeep.

The Necromancer walked toward Gavin, his lieutenants following, and Gavin approached. When they were about thirty feet apart, both parties stopped.

"So...Gavin Cross, the Archmagister of Tel," the Necromancer remarked. "You've interfered in my plans entirely too much for one so young."

Gavin shrugged. "You must be the Necromancer of Skullkeep, and as for interfering in your plans...well, I needed some way to pass the time. It's so much fun I've decided to make a hobby of it."

The Necromancer's hands clenched into fists, and Gavin fought to maintain his non-expression, glad to see his barb draw blood.

"You were a fool to face me, Gavin Cross," the Necromancer said. "There's nothing to stop me killing you where you stand."

"Just this," Gavin replied, now allowing himself a smirk before he invoked a Word of Interation. "*Thraxys!*"

Gavin fully expected to see the Necromancer and his lieutenants collapse to the ground, dead. After all, that's what happened every other time he'd used that specific Word. Alas, this time was not like all the others. The Necromancer simply remained where he stood, by all appearances, utterly unaffected. As for the lieutenants, the moment Gavin's invocation attempted to take hold of them, ruby auras flashed into existence. They grimaced and clenched their fists but otherwise remained alive.

"Well," the Necromancer remarked, his tone gloating, "I don't think that went according to plan for you. I know how much you like that particular Word, so I gave my lieutenants a death ward before we arrived...on the off chance we'd meet you."

"What about you?" Gavin asked. "Don't you need a death ward, too?"

"Silly boy, I have long since become death incarnate." The Necromancer used one hand to throw back the hood of his robe while his other opened it. At first, he appeared to be a normal man, but the semblance of normality quickly faded, and Gavin found himself looking at an upright skeleton with scraps of desiccated skin hanging off it.

Gavin's first thought was that Othron had been a traitor all this time, but then, his rational mind took over. The lich standing before him, while similar to Othron in that they were both desiccated corpses physically, didn't have the same bone structure or voice. Apparently, there was more than one lich in the world.

"So, that's how you're still alive after all these years," Gavin said. "You're a lich like Othron. He never mentioned training anyone, though."

The Necromancer growled. "Do not speak that one's name to me! He rejects the power this state permits and wants nothing more than to hide from the world in the ruins of his king's keep. I will conquer Tel and return to Vushaar, and my first act in that realm will be the destruction of that worthless stack of bones."

"You won't conquer Tel as long as I live," Gavin countered. "I challenge you to a Wizards' Duel, right here and right now."

"Why not? I'll enjoy killing you either way, so I might as well have a bit of sport with it."

They squared off as the Necromancer's lieutenants stepped back to give them space. Soon, magical effect after magical effect shattered the relative calm of the northeast plaza as they hurled power at one another. First, Gavin was on the defensive, countering an invocation. Then, he riposted with an invocation of his own that the Necromancer countered. Fire, ice, acid, lightning—every element at an arcanist's command and more flew between the two combatants.

And yet, it was all for naught. It seemed Gavin and Necromancer were evenly matched.

But Gavin had not started the duel at his full strength, and it was only a matter of time before his extreme power expenditure in Arundel caught up with him.

After what seemed like an eternity, with neither giving an inch, a piece of one of the Necromancer's invocations slipped through Gavin's defense. It was a core of earth wrapped inside a vitality-leeching effect. The earth core gave it a physical hit, and the leeching effect drained what little of Gavin's strength remained. He collapsed to his knees as he fought to remain conscious. Dimly, he thought he heard someone scream his name, the voice so familiar his mind told him he should pay attention, but he was weak, so weak.

It was all Gavin could do to lift his head and face his opponent.

"At last," the Necromancer gloated. "Tel Mivar shall be mine!"

The Necromancer lifted his hands and invoked a Word of Transmutation, flinging a seething orb of amber-colored power at Gavin. Just as the orb neared him, Gavin felt something slam into his back, and black-leather-clad arms wrapped around his torso. Gavin forced himself to focus on the orb, intent on dispelling it, but he had nothing left. Just before the orb struck him, Gavin felt it seem to spasm through his *skathos*, and then, everything went black.

The Necromancer soon found himself surrounded by his lieutenants as they cheered his success. He wanted nothing more than to bask in his victory, but there wasn't time for that yet.

"You did it, Master!" the lieutenant who had advanced the plan of attacking Tel Mivar cheered. "The Archmagister is no more!"

A quiet, contemplative wizard who always seemed to be the reliable bedrock for the Necromancer slowly shook her head as she said, "I wouldn't be too sure of that."

Turning to face her, the Necromancer asked, "Oh? And just why is that? I ended him and whoever that was trying to save him with a disintegration effect."

"If you disintegrated him, Master," the wizard replied, "where is the pile of ash? Disintegration always leaves a pile of ash. Besides, look at the streetlamps. They only burn when there is a living Arch-magister named by Bellos, and they're still burning."

The Necromancer pivoted, his eyes seeking out the nearest street-lamp. And...she was right. Somehow, the upstart puppy still lived!

An inarticulate scream of utter rage erupted from the Necro-mancer, and he grabbed the lieutenant who'd pressed for this futile attack, practically shouting, "*Idluhn!*"

The lieutenant erupted in flames and died screaming.

"Why?" the Necromancer raged as his former lieutenant burned. "Why do the gods hate me so? All I want to do is build a coalition capable of defeating Lornithar. I want to *save* this world. But *no*! I am defeated and opposed at every turn! Must I challenge the gods them-selves to make this world safe? Is that what it will take?"

Unseen by the cluster of people surrounding the Necromancer, a black-robed figure slipped away from the crowd and walked toward the Temple of Valthon. The moment the figure set foot on the first of the Temple's steps, the black began draining away like ink washed off in the rain. Half-way up the steps, no black remained, and a seem-ingly old man with wildly unkempt hair stumped up the steps, clad in a gray robe that was tattered and frayed around the hem.

"Heh," he scoffed. "If he thinks I'll allow him to interfere with plans I've built and carried across millennia, Drannos Muldannin is a bigger fool than I thought he was. I've spent too much time and effort ensuring a true Wizard of House Kirloth is alive and well to allow him to ruin everything we've built in the wake of the Godswar." By now, the old man approached the vacant greeter's desk. "And I told them all thousands of years ago. Nesta and I are *not* gods; we're merely the caretakers the old gods assigned to watch over things."

Without another word, the old man snapped his fingers, dispelling the lock Gavin had placed on the Temple and faded away like mist on the wind.

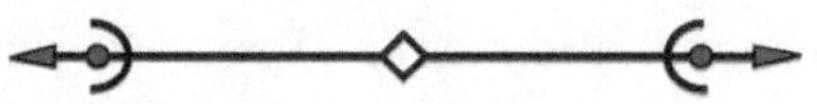

CHAPTER 37

Something hot and sticky warmed his cheek, neck, underside of his forearms, and the inside of his hands. The sun beat against the back of his neck, his forearms, and the backs of his hands. His awareness returned at a slow, crawling pace, and the next thing he realized was that someone was lying against his side. Then, a bone-deep throbbing ache forced itself into his awareness, and he almost wished he could go back to not awake. The nothingness of it was much more pleasant.

A thought exploded at the forefront of his mind. He was Gavin Cross, Head of House Kirloth and Archmagister of Tel. His city was under attack, and he'd been dueling the Necromancer of Skullkeep. What was really odd, though, was that Gavin couldn't hear any sounds of battle around him. Nor did he smell the awful stench of undead he knew should be there.

Lifting his head and forcing his eyes open, Gavin saw a prostrate form at his side. From the length of hair and the body shape, he assumed it was a woman. The hair was glossy black, and what skin he could see seemed to bear an olive complexion. She wore a gray t-shirt, blue denim jeans, and tennis shoes. He pulled his eyes away from the woman at his side to take in more of his surroundings.

He and his companion occupied what appeared to be an alley. Gavin would've scoffed at waking up in another alley, except he hurt too much. He looked in front of him and froze at the sight across the street.

There was an aged storefront directly across from the alley. A large placard above the storefront's entrance held the business's well-maintained sign: "Cross General Store, Est. 1743."

It was then that Gavin knew...everything. He remembered his parents. He remembered his childhood, wedding, and the birth of his daughter Jennifer. He and his wife named her Jennifer Anne. Jennifer was his wife's mother's middle name, and Anne was his mother's. His father's name was Richard. His family had first settled in the region in the early 1700's, founding the town and protecting it during the War for Independence and all the turmoil since.

He was home.

The home where he'd grown up. It hit him like a haymaker from a pro heavyweight boxer. Graham, Virginia. The United States of America. Earth. And he was one of the most powerful arcanists to have ever lived...in a world that believed magic didn't exist.

Gavin put his head down on the alley's pavement, closed his eyes, and sighed.

"Oh, boy..."

WHAT'S NEXT?

The story continues in "Home Sweet Home," and it's available now!

ISBN: 978-1-7334735-8-3

* * *

Want to keep up-to-date on my projects and receive exclusive content?

Sign-up for my newsletter:
http://kfplink.com/g8i

RATE THIS BOOK

Did you enjoy this story? If you did, please consider leaving a review.

Reviews are the lifeblood of visibility for independent authors, especially on the eBook retailers. The more reviews a book has, the more visible it will be on the retailers' sites.

I appreciate all reviews...good, bad, or indifferent.

If you would like to leave a review, visit this book's review page (http://kfplink.com/961a1).

First and foremost, thank you for reading...both the novel and these notes! I hope you enjoyed *Archmagister*!

The past few months have certainly been...unusual, to say the least. I'm never really sure what I should write here, and these are such trying, uncertain times for many people of the world.

I have been extremely fortunate that the pandemic hasn't really impacted me, aside from shortages in the stores and certain favored haunts shutting down. I know I am far, far more the exception than the rule.

I am already at work crafting the next volume of this series, "Home Sweet Home," and I hope to have it ready for my new editor (whoever that turns out to be) by the end of May.

So far, the three editors I've had have all lived in different states, and the editors I'm considering also live in different states from those I've worked with before. If this trend continues, I feel like I should try to assemble the complete set...work with an editor from every state in the country by the time I retire. :P

As amusing at that thought is to me, I'm sure it's the kind of professional goal I should have. I'd much rather find *the* editor, the one with whom I have excellent rapport and work with across the remainder of my career.

If someone were saying this to me, I'd give the person an encouraging smile and say, "I like working with an optimist."

We'll see how it goes.

I offer my best wishes to you and yours, especially with the world as it is right now, and I hope you're able to stay as safe and healthy as possible.

If you're still reading this, thanks for the dedication...or perhaps the curiosity. :) As I said above, I hope you enjoyed reading *Archmagister*. Thank you.

TYPOS

Typos and little slips in grammar are the bane of any author. Unfortunately, they are almost impossible to eradicate completely. I can show you many traditionally published books—twenty years old and more—that have a 'whoopsie' here and there.

That being said, if you find a typo or something that seems to be an error in grammar, please do not hesitate to contact me at typos@knightsfallpress.com.

I will periodically collate any emails and produce an updated PDF and eBook files, and I'll make an announcement in my monthly newsletter when the updates have been published.

ACKNOWLEDGMENTS

There's an old saying: it takes a village to raise a child. I don't know if that's true or not, but it certainly seems true where publishing a novel is concerned. You would not be reading this were it not for contributions from several people.

Did you like the cover? The background image was created by Jakub Skop (https://www.behance.net/JakubSkop).

I'm sure there are many who will see this next paragraph and think, "Goodness, he's acknowledging his parents and grandparents *again*?" My greatest regret is that I cannot hand my grandfather, Bob Miller, a paperback copy of my novels. So, yes...the Acknowledgements page of *every* book I publish will have the paragraph that follows. Consider yourselves forewarned.

Without my grandparents, Bob & Janice Miller, I honestly don't know where I'd be today; my grandfather taught me to read and love reading, and my grandmother taught me to develop and exercise my imagination. This novel (not to mention my life in general) certainly would not have happened without my parents, Vernon & Judy Kerns.

THE NOVELS OF ROBERT M. KERNS

For a complete and accurate listing of all publications, both currently available and forthcoming, please visit Knightsfall Press.

Knightsfall Press - Books

https://knightsfall.press/books

SO...WHO'S THE AUTHOR?

Robert M. Kerns (or Rob if you ever meet him in person) is a geek, and he claims that label proudly. Most of his geekiness revolves around Information Technology (IT), having over fifteen years in the industry; within IT, he especially prefers Servers and Networks, and he often makes the claim that his residence has a better data infrastructure than some businesses.

Beyond IT, Rob enjoys Science Fiction and Fantasy of (almost) all stripes. He is a voracious reader, with his favorite books too numerous to list.

Rob has been writing for over 20 years, and *Awakening* is his debut novel.

Connect with Rob at knightsfall.press.

facebook.com/RobertMKerns

amazon.com/author/robertmkerns

bookbub.com/authors/robert-m-kerns

www.ingramcontent.com/pod-product-compliance
Lightning Source LLC
Chambersburg PA
CBHW050241110726

47898CB00007B/2232